The Secret Life of Mac

Center Point
Large Print

Also by Melinda Metz and available from
Center Point Large Print:

Talk to the Paw

**This Large Print Book carries the
Seal of Approval of N.A.V.H.**

The Secret Life of Mac

Melinda Metz

CENTER POINT LARGE PRINT
THORNDIKE, MAINE

This Center Point Large Print edition
is published in the year 2019 by arrangement with
Kensington Publishing Corp.

The text of this Large Print edition is unabridged.
In other aspects, this book may vary
from the original edition.
Printed in the United States of America
on permanent paper.
Set in 16-point Times New Roman type.

ISBN: 978-1-64358-162-0

Library of Congress Cataloging-in-Publication Data

Library of Congress Cataloging in Publication
Control Number: 2019002484

For Robin Rue—so smart, so kind, so funny—with so many thanks, and in memory of my dad, limerickist extraordinaire

CHAPTER 1

MacGyver caught the silver tab between his teeth and slid the zipper free. With a flick-whap paw combo he opened the lid of the suitcase, then leapt inside and stretched out on the pile of folded clothes. Nice nap locality. But it could be improved. He'd never understand humans' desire to make things flat. With a little huff of exasperation, Mac stood and gave the clothes a good fluffing, then lay down again. His claws extended, digging into the softness of a silky sweater. Sweet sardinsies, that felt good.

"Mac! No!" his person, Jamie, cried. She swept him out of the perfect nap nest he'd created, then with a *smapt* and a *zzzzpt* shut it away. As if he couldn't reopen it just as easily. "I'm going on my honeymoon. Hon-ey-moon! The look I'm going for is romantic, not crazy cat lady covered in cat hair."

He ignored her blah-blahs. He understood humans used them to communicate, but that was because their noses were basically useless face blobs. His nose told him more than a billion blahs, and right now his nose was informing him that Jamie was happier than she'd ever been.

And who was that thanks to? It was thanks to him. MacGyver. She'd needed a packmate— he hated to say it, but she was like a dog that way—and he'd gone out and found her one.

He began to purr with pride. "You don't care what I'm saying, do you, my little beastie?" She turned toward the door, and Mac saw David, the packmate *he'd* found, coming toward them. "Mac has done a style consult on everything in my suitcase. Everything I wear will now be accessorized with beautiful tan-and-gold tabby fur," Jamie told him.

"That's why my suitcase has a lock," David answered. Mac felt Jamie's body shake as she began to laugh. "What's so—" David began. Then he reached down and ran his fingers over one of the three ties Mac had been playing with before he'd been ready for his nap.

David studied the suitcase. "Still locked. Your cat split the zipper open wide enough to work the ends of the ties out."

"Not *my* cat. *Our* cat. We're married now. What's mine is yours, and that includes Mac," Jamie said.

"I just bought *our* cat that Octo-mouse, with eight crinkly legs guaranteed for hours of feline pleasure." David glared at Mac. "Eight crinkly legs, and you couldn't leave my stuff alone." He shook his head, running his fingers over a long claw snag in one of the ties.

8

Mac ignored David's blah-blahs, too, and the glare. He'd smelled David before Mac had decided to take things into his own paws, and David had smelled just as bad as Jamie, sometimes even worse. He was desperate for a packmate, whether he knew it or not, and Mac had found him one. Now he was as happy as if he'd been rolling in catnip.

"Mac loves his present. He just also enjoys a DIY project now and then," Jamie said as David dialed his combination into the useless suitcase lock.

The doorbell rang, and Diogee immediately started to bark. The bonehead had never figured out stealth was key to a successful attack. All the dog was doing was alerting whoever was out there to his presence. Mac leapt out of Jamie's arms. Diogee was part of his pack now, a sacrifice that had to be made for Jamie's happiness. That meant Mac had to do what he could to keep the dog safe from his own stupidity.

When Mac reached the door, he gave Diogee's ropey tail a little whack, partly to get him out of the way, and partly because it was fun. He opened his mouth wide and used his tongue to flick air inside. That gave him extra intel. It was a woman outside, and she was unhappy. Big-time unhappy.

Jamie opened the door a crack. "Briony, hi. I have to grab my cat. MacGyver is a complete escape artist; I'm talking a climb-up-the-chimney escape artist. We had to block up the fireplace. Also, the dog, Diogee, *will* jump on you. I know I should be able to tell him no. And actually, I *can* tell him no, but it has no effect. But he's friendly. Okay, brace yourself." She scooped Mac up under one arm, pulled the door open, and backed up.

As soon as the woman stepped inside, the bonehead planted both paws on her shoulders, but before he could wash her face with his enormous tongue David was able to grab him by the collar and pull him away. He hauled Diogee upstairs, and a few seconds later pathetic howls filled the house. The bedroom door was easy to open with even the most basic skills. But Diogee didn't have even the most basic skills.

Mac took another deep breath. Yes, this woman was extremely sad. She needed Mac's help. He had things to do, escapes to make, naps to take, but clearly, he'd have to get involved here. The woman had to be smarter than Diogee, but obviously not smart enough to solve whatever was wrong. That would require a master.

Fortunately for her, she'd come to MacGyver's door.

About five minutes after arriving at her cousin Jamie's front door, Briony Kleeman found herself at the kitchen table. Jamie was filling the teakettle, while her cat, MacGyver, sat on the counter, staring at Briony with his unblinking golden eyes.

Briony wasn't quite sure how she'd gotten there. She wasn't quite sure how she'd gotten to Los Angeles at all. Less than a day ago, she was walking toward the altar of the little white Peace of Prince Lutheran Church in Wisconsin. Her hand was resting on her father's arm. Her feet were walking over rose petals scattered by her three-year-old cousin. Her train, trimmed with lace from her great-great-grandmother's wedding dress, was being carried by Caleb's niece. Everything was just as planned.

She looked at Caleb. He was smiling as he watched her walk toward him. Then everything went wobbly. The floor. Her father's arm. The faces of the guests. Caleb. A mix of dizziness and nausea flooded her, and everything went dim, then dark.

"Briony," Jamie said, her voice jerking Briony away from the memory of that horrible morning. "What kind of tea do you want? I have orange spice, lemongrass, chai black, Earl Grey, mint, and a bunch of others. I've recently become a tea convert. Not that I'd ever give up coffee. And you can have coffee if you'd rather. Also, I have some juice, cranberry and orange. And some sparkling water. And some unsparkling water. So, what'll you have?"

Too many choices. Briony couldn't remember

half of them, probably because part of her felt like she was still back in the church with the world slipping out from under her. "You choose."

"You sure? Some of the teas aren't, you know, everyone's cup of tea," Jamie answered, her brown eyes filled with concern.

"I just feel . . . Somehow I . . ." Briony shook her head helplessly. "I just can't make a decision. Even about what to drink. I know it's stupid."

"It's not stupid. You must be exhausted," Jamie said.

"Yeah, I thought I'd fall asleep on the plane, but I couldn't," Briony admitted. Instead of an in-flight movie, she'd seen that walk down the aisle again and again and again, unable to force it from her mind.

"No worries. I'll pick for you." Jamie stood up, opened the cupboard over the coffeemaker, and began studying the boxes of tea.

Briony let out a little sigh of relief. Jamie was picking up where her parents left off. Since the Incident in the Church, as Briony had started calling it to herself, all decisions had been made for her. She was whisked to the airport, her parents promising to handle everything. Then she was on the plane. Then she was handing a cabdriver a piece of paper with Jamie's address written on it. And now she was here, with Jamie acting like it was completely normal to be taking care of Briony, even though they hadn't seen each other since the family reunion that was, what, probably eleven years ago.

Jamie set a mug of tea in front of her. "It's Get Relaxed. I don't know why, but something is telling me you could use it. My instincts are really keen," she joked.

The mug shook in Briony's fingers as she raised it to her lips. She set it down without taking a sip. "You're right. I'm still . . . a little shaken up." Understatement of the millennium. She felt like a tennis shoe in the spin cycle of a beat-up old washing machine. "Thank you so much for letting me stay here. I really—"

"Stop. Stop, stop, stop. You've already thanked me one hundred and three times by my calculations." Jamie put one hand over Briony's. "You're completely welcome here. Sometimes you need to get away. And Storybook Court is a good place to get away to. Trust me. Besides, we were going to board the fur babies, and now they can stay at home."

Tears stung Briony's eyes. Jamie was being so nice to her, as if she didn't realize Briony was a terrible person. "Do you want to talk about it?" Jamie asked. "I know we don't know each other that well. You and your family moved to Wisconsin when you were, I think, about ten? But remember that time I was babysitting you when I was sixteen and I took you to my boyfriend's house, I mean horrible ex-boyfriend's house, when I knew he and his family were out, and—"

"We broke in! You let me put salt on his toothbrush. And tape on the toilet paper in his bathroom. That was one of the best nights of my life! For that one night, I felt like a badass. A nine-year-old badass!" Briony exclaimed, the memory distracting her from why she was at her cousin's. She couldn't help smiling. "That was so fun."

"Until your parents got so mad at me!" Jamie exclaimed. "And they didn't even know what we did. They just knew I took you out of the house. I told your mom and dad we walked to the Dairy Queen. Which we did. After. And just that freaked them out!"

"Yeah, they were a little overprotective," Briony answered.

"A little? I bet you weren't allowed to cross the street by yourself until you were in college." She took a swallow of her tea. "So, *do* you want to talk about it?"

The rose petals. Her dad. Caleb smiling. For a moment, Briony felt like she'd forgotten how to breathe. "No," she managed to say. "If that's okay," she added quickly.

"Of course it's okay," Jamie answered.

"So, the animals," Briony said. She wanted a nice, safe topic. "What do they eat? Where do

14

they sleep? What do I need to do? I've never actually had a pet."

"Really? I thought I remembered a hamster."

Briony shook her head.

"You were deprived," Jamie told her.

"Clearly, you don't remember my bedroom. I had every toy ever invented. At least the educational ones that didn't have any sharp edges, or pieces you could swallow, or other hazards," Briony said.

"Like I said, deprived." Jamie stood up and walked to the fridge. She slid a piece of paper out from under a magnet that said "Give Peas a Chance" and handed it to Briony. "This is everything you need to know. I have to warn you, Mac always wants breakfast at seven thirty, and he won't be denied. It's fine if you want to attempt to sleep in, but that's all it will be, an attempt. He eats at seven thirty at night, too, but you can feed him early if you're going out. Early feeding is no problem. And Diogee doesn't really chew. He just kind of vacuums food up. Which means sometimes he vomits. Not that often. But I just don't want you to worry if it happens. Also, Mac is a sneaky little bugger."

Mac gave something that was part meow and part growl. "Yeah, I'm talking about you," Jamie told him. She leaned back and gave him a scratch under the chin. "It's probably safest to

15

shut him in one of the bedrooms before you try to go outside. Not that any room can really contain him, but it will give you a head start. Oh, and Diogee does this thing David calls the Shoulder Popper. If you're walking him, and he sees a squirrel or—"

"You're going to terrify her," a dark-haired man said from the doorway. He looked sort of like Ben Affleck, but younger. "Just remember. You're the alpha. You have the power," he told Briony. Jamie gave a snort. He ignored her. "You provide the food; that means you're in charge," he continued, then grinned and put out his hand. "I'm David, Jamie's husband."

"That still sounds so weird," Jamie said. "So weird, and amazing, and wonderful, and yummy." She walked over to David and put her arm around his waist. Her face glowed when she looked at him, the same way his did when he looked at her.

Briony had to drop her gaze. She was happy for her cousin, but it hurt to see a couple so completely in love. She'd thought she was completely in love with Caleb. Hadn't she been? But how could she have been? You don't leave someone you completely love at the altar. You don't have a panic attack walking down the aisle toward him.

"I'm going to go bring the car around," David said. "Sorry we have to leave when you just got here. When we get back, we'll all go out to dinner," he told Briony before he headed out.

"You shouldn't have been sitting here having tea with me," Briony said, feeling stricken. Her cousin was trying to start her honeymoon. "I don't want you to miss your flight."

"We won't. Don't worry. So, you have the instructions for the pets. The guest room's upstairs to the left. David also made you a list of the best restaurants and stuff in the neighborhood. Even though I think I know LA at least as well as he does. I did a lot of exploring when I first moved here."

"I know!" Briony exclaimed. "I got your book!" Jamie'd done a book with photos of people from all over LA and stories about the jobs they had.

"You did? Aww, that's so sweet," Jamie said. "Here are the keys. Okay, what else? We also left you a list of neighbors who'll be able to answer questions. I'm sure Ruby will call to see if you need anything. If Diogee's too much for you to handle on a walk, Zachary across the street will take him. It's also fine to let him out in the yard. He used to have a dog door. But Mac and a dog door—no. It's been permanently closed." She took a deep breath and rushed on. "You have David's and my cell numbers, right? What else? What else?" Jamie stared around the room.

"Okay, Jamie, you're entering the Lunacy Zone," David said as he returned to the kitchen. "You should have seen her the last few weeks before the wedding; she left a trail of lists wherever she went and was on the phone and the computer constantly—and at the same time— while also talking to herself," he told Briony. Briony hadn't gotten like that. Caleb had found the best wedding planner in the state and she'd taken charge like a general going into battle. "I'm going to go grab our suitcases," David added.

"Can I help?" Briony asked. She just wanted them gone. They'd both been really welcoming, but she hadn't been alone since she started dressing for the wedding yesterday—yesterday! She still had her wedding hairdo and had on the maxi dress she'd been planning to wear on the plane to her own honeymoon. She needed privacy to cry or scream or collapse or something.

"No, thanks. I've got it." David left again.

"My car!" Jamie exclaimed. "I knew I was forgetting something. You should use my car. Bright green Bug. Parked on Gower. That's the street that runs past the fountain in the courtyard. You can see the car from there. No parking in the complex." Jamie pulled a set of keys out of one of the cabinet drawers and put them on the table.

"Great. Thanks. Thanks so much. I'm sorry I showed up just when you're—"

Jamie held her hand out, palm facing Briony. "Stop. I told you your timing is perfect."

"Okay, we're all set, Jam!" David called.

"He calls me Jam sometimes," Jamie said. "He's so cute." She stood and swept Mac into her arms. "Okay, best kitty in the world. You be good for Briony. I'll see you soon, and I'll bring you a present." She buried her face in his fur for a moment and gave him a cuddle. "I'm going to put him upstairs and say good-bye to Diogee, but expect Mr. MacGyver to be back down in a few," she told Briony.

"Okay," Briony answered. She followed Jamie out of the kitchen, then went outside where David was waiting by the car. He'd been just as nice as Jamie had, but what could he think of her after what she'd done to Caleb? She pushed the thought away. Everything wasn't about her. "So a month in Morocco. Wow." Her mom had filled her in on Jamie and David's plans.

"It's all thanks to a movie producer who loves my mojito cupcakes," David explained. "When he heard I was getting married, he offered me and Jamie the use of his vacation place in Essaouira."

"Can I admit I don't know where that is?" Briony asked.

David laughed. "Neither did I. It's on the

Atlantic coast, about a three-hour drive from Marrakesh. We wanted to—"

"Morocco, here we come!" Jamie exclaimed as she rushed out the front door. She practically skipped over to them. "I hope Storybook Court is as wonderful for you as it was for me. Coming here changed my life." Jamie smiled up at David.

Go; just please go, Briony thought. All the happy physically hurt. She should be going on her honeymoon now. With the perfect guy. What was wrong with her?

Finally, the happy—happy, happy, happy—couple was in the car. The car pulled away. Briony watched until it disappeared around the gentle curve at the end of the street.

Then she went inside.

Shut the door.

Locked it.

Closed the round wooden shutters that matched the adorable hobbit hole of a house, blocking out the bright Southern California sunshine.

Then lay down on the sofa.

All she wanted was oblivion. But her mind wouldn't stop spinning, slamming images at her—Caleb smiling at her from beside the altar, her great-aunt MeMe's mouth flying open as Briony started to fall, her parents pretending not to be horribly disappointed in her as they took her to the airport.

Something plopped down on her belly, jerking her out of her mental horror movie. Briony cracked open her eyes. The cat—MacGyver—stared back, then began to purr. It was . . . nice. The cat's warmth radiated into her, and the purr's vibrations somehow relaxed her muscles.

A few minutes later, the dog—Diogee—ambled over and managed to squeeze his ginormous body onto the end of the sofa. A spot of warm drool quickly formed above one of her knees. That shouldn't have been soothing. But it was—gross and soothing. And the sound of his snoring as he drifted off seemed to invite sleep to come to her. She closed her eyes again, grateful to the two animals, even though she didn't deserve even their small comforts. Not after what she did.

CHAPTER 2

The woman's breaths were slow and even. The bonehead was making those wheezy snorts that meant he was asleep, too. But Mac was full of energy. It was time for adventure.

He leapt down to the floor then gave the mutt a claws-in whap on the butt. Diogee came awake with a snort, two long strings of slobber hanging from his mouth. The bonehead was disgusting, but he could be useful. Mac trotted into the kitchen, launched himself onto the counter, and deftly released the latch of Diogee's treat jar. He used one paw to flip out a biscuit. Diogee was already down below, whining for it. No cat would ever whine. Or eat something that smelled like dust.

Mac looked over at the round window that was too high for him to reach, or so his people thought. He aimed, then—slap shot—whapped the biscuit off the counter and onto the floor directly underneath the window. Diogee raced over and lowered his head toward what the dog thought of as a treat. Perfect. Mac jumped onto his head. Diogee jerked his head up, surprised. And alley-oop, Mac got a boost to the window ledge. He head-butted the window open and escaped into the night.

He paused for a moment on the lawn, savoring every scent. Mac loved the familiar smells of home, but he was ready for excitement, and his own backyard wasn't the place to find it. Not tonight. He loped through Storybook Court, past all the houses he'd come to know so well. Most of the humans were smelling content. Thanks to him. He'd helped where he could. It was the duty of a higher creature.

Mac came to an abrupt stop, nostrils twitching. Sardinsies. Sardinsies were close. He began to run, streaking toward the delicious odor. He left the boundary of the complex behind and entered new territory. Unfamiliar scents all called to be investigated. He'd get to them. Later.

For now, all his attention was locked on the smell of the sardines. He zeroed in on the scent and only stopped when he reached a bungalow with walls blocking his way to his beloved. But not for long. The first option Mac noticed for breaking in was the chimney. There might be an easier way, but he wasn't going to wait to find it. He climbed a palm tree near the side of the house that gave him access to the roof. Then it was down the chimney, bracing each forepaw on opposite sides of the tunnel. Same with the back paws. Then one, two, three, four, five, he was in.

The sardines were close, so close. But so was a human. A male sat facing the television, his back to Mac. On the table beside the chair was an open can of the yummies.

Mac went into stealth mode, lowering his body until his belly brushed the carpet. The bonehead would have galloped up and started whining to be given a morsel. Mac didn't beg. Mac took. He crept forward until he was in position, then reared up on his back legs and started to swipe the can off the table.

"Hey! What do you think you're doing?" the man yelled, snatching the beloveds out of reach. Humiliation flooded Mac. He turned and slunk toward the chimney, tail between his legs. Like a dog. He didn't want to remain at the site of his epic fail for another second.

The man let out a sigh. "What the hell. Someone might as well have a good night." The smell of sardines grew slightly stronger. Mac looked back. Two glistening little beauties were cradled in the man's outstretched hand.

He turned, raising his tail halfway up. He pressed his ears back as he assessed the situa-
-tion. The sardines' little eyes seemed to be pleading for him to come closer. The man remained motionless. It could be a trap. But Mac wasn't afraid of traps. There hadn't been one invented he couldn't escape.

A few seconds later, the first oil-slick little

fish was sliding down Mac's throat. He could almost feel its little tail wiggle. Perfection.

"You like that, huh?" the man blah-blahed. "I like 'em too. Especially because I get to eat them with good company. Unlike in the dining room." He ate a sardine as Mac crunched the little bones of his second fish.

Mac was filled with sardine-eating joy, which increased when the man handed over a third. But once he'd swallowed, it occurred to him that the man wasn't feeling equal bliss. Even if he lived a thousand lives, Mac didn't think he'd ever completely understand humans. He pulled in a long breath, fighting to ignore the odor of sardines. Mac let out a little huff. He already had an unhappy person at home to deal with. But when the man handed Mac another sardine, Mac knew he had to find a way to help this human, too. He deserved it.

Nate Acosta stepped into the dining room. He was met with the subtle scents of citrus and bergamot from the aromatic oil vaporizing into the air ducts. His granddad had noticed similar systems in Vegas casino ventilation systems and installed one. He wanted the dining room and the rest of the community center to feel like an elegant luxury hotel and believed scent was as important as décor.

The room looked good. The servers attentive.

The residents and their guests enjoying the feta turkey burgers and peach slaw. He made a mental note to stop in at the kitchen and compliment LeeAnne, the chef. It had been a coup when he'd lured her away from Suncafe.

His gaze snagged on the fiddle-leaf fig in the corner. It was starting to get bushy. He needed to find some time to do some pruning and maybe some notching. July was a good time of year for it. The plant would have had time to build up some good energy resources. He squinted, envisioning the umbrella shape he wanted, as he tried to decide where he wanted to encourage branching.

A burst of laughter drew his attention to a table by the window. Looked like the new tenant, Archie Pendergast, was settling in. He was dining with Peggy Suarez, Regina Towner, and Janet Bowman, three of the most popular ladies at The Gardens. Rich Jacobs, the community's resident limerickist, with the business cards to prove it, was also at the table, scribbling in a small notebook with one hand while munching on the burger held in his other.

"Want to hear my latest?" Rich called to Nate as he headed toward the group.

"Always," Nate answered. He took the empty seat, the one that usually belonged to Gib Gibson. Gib hadn't come to eat in the dining room in three nights. Nate suspected that seeing

27

Peggy flirting with Archie turned Gib's stomach. It was obvious to Nate, if not to Peggy, that Gib had a thing for her.

Rich held up the notebook, cleared this throat, and began to read. " 'There once was a man named Pendergast/Who made all the ladies sigh and gasp/They were all quite keen/To be his fair queen/But he'd ne'er be caught in an iron grasp.' "

Archie ran his hand over his thinning white hair. "You're making me sound like a cake-eater, Rich."

"A what?" Peggy asked, leaning in close to him with a smile that showed off her dimples. Yeah, that was exactly the kind of thing Gib wouldn't want to have to watch.

"You know, a ladies' man," Archie answered. "I was married to the same woman for almost fifty years. She was my one and only."

Peggy, Regina, and Janet gave a synchronized sigh. They were goners. Nate could tell they'd all paid special attention to their looks tonight. Peggy was wearing a skirt Nate was pretty sure was new, full, with a large floral pattern around the hem. Regina's blond bob looked like it had new, though subtle, highlights, and Janet had completely changed her hair color, going from a deep burgundy to a nothing-subtle-about-it bright cherry red with lipstick to match.

Hearing about Archie's devotion to his late

wife had clearly made him an even more romantic figure. It didn't hurt that he was fit for a guy in his late seventies and he took care with his appearance. So far, he'd come to dinner every night in a jacket, pressed white shirt, and bow tie. Unlike, say, Rich, who favored wildly colored track suits with equally wildly colored sneakers.

"I'm so sorry for your loss." Regina reached across the table and put her hand on Archie's arm.

"Reggie, would you like to try this wonderful new lotion I just discovered?" Janet asked, rummaging in her purse. "You were saying this morning that you hated how scaly your skin had gotten." She held out a small tube to Regina, who managed to simultaneously glare at her friend and smile at Archie.

"Applesauce!" Archie said. "Her fingers are as soft as silk."

"Thank you," Regina answered, slowly drawing her hand away. She was smiling at Janet now, a triumphant smile.

"It's so wonderful you had a marriage like that. Poor Regina was married four times," Janet told Archie.

Nate hoped the competition for Archie's attention didn't get to be a problem. There'd been a few times when a new tenant had upset the equilibrium of the place. He'd keep an eye on it. Before Regina could take a swipe back at Janet, he said, "I hear you three ladies are getting up an art show."

"That's right. We want to show off what we've been learning in class," Peggy answered. "We're even getting a local art critic to come in to judge."

Archie wagged his bushy gray brows. "I'm sure there won't be anything prettier in the show than you three ladies." That got blushes and giggles from all three women. Nate was glad he'd included them all.

"Be careful, Grandpa. You don't want to break any hearts."

Nate looked toward the sound of the high, sweet voice and saw Eliza, Archie's grand-daughter, heading toward them. Her white blouse was buttoned all the way up to her throat, and her flowered skirt hit below the knee. She reminded him of an old-fashioned school-teacher, one the boys in class would all have had crushes on.

Peggy tossed her thick silver braid over one shoulder. "Don't worry on my account. I'm always the one who does the heart breaking." She winked at Archie, and he winked back. Something else Gib wouldn't want to see. Nate made a mental note to check on him. If he knew Gib, the man was living on beans, sardines, and any other foods he could eat straight out of a can. Plus a few beers. Skipping meals in the dining room once in a while was no big deal, but he didn't want Gib to make a habit of it.

"Eliza, have a seat." Nate stood up to make room. Archie's granddaughter had been at The Gardens at some point every day since Archie arrived. She had to be pleased to see how well Archie was doing. Moving to a retirement community could be a tough transition, but Archie had very quickly made a place for himself. In a little more than a week, he'd gone on a movie trip, attended a Social Security chat, and been a game-night star.

"Would you mind if I sat next to Grandpa?" Eliza asked Peggy.

"That's not—" Archie began, but Peggy was already moving to the chair Nate had vacated.

"Thank you." Eliza sat, then reached over and straightened Archie's bow tie. He gave her fingers a squeeze.

"I like seeing a granddaughter looking after her grandpa." Rich popped a forkful of slaw into his mouth. "I have three, but they're scattered all over the country. We exchange messages on Facebook and we do FaceTime. But it's not the same. At least my grandson's nearby, over at UCLA. I've offered to pay the girls' way here for a visit, but no go. They're all too busy." A gleam came into his eye. "I think there's a poem in there." He took his little pencil from behind his ear and flipped to a new page in his notebook.

"I think it's wonderful that you use FaceTime and Facebook to stay in touch," Regina commented.

"You almost made me drop my pencil," he told her. "Here I had the impression you didn't think I had one admirable quality."

"You don't have many," she answered. "Those shoes, Rich."

Nate checked out the sneakers. Today's were cheetah print. Purple cheetah print, with twisty no-tie shoelaces in neon orange.

"I think it's great that you've kept up with current technology, too," Eliza said. Rich gave a grunt, already writing in the notebook. "My grandpa won't even own a computer."

"Too dang complicated. And unnecessary," Archie insisted, then used two fingers to smooth down his mustache.

"I could teach you the basics," Peggy volunteered. "I couldn't live without Google."

"Goggle at Google," Rich muttered, erasing a line.

"I might just take you up on that," Archie told Peggy.

"If you want to learn how to use a computer, I'm the one who should teach you," Regina said. "I was a programmer for almost forty years."

"You know too much to make a good teacher," Janet said. "You'd give him way too much information."

"I'll probably need help from all three of you shebas to understand one of those machines," Archie answered.

He knew how to be diplomatic. That was good, Nate thought. He checked the clock. He wanted to hit the kitchen to compliment LeeAnne. He'd discovered compliments were her kryptonite. When he was trying to hire her away from Suncafe, a higher salary or more staff wouldn't do it. What got her was appreciation. "I'm heading out. Have a good night, everyone. Good to see you, Eliza. Have you eaten? I should have asked before. I can get you a plate." Nate encouraged the residents' families to stay for meals.

"No thanks. I can share with Grandpa." She picked up his burger and took a bite.

That was a little weird. But kind of sweet, too. It was probably something that had started when she was a little girl, sharing a PB & J with her grandfather.

"Okay. Hope to see you soon."

"Oh, you will," Eliza said.

Nate gave the group a wave and started across the dining room, shooting a look at the fiddle-leaf fig. His fingers were itching to get to work on it. Maybe he should use some waxed string to coax the branches into place. . . . But there wasn't time to tend to the plant now. He had a ton of paperwork waiting for him.

As soon as he entered the kitchen, he knew he'd timed things wrong. LeeAnne and her crew were getting dessert ready for the servers. Not the time to hand out a few compliments. He sat down at the big table where staff had meals, and without asking Hope put down a plate with a burger and slaw in front of him. A moment later, she returned with an iced tea, lemon, and light sugar, his beverage of choice.

Hope wasn't giving him special boss treat--ment. Her biggest skill was seeing what was needed and doing it. She did a little of everything, from getting orders for the residents who were no longer able to eat in the dining room to meeting with vendors and placing orders. "What's dessert?" he asked.

"Chilled cherry soup," Hope answered. "With fresh tart cherries."

"Also known as Hungarian *meggyleves!*" LeeAnne called from behind one of the kitchen islands.

The servers started taking the bowls out and LeeAnne was speaking to him, so Nate figured it was safe to start the compliments, completely sincere compliments, but ones that he couldn't forget to give if he wanted to keep the kitchen running smoothly. "How did you find fresh tart cherries?" He remembered from a cherry pie crisis that it was almost impossible to get them in SoCal.

"You have to get to the farmers' market before dawn. You have to be fast. You have to be wily. The before-dawn part was a challenge. The rest comes naturally." LeeAnne grinned. "Hope reminded me that it's Gertie's birthday, and I wanted to do it for her. She loves her Hungarian food."

Nate made a mental note to look into giving Hope a pay bump. She deserved it. She was a hard worker with a good attitude and somehow managed to carry almost a full load at UCLA while working almost full-time.

"Hope, would you mind sticking my dinner in a bag? I need to get to my office."

LeeAnne jerked her head toward him, her dark eyes narrowing. "No bag, Hope. If he's planning to eat my food, he's going to give it the attention it deserves."

Rookie mistake, Nate thought. He ran the place, and he didn't have to take orders from LeeAnne or anyone else, but failing to give her food attention was bad management. Who knew how long he'd have to spend getting LeeAnne calmed down if he refused to give her food due appreciation. "Sorry. Just a lot to do. But you're right. I need to take time to savor."

"You bet your sweet butt you do," LeeAnne told him.

Nate wondered if he should discuss the sexual harassment policy with her again. But he'd never heard her say anything like that to anyone else, so he let it slide. He could feel her watching him as he took his first bite of the peach slaw. "Nice little kick," he commented.

"People get older, their taste buds get less sensitive. That's why I do it." He could tell LeeAnne was trying not to smile. Ego stroked. Mission accomplished. He hid a smile of his own. He knew he was the person who had given LeeAnne the info about taste bud sensitivity.

"Hope's going to oversee cleanup. I'm outta here." LeeAnne stripped off her white chef's coat. The lime-green tank top she had on underneath showed off the tattoo of a tree with cooking utensils instead of leaves.

"Have fun. She and Amber are going to Black Rabbit Rose, that magic place," Hope added to Nate.

"I've been meaning to check it out," Nate said.

LeeAnne snorted as she began putting on the silver rings she wore on each finger when she wasn't cooking. "Sure you have. Dude, it's been open for almost two years."

"That long? My problem is when I get off work all I want to do is crawl into bed," Nate admitted. "How do you do it?"

"Because I don't work all day and half the night," LeeAnne told him. She pulled off her bandana and shook out her hair, which started out dark purple up top and gradually lightened to lavender. "I have a life, unlike you. You're twenty-eight and you act like you're one of the residents. Oh, except the residents have much more of a social life than you do." She started toward the door, then whipped back around and pinned Nate with a severe look. "When is the last time you even spoke to a woman?"

"I thought I was speaking—"

LeeAnne pointed at him. "No. You know exactly what I mean."

"Does our newest resident's granddaughter count?" Nate asked. Eliza was around his age, he figured. Pretty. Devoted to her grandfather, and obviously responsible. She was putting in the time to make sure he was in a good place.

"Would you date the granddaughter of a resident?"

She had him. "No."

"Then no."

Nate tried to calculate the last time he'd gone out with anyone. "This place takes a lot of time." It sounded pathetic even to his own ears.

LeeAnne just shook her head and left, letting

the door slam behind her. Hope adjusted the tie holding her ponytail in place. "If it makes you feel any better, I'm twenty, and after I finish my homework tonight all I'm doing is going to sleep."

"Are you getting too many hours? We can make adjustments in your schedule."

"No!" she cried. "No," she repeated more softly. "I need the cash. I have that scholarship, but—" She waved her hands helplessly.

"You can have all the hours you want. Everything runs smoother when you're here," Nate reassured her.

She smiled, a beautiful smile. She was great, responsible, reliable. If Hope were a few years older . . . He wouldn't do anything. Because she was an employee. He grabbed his plate and stood up. "Don't tell LeeAnne," he loudly whispered as he started for the door, making Hope laugh.

Ten minutes later, he was deep into the monthly accounts.

Three hours later, he stretched, trying to loosen up his shoulders. Maybe now he could go back to the dining room and at least make a plan for the fiddle-leaf. Except he hadn't gone through the mail in days. He picked up the first envelope and ripped it open. Somebody trying to sell him a line of senior living fitness equipment. Recycle. He'd upgraded the gym a little more than two years ago. Next. Another letter from that real estate guy who wanted to buy the place, probably to put up some luxury loft apartments. He'd been e-mailing, calling, and sending letters for months. Nate wasn't going to bother answering. He'd already said no. Recycle. And next.

About a half an hour later, he was done with the mail. But if he didn't at least get a start on the monthly letters he sent to each resident's family, he'd never get them all out on schedule. His cell started playing the violin screeches from *Psycho*, his sister's ringtone. He loved her and everything, but she could make him, well, psycho, and the ringtone helped him keep things in perspective.

Nate hesitated. If he answered, it could take hours, hours he needed. But one of the kids could be sick, or—He grabbed the phone. "What's up, Nathalie?" he asked his twin.

"I was talking to Christian, and I asked if he wanted kids," she began.

"Hold up. You've gone out twice with this guy, right?" It was sometimes hard for Nate to keep up.

"Three times. Anyway, I think it's important to talk these things through. And he said no. He didn't want kids. Which I'm okay with. The two kids I have are great. But I wanted to know if he would want his own biological child.

So, we keep talking, and it turns out he doesn't want kids. At. All. And yet, even though I put that I have kids on my dating profile, he wanted to meet. When was he going to tell me this no-kids policy of his? What exactly does he think I should do with my kids?"

Nate rolled his eyes. Wasn't his sister supposed to have a girlfriend she talked over things like this with? Or their mother! That would solve two problems at once. Their mother needed attention. She lived right on The Gardens grounds in the house that had been in their family for generations. Nate stopped by almost every day, but she needed a *lot* of attention. She'd love it if Nathalie wanted to talk relationship issues with her.

"Maybe Mom would be a good person to discuss—" he began.

"Mom?" Nathalie repeated. "*Mom?* I bring up anything about a guy and she starts crying. It's been years since Dad left. You'd think she'd be somewhat over it, but obviously not. Anyway, she thinks now that I have kids I don't need a man for anything."

Nate opened up a Word document. He decided to write to Gertie's son first. He could tell him about the—*what had LeeAnne called the cherry soup?* Muh-*something.*

"What do you think I should do about Christian? Should I confront him? Or should I do some kind of desensitization, where I have him spend little bits of time with the kids that gradually get longer and longer?"

No. Meh-*something.* *Meh—Meh—*"Meggy-leves!"

"You're not working while I'm talking, are you, Nate? This is a crisis. I need your full attention."

He considered pointing out a crisis was a tornado, or a ruptured appendix, or a lost job. But that would add probably forty minutes to the call, with Nathalie getting all teary because no one understood her and her life as a single mom.

Nate shut his laptop, let his head drop back, and closed his eyes. "You now have my complete attention. Continue." He began mentally composing the first letter in his head as his sister rambled. Dealing with Nathalie often meant letting her vent.

And vent.

And vent.

A soft rustling sound made him open his eyes and straighten up. A cat was on his desk. The gold-and-tan tabby looked him in the eye, then batted a pile of invoices onto the floor. He looked at Nate again, then sent his calendar flying.

"Nathalie, I have to go. We can talk more tomorrow. A cat got into my office and he's causing havoc." He hung up before she could protest. When the shrieking violins started up a few seconds later, he ignored the call. He knew he wasn't needed to drive one of the kids to the emergency room or call the fire department or anything like that.

The cat whacked the temperamental miniature rose Nate had been babying to the ground. Soil from the pot spilled over the carpet. *Damn it.* He'd just gotten the pH right in the zone. "Hey. Knock it off!" The cat looked at him, blinked slowly, sent his stapler flying, then escaped through a tear in the bottom of the window screen. A tear that hadn't been there when he was in the office before dinner. He knew he'd have noticed it. That's what a lot of this job was, noticing the small things.

He got up and dealt with the aftermath of the catnado. He was about to sit back down, but what the hell. It was almost ten. He'd go home. Maybe even have a beer. He'd been at the office until after midnight for three days running. He'd catch up tomorrow.

Yeah, he deserved this.

CHAPTER 3

Briony's father tapped her on the nose. "What do we do when we cross the street?" Tap. "What do we do when we cross the street?" Tap. "What do we do when we cross the street?"

The taps got a little harder. The lines on her father's face deepened as his expression grew angry. "And what do we do when we accept a proposal?" Tap. "We." Tap. "Get." Tap. "Married."

This didn't happen, Briony told herself. *I'm dreaming. I need to wake up.*

"We get married!" her father yelled, and her father never yelled. His face had turned a deep red, almost purple. He looked like he was about to have a stroke. Tap, tap, tap.

Wake up, wake up, wake up, Briony thought. She managed to open her eyes and found herself staring up at a striped cat. He was sitting on her chest, tapping her nose with one soft paw. It took her a moment to orient herself. She was in her cousin Jamie's house. That was MacGyver, her cousin Jamie's cat. He gave her nose another tap.

"What?" she muttered. "It can't be time to eat again."

But when she said the word *eat,* Mac meowed. Briony Jamie slowly sat up and grabbed her cell phone off the coffee table. Seven thirty-two. She'd been asleep for almost eleven hours. She'd curled up on the couch again that morning, right after she fed Mac and Diogee breakfast and let Diogee out for a pee break. She put the phone back down. She didn't want to see how many texts and voice mails she had. She knew she had to get in touch with, well, basically everyone, but not now. Not yet. She'd texted her parents that she'd arrived safely as soon as the plane landed. Everything else could wait.

She pushed herself to her feet with a groan. Diogee began to prance in place, starting up a barrage of barks that made her eardrums vibrate. Mac gave a louder meow. "I'm up. I am your pet sitter, and I am going to take care of you." She swooped the cat up in her arms, then let the dog out. She made sure the door was firmly shut, then set Mac back down. He trotted toward the kitchen, tail straight up. That tail felt like a command—*follow me.* She followed him.

"How about turkey and sweet potato?" she asked when she'd opened the cupboard jammed with pet food and treats. Her mouth had a nasty taste. She hadn't brushed her teeth since she arrived, and she never missed brushing. She

44

took a step toward the fridge to get the water pitcher, and Mac let out a yowl of outrage.

"Right. You first. What was I thinking?" She served up his dinner, let Diogee back in, fed him, gave both animals fresh water, got a drink of water herself, then allowed herself to return to the sofa. She couldn't deal with moving to the guest room yet. It felt too far away.

As she stretched out, the emotions from the dream came back to her. Her father yelling at her made her feel sick inside. It hadn't really happened, she reminded herself. Her father and mother had arranged everything after the Incident, neither one giving even a word of criticism. But the emotion from the dream stuck with her. They should have both yelled. All that money wasted. And what she did to Caleb.

She looked over at her cell. She should call them. She should call Caleb. She should call Vi and the rest of her bridesmaids. She should call the wedding planner. She should call— She squeezed her eyes shut. Not now. Not yet.

Once Mac was sure Briony was asleep again, he made a Diogee-assisted escape out the window; then he loped over to the cedar tree and gave it a good scratching to obliterate the dog's stench. He peed everywhere the second he got outside. He hadn't been able to wrap his bonehead around the fact that the yard was Mac's. The yard, the house, the people in the house, the neighborhood, all Mac's. Even Diogee was Mac's, not that Mac wanted him.

Now that that chore was behind him, it was time for Mac to get to work. He had to check in on the Sardine Man. He started toward the man's bungalow, enjoying the mix of smells in the night air. *Oh, Holy Bast.* The Sardine Man was having sardines again. Mac began to run. He could almost feel the little bones crunching between his teeth.

He turned onto the street where the man lived, then forced himself to stop. His mission wasn't to obtain sardines. His mission was to help the Sardine Man. Whiskers twitching with impatience, he considered the possibilities. A present. Jamie didn't always appreciate the gifts Mac brought her. Sometimes she even tried to throw them away. She wasn't all that smart. Fortunately, she had him to look out for her.

The Sardine Man had better taste. Jamie gave Mac a sardine now and then as a special treat, but she never ate them herself. Her nose wrinkled up when she touched them. But the man appreciated them, so it was possible he would appreciate a gift.

Mac turned toward the closest house. He could tell no one was inside. Maybe there'd be something in there the man would like. Mac could have gone down the chimney, but the sardinsies were calling to him, so he used one claw to slice the screen that surrounded the porch. Jamie would call him a bad cat. She didn't understand that being a bad cat was fun. And useful. Yes, even though he loved her, he had to admit she wasn't anything close to his intellectual equal.

Mac wriggled through the slit he'd made in the screen. After checking a few rooms, he found something that might work. He'd given something like it to David once, and David seemed to enjoy it. He hadn't thrown it away. Mac caught the soft object between his teeth. Then he was off to the sardines.

No, he was off to the man. The man was his mission.

Since Mac was acquainted with the man, he went directly to the front door. He rose up on his back legs and batted at the button until he heard a bing-bong.

"I'm not home," the man blah-blahed. Then Mac heard the man's footsteps coming toward him. The door opened a crack. "Oh, it's you." The door opened wider. Mac deposited the gift on one of the man's sneakers. The man picked it up and turned it over in his hands, staring at it.

Job done, Mac headed for the sardines.

Nate rang Gib's doorbell. "I'm not home!" he yelled, but Nate could hear him walking toward the door. Good. Gib was a sociable guy—usually—and if he'd really been planning to leave Nate standing on the front step it would mean things had gotten very bad for him.

"Oh, it's you," Gib said. He opened the door. "Want a beer?"

"Sure." Nate followed Gib to the kitchen. He handed Nate a Schlitz from the fridge, then poured a saucer of milk. "Did you get a cat?" Nate asked.

"I don't know how he got in yesterday. He rang the damn doorbell today. But he hasn't moved in."

"O-kay." Nate headed into the living room with Gib, and sitting in Gib's favorite recliner was a tan-and-gold-striped cat, the same cat who had half-destroyed his office the night before.

"I hope you didn't want sardines. He ate the last one." Gib picked the cat up and sat in his chair. The cat settled down in his lap.

"I don't like to eat anything that can look at me," Nate said. He popped open his beer and grabbed a handful of pretzels.

"He might have licked the salt off some of those," Gib informed him.

Nate didn't know what to do with the pretzels. He ended up shoving them in his pocket as he sat down on the couch across from Gib and that cat. The cat stared at him a long moment, then slowly blinked.

"If you're here to tell me I should be eating in the dining room, it's none of your business."

Gib was sharp. Nate decided to be equally direct. "The food's better. But I get it if you don't want to see Peggy flirting with Archie."

"That's nothing to me." He picked up a pretzel with elaborate casualness and popped it in his mouth.

"You said the cat might have licked those," Nate reminded him.

Gib stopped chewing, hesitated, then swallowed. "Why'd you think I'd care if Peggy's throwing herself at Mr. Bow Tie?"

"I didn't say throwing herself at him; I said flirting with him. And I thought you cared, because, let's see, I have eyes. I see how you look at her. By the way, if you don't water that peperomia in the next couple days it's a goner." Nate made sure all the residents had a plant. He usually would have gone into the kitchen and gotten the water himself, but he wanted to stay with this conversation. Not that Gib was saying anything. He was looking down at the cat, scratching him under the chin until he started to purr.

"You're saying everyone knows? Even her?" Gib finally asked, not looking up.

"Doubtful. I probably look closer. My granddad always knew everything that was going on at The Gardens. It seems like the way the job should be done," Nate answered. "I've

49

seen that cat before," he added, figuring he'd pressed Gib hard enough. Like he'd said, he'd noticed Gib looking at Peggy, but he might have missed how deep Gib's feelings went. "He trashed my office."

The cat gave Nate another slow blink. Like he knew Nate was talking about him.

"My advice? Invest in a few cans of sardines." Gib took a pull on his beer. "I used to look at her back in school. You know we went to high school together." Guess he didn't want to avoid the subject.

"Yeah, you said." That had come up almost as soon as Peggy came to live at The Gardens a few years ago.

"Never talked to her back then. At least now I talk to her. Or I did until Mr. Bow Tie."

"He's the flavor of the month," Nate said. "New people always get a lot of attention. You know that. And I don't think Peggy has stopped talking to you."

Gib shrugged and continued petting the cat.

"What I don't get is you hiding out," Nate told him. "You're cutthroat when you play gin rummy, but you're giving up without even trying on something you actually care about."

Gib jerked his chin up. "I've been trying this whole time."

"Oh. I didn't realize that. So, you asked Peggy out and she turned you down?"

50

"No. Not exactly."

"You called her and she hung up on you?"

"I can tell when a woman's not interested, and she's not interested. I'm fine as a friend, but that's it," Gib answered.

"Maybe she thinks the same thing about you. It doesn't sound like you've done anything to show her how you feel."

"Who are you to be giving romantic advice anyhow?" Gib demanded. "When's the last time you spoke to a woman who wasn't over sixty?"

Et tu, Gibson, Nate thought. "Keeping this place going is more than a full-time gig," he said.

"Bull crap. That assistant manager you've got can handle things. You have good people in all the departments. You don't have to be here every minute."

"Just so you know, I realize that you turned the conversation around to me because you don't want to talk about yourself."

"Just so you know, *I* realize that you're turning the conversation back around to me so you don't have to talk about *yourself,*" Gib countered.

"To avoidance." Nate clicked his beer bottle against Gib's.

Gib nodded, then took a long swallow.

"Look, if you don't want to eat in the—" Nate stopped, his gaze snagged on a shiny piece of cloth on the table next to the sardine can. "Are those . . ." He leaned in for a closer look. "Are those panties?"

Gib nodded. He picked up the panties between two fingers and held them up for Nate to see. A thong. Silk. Pink. Very small.

"Maybe you *do* have the creds to lecture me about women," Nate said, eyes still locked on the thong.

"He brought it." Gib jerked his thumb toward the cat.

"*He* brought it," Nate repeated, staring at the cat now. The cat licked his paw and swiped it across one ear. It's like he was saying, "Yeah, I've got it going on."

Nate got himself back on topic. "Gib, if you don't want to eat in the dining room, that's your business. But let me at least have meals sent over. You can't live on sardines and beer."

"Sardines are all protein," Gib answered. "And beer lowers blood pressure."

"Are you making that up?"

Gib grinned. "I definitely feel more relaxed when I have a beer." The cat rolled onto his back and began kneading the air with his claws.

"How many beers did you give him before I got here?" Nate asked. "He gets any more relaxed, he's going to slide onto the floor."

"Sardines are his alcohol." Gib lightly tickled the cat.

52

"You thinking of taking him in?" Nate asked. He encouraged the residents of The Gardens to have pets. There were documented health benefits. "I read an article that said having a cat is as emotionally satisfying as having a romantic relationship. And since you're not going to pursue anything with—"

"If that's true, you're the one who should take him," Gib interrupted. "I'm an old man. I'm past romance."

"Unlike Mr. Bow Tie," Nate commented.

"Anyway, he has a home. There's a phone number on his collar. His name too. MacGyver," Gib said. The cat sat back up and gave a short meow.

Nate took out his cell. "Somebody might be worried about our buddy. Let's give them a call." He punched in the number as Gib read it aloud. The phone rang several times; then voice mail picked up. When he got the beep, Nate started to leave a message. "Just wanted to let you know that your cat is over at The Gardens. We can keep him here, and you—"

"What?" a woman exclaimed, her voice husky. She cleared her throat. "Did you say my cat?"

"Yeah. MacGyver. Striped. Tan and gold," Nate answered.

"But he's here. He was here. I fell asleep. Mac. Kitty, kitty, kitty? I don't see him!"

"Because he's here," Nate said.

"But he couldn't have gotten out. Kitty, kitty, kitty? Kitty!" She sounded like she was getting hysterical. "All I was supposed to do was watch the cat and dog. How hard is that? I keep ruining things."

"Calm down. He's here. He's fine. He's hanging out, eating sardines over here at The Gardens. The retirement community over on Tamarind Avenue, where it intersects with Sunset."

"I don't know where that is. I just got here. I'm in, I'm in, what is this place called? Storybook Court! Are you anywhere near here?" the woman cried.

"Very close. We back right up to it," Nate told her.

"Give me the address. I'll be right there."

After Nate told her Gib's address and gave her directions, she hung up without another word. "The cat sitter, at least I think that's who she was, is coming over. She didn't know he was gone."

"Not much of a cat sitter."

Five minutes passed. Then ten. Then fifteen.

The cat, MacGyver, stood and stretched, glanced at the empty sardine can, then leapt to the floor. He sauntered over to the door and gave one short meow. "No can do," Gib told him. "Someone's coming to pick you up."

"She should have been here by now," Nate said. "She's only coming from Storybook Court."

MacGyver looked over his shoulder at him and Gib and gave four rapid-fire meows.

Gib laughed. "He thinks we're idiots. He's telling us to open the damn door already. I'll get him some more milk. That'll distract him." He headed to the kitchen. The cat continued to stare at Nate, like he was trying to control Nate with his mind.

"Here you go," Gib said when he returned. He set the saucer of milk next to the cat. MacGyver gave it a sniff, then let out another burst of meows.

"Go on. Drink your milk," Gib told him. MacGyver let out a little huff, then turned around, trotted toward the fireplace—and climbed up the chimney.

"I'll be damned." Gib shook his head. "I'll be damned."

Nate rushed after the cat, crouched down by the fireplace, and used the flashlight app on his cell to survey the interior. "He made it out."

The doorbell rang. Then there was a torrent of knocks. Then the doorbell rang again.

"I'm not home!" Gib called as he started for the door. It flew open before he could reach it, and a woman burst inside.

"Where is he? Where's the cat?" she cried.

Gib stared at her. Nate tried not to stare, but it was impossible. Makeup streaked her face. Her auburn hair was half up in some kind of complex loopy bun kind of thing and half tumbled around her shoulders. Her long sky-blue dress was wrinkled and grass stained, with a tear that went all the way up to her nicely toned thigh. She was missing a shoe, showing perfectly painted pink toenails on one pretty foot.

"The cat . . ." Nate hesitated. The woman was clearly teetering on the edge. He didn't want to just blurt out that the cat was gone.

"The cat's gone," Gib blurted out.

"What?" she exclaimed, her big blue eyes bright. Tears hung from her long lashes but didn't spill down her cheeks. "What? Somebody called and said he was here."

"I called," Nate began.

"And you let him out?" She whipped her head toward him, then took a step back, like she'd been punched. She was only silent for a moment; then she was rushing on again, speaking even faster than before. "You knew I was coming. I have this one thing I'm supposed to be doing. One thing. Watch the pets. And MacGyver's gone? How could he be gone? I got here as fast as I could. I got a little lost. Then one of my shoes came off. And I slipped. And how could you have let him out?"

"He went straight up the chimney," Gib explained.

"What?"

Nate nodded. "Somehow he managed to climb it. He's probably on his way home."

"Probably? Probably!" she yelled. "You're telling me probably." She whirled around and raced out the door. "MacGyver! Kitty, kitty, *kitty!*"

"I wouldn't come to that," Gib commented. "And that cat won't, either. Too smart."

Nate started to follow her. Just what he needed, another crazy female to deal with, as if his sister and his mother weren't enough. But before he could reach the door, his cell rang. He glanced at the screen. His night manager. "Talk to me," Nate said.

"We've got a problem over here at the community center," Amelia told him. "Big problem. I'm talking titanosaur *Argentinosaurus huinculensis*'s big brother big. And that sucker was more than ninety-six metric tons. You need to get over here. Now."

CHAPTER 4

Y ou. You! You're here." Briony shook her head as she stared at MacGyver, who was curled up in the armchair next to the sofa. She began walking through the house. Back door shut and locked.

She paused. There was a window ajar! But it was way too high even for an incredibly agile kitty to reach. She continued through the house, not seeing any possible escape route. But MacGyver had gotten out somehow.

Briony stepped into the master bath. The window was closed and latched. She turned around and froze, catching her image in the large mirror. "Oh, god." She took a deep breath, then flicked on the light to get a better look. "Oh, my god."

The beautiful maxi dress she and her best friend and maid of honor, Vi, had spent a full day shopping for was a mass of wrinkles—not surprising, since she hadn't taken it off since she changed out of her wedding gown. It was grass stained, with a rip that went up so high it was almost obscene from when she took that spill.

And her hair. Her hair! The elegant updo that

had taken her months to choose was a disaster. Part of it mashed to her head, still up. Part of it down, in tangles. Her lipstick was long gone, but her mascara was still there, under her eyes instead of on her lashes. She was a wreck.

Her legs went wobbly and she sat down on the edge of the tub. She was a complete wreck. It had to stop. First, a shower. She began deconstructing the do, placing the pearl pins beside the sink. Once that was done, she went and got her bathrobe out of her suitcase. That was something else she needed to do—unpack. But first, the shower. No first, teeth. She returned to the bathroom and brushed her teeth three times, then stripped and got in the shower. She washed her hair, conditioned it twice to help get out the tangles, then stood under the stream of hot water until it started to turn cold.

She got herself dressed in the skinny black pants and striped shirt that all the magazines said would be perfect, so Audrey Hepburn, for a Paris honeymoon. She dried her hair and pulled it back, put her old clothes and toiletries away, then returned to the mirror and studied herself again. Much better. She could now go outside without embarrassing herself. She just had to hope she never saw either of those two men again. Especially the one with those brown eyes so dark they—

What was she thinking? She didn't want to see

either of those two men again, because they'd both witnessed her insane behavior. Both of them.

Okay. Getting herself looking presentable was only a baby step. Now she needed to . . . She needed to . . . What was the next step? The answer hit her like a slap. Apologize to Caleb. She hadn't even spoken to him since she went down on the way to the altar. She'd let her parents make the apologies to the guests. They must have said something to Caleb, too. But who knew what.

Yes, that was definitely the next step. Right? Yes. Apologize, and return the ring. It was inside the zippered compartment of her purse. She'd taken it off during the flight. Slowly, she formulated a plan. The ring needed to be insured. The post office was closed. But there had to be a FedEx. She'd Google it and go. She'd put a note in the package. She wasn't ready to actually speak to Caleb. It was the right thing to do, but she couldn't, not yet. So that was the plan.

She nodded at herself. She nodded again. She nodded a third time. It was the right decision. She could do this. She made herself go get her cell and look up the closest FedEx. Only a couple blocks away. She could walk it. She picked up her purse, checked to make sure the ring was inside, which of course it was.

Briony stood motionless, purse clutched in hand. *Come on. Next step. Leave the house. Walk to FedEx.* "Okay, guys. I'm going out for a little," she told MacGyver and Diogee. Diogee started whining with excitement. "Alone. This time." She had to take the dog for a walk too. But that was farther down the list. "Please be here when I get back," she added to the cat.

Remembering Jamie's instructions, she put him in the guest room before she tried to go out the front door. Once she was outside, she locked the door behind her, then stood motionless again. *Plan. Follow the plan,* she told herself. And began walking. Just putting one foot in front of the other. This much she could handle.

She spotted the FedEx/Kinko's office on the corner, right where Google said it would be. She went inside and took a priority envelope from the small counter. Next step. Fill out a label. Her fingers shook as she began to write Caleb's name. She gave her hand a couple hard shakes and continued. The writing didn't look great, but it was legible.

Keep going, she told herself. She had to take two deep breaths, breaths that came out quivery, before she could remove her engagement ring from her purse. She wrapped it in a piece of Kleenex from the little pack her mother always stuck in her purse when Briony wasn't looking, then slid it into the envelope. Now the note. Why hadn't she written the note before she left? This wasn't the place to write a real apology, a real explanation. Finally, she just scrawled the words *I'm so sorry* on a piece of scratch paper left on the counter, added it to the envelope, sealed it, and brought it to the front counter.

"Are you okay?" the guy asked.

Briony nodded, without looking at him. He sounded nice, and she was afraid if she tried to speak to someone who was the littlest bit kind she'd end up sobbing. This was . . . She felt like . . . It was like she was walking down the aisle again. Except instead of everything going wobbly, her bones felt like brittle sticks of ice, like they could just snap, snap, snap, and she'd hit the ground. And never get up.

"You don't look okay," the guy said.

"How much?" Briony managed to get out.

"Nine-ninety."

She shoved a twenty at him and bolted, ignoring his calls about her forgotten change. She needed to get inside. She needed to be someplace where she could lock the doors and shut off the lights and breathe. She needed to put all her focus on breathing.

Few blocks, she told herself. *You're just a few blocks from Jamie's. Keep moving. Keep on moving. Step, step, step, step.*

She turned the corner and Storybook Court

came into view. She could hear the fountain in the courtyard. *Not far. Not far.* She used all her will to keep going until she reached it. Then she collapsed down on the stone edge. The palm trees wavered in her vision. Her head felt like a balloon tethered to her body by a thin string.

Briony pressed her hands against her chest. It was rising and falling. Her lungs were working. Even if it didn't feel like it, she was getting the oxygen she needed. She squeezed her eyes shut and kept her hands in place. She was breathing. All she had to do was sit here, continue to breathe, and at some point she'd be able to walk again. She'd get herself back to Jamie's. She'd be okay.

Breathein. Breatheout. Breathein. Breatheout. Breathein. Breatheout.

Too fast! Too fast! Slow it down, Briony ordered herself. But she couldn't.

Breatheinbreatheoutbreatheinbreatheout-breatheinbreatheout.

"Could you give me a hand with these?"

Breatheinbreatheoutbreatheinbreatheout-breatheinbreatheout.

"Do you mind giving me a hand? I love Storybook, but not being able to park is a bother. So could you give me a hand?"

Briony felt like she was getting the words on a delay. No, not the words. The meaning of the

64

words. Someone was asking her for help. She slowly opened her eyes. A woman with short black hair streaked with gray was standing in front of her. She held bags of groceries in both hands and had a couple bolts of fabric jammed under one arm.

"I'm Ruby, a friend of David and Jamie's. And you're Briony, Jamie's cousin, right?" Ruby held out one of the grocery bags and Briony found herself reaching for it.

"Briony. Jamie's cousin. Right," Briony was able to say.

"Jamie texted me that you'd be staying with Mac and Diogee. I was planning to give you a call once you'd had time to settle in," Ruby said. "My place is really close. If you could just carry that." Ruby started off. And Briony found herself following the woman. They stopped in front of what looked like a fairy-tale witch's cottage, complete with a large black wrought-iron spider as the door knocker.

Ruby unlocked the door and waved Briony inside. "Just dump it on the kitchen table. Kitchen's to your left."

Briony again found herself following Ruby's instructions. Somehow when she wasn't paying attention her breathing had slowed down a little.

"Sit, sit," Ruby told her after Briony put down the groceries.

Briony sat. "I'm sorry."

"For what? Helping carry stuff?" Ruby answered as she put down the material and the other bag of groceries. She grabbed a dish towel and ran water over it, then wrung it out.

"For—" Briony waved her hand at herself.

"That's nothing to apologize for." Ruby handed her the damp dish towel. "Put it on the back of your neck. Jamie mentioned you'd had a panic attack recently. I'm assuming that's what's happening. Am I right?"

Briony nodded. "I . . . yes." The family doctor had checked Briony out after she passed out going down the aisle. The doctor was at the wedding, so she was able to do it right away. She said there wasn't anything physically wrong with Briony and had explained that a panic attack could explain all the symptoms Briony had experienced in the church.

"Try the cloth. David used to get panic attacks. He said this helped."

"David?" She'd only spent a few minutes with Jamie's husband, but it was hard to picture him collapsing with his heart trying to break free from his chest, all because of anxiety.

"Cloth," Ruby urged. Briony pressed the dish towel against the back of her neck. The little strip of coolness did help. She closed her eyes and focused on it.

"Thanks," Briony said without opening her

eyes. Her breathing was almost back to normal. "Thanks," she repeated. "I should be able to go in a minute."

"Nuh-uh. You owe me. I have coffee with Jamie almost every day and I'm already missing her. You have to at least have something to drink and visit a little. I'm thinking lemonade. Lemonade in a tall glass is perfect for a July night."

Briony opened her eyes. Ruby was smiling at her and it was impossible not to smile back. "I can drink lemonade."

"Good." Ruby opened the fridge and pulled out a pitcher. She took two frosted glasses from the freezer.

"David had panic attacks?" Briony asked. She felt like she should say something, and that was the first thing she thought of.

"Just for a stretch, when he and Jamie were first getting together," Ruby said. "It's like a part of him didn't ever want to fall in love again after Clarissa. Hence the panic attacks when he started to feel something for Jamie."

"Clarissa?"

"David's first wife. I just assumed Jamie had told you about her when she talked about David. And I know she had to have talked about David. Talking about David is one of her favorite things." Ruby hummed a little of the *Sound of Music* tune as she set the lemonade on the table. "Jamie actually reminds me of Maria a little. Don't tell her. No, go ahead. She'd probably love it. She just dives into things in a joyful Maria-the-hills-are-alive kind of way."

"We haven't been in touch much since we were kids. Just Christmas cards, Facebook posts," Briony admitted. "And she and David had to leave almost as soon as I got here. It was a last-minute plan." Briony wondered how much Jamie had told Ruby. She'd told her about the panic attack. Had she told her Briony had left her fiancé standing at the altar? She felt her face flush, hating the thought of Ruby knowing what a bad person she was. She took the cloth from the back of her neck and ran it over her cheeks.

"Want me to rewet it for you?" Ruby asked.

Briony shook her head. "It helped, though. I really am feeling much better." As much better as she could expect to feel. She'd managed to send back the ring at least. But she owed Caleb so much more. Thinking about him sent her heart rate back up. She had to get her brain somewhere else, fast. "MacGyver got out somehow," she blurted. "He's back. I don't know how he got in. Or out. But at least he's home."

"MacGyver. We're all lucky that cat hasn't learned how to use duct tape," Ruby said.

"What?"

"Never mind. I'm not surprised he got out.

MacGyver is always getting out of places. And into other places." Ruby leaned closer, dark eyes full of concern. "Is that what started the attack? Freaking out about Mac?"

"No. I was upset. Really upset. But nothing like how you found me. That was . . . I just sent my . . . fiancé, my ex-fiancé . . . his ring. . . ." And her breath was starting to come in pants again. She tried to take a sip of the lemonade but couldn't.

"Wonder where Mr. MacGyver got to this time. Jamie probably didn't get to tell you about all the adventures that kitty's had. He created total pandemonium in the court when he and Jamie first moved it, stealing stuff from everyone."

Getting back to the subject of MacGyver helped. Which was probably why Ruby had brought him back up. "He was at one of the bungalows in The Gardens. That retirement community near here," Briony said. Ruby nodded. "I got a call from the man who runs the place. But when I got over there, Mac was already gone. They said he'd climbed up the chimney. Jamie said he could climb up a chimney, but that seems impossible."

"*Impossible* is not a word that applies to that cat," Ruby told her. "I'm curious. Was the owner of the place cute?"

"Cute?" Briony repeated.

"Yeah. The guy who called you about Mac. Was he cute?"

"Yes," Briony answered, without hesitation. Those almost-black eyes. The cleft in his chin. The longish dark brown hair. Great shoulders. Nose that looked like it might have been broken once. When she'd first looked at him, she'd actually taken a step back. It's like he'd thrown a pheromone bomb at her.

Ruby laughed. "Mac's a matchmaker. Did you know he got Jamie and David together? You'd better watch out. He's probably planning . . ." Her words faded away; then she reached out and put her hand on Briony's wrist. "You just went pale. That was incredibly insensitive of me. I wasn't thinking."

"It's okay," Briony told her. "So, I guess Jamie told you about where and when I had the first panic attack."

Ruby nodded. "Because she was worried about you. She wanted me to check in on you. Sorry again about making that joke about Mac playing matchmaker. I was thinking I was just making some nice, safe kitty chitchat, then *bam!*" She smacked her hands together.

"It's really okay. I'll have to remember to tell Mac that matchmaking for me is pointless. I already had the absolutely perfect guy. And I left him at the altar." At least she seemed to have completely recovered from the panic attack. She was talking about Caleb without palpitations.

"Have you considered that your panic attack didn't have to do with him?" Ruby asked slowly. "Maybe it was just wedding stress. Planning a wedding is intense."

"I had a planner. And my parents. And Caleb. I hardly had to do anything," Briony answered. "And it was . . . it was seeing Caleb there. Waiting for me. That's what started it. And even now, thinking about him, all I feel is bad. For what I did to him. But I don't feel like I want him back. I could barely even write him a note without having a meltdown. Actually, I guess a meltdown is exactly what I did have." She spoke faster and faster, saying things to this stranger she hadn't said to anyone. "I can't explain it. Like I said, he's perfect. Everybody thinks so. He's smart; he's handsome; he's considerate; he has a good job; my parents like him; my friends like him. Who has a panic attack when they're about to marry someone perfect? What you told me about David's panic attacks made sense. But mine? No. Caleb's family is perfect, too. They were so great, so welcoming. I don't know what's wrong with me. Something has to be wrong with me."

"I don't think anything's wrong with you," Ruby told her.

"No, there is," Briony insisted. "Rejecting

someone like Caleb? If you knew him, you'd think I was crazy. Crazy and heartless. Not that he won't find someone else. Someone better."

"When I first started college, I was a biology major," Ruby said. "And I know that sounds random, but there is a point to it. I had this idea that I wanted to cure cancer or something like that. It was all really vague in my mind to be honest, but I don't think I even realized that. Anyway, when I had about a year left until I graduated, I started getting these headaches. Really intense. Really often. It's not like I was having an especially hard time with my classes, well, except for physics. Anyway, to cut to the chase, I switched my major to theater, and they went away. I ended up working in movies, first doing makeup and now doing set decoration. Biology is the perfect major for a lot of people. Just not me."

"But changing majors isn't like leaving someone at the altar. It didn't hurt anyone. Or cost a ton. Or—"

"Would it have been better if you realized earlier you didn't want to marry what's his name—Caleb? Yes. But you didn't. All you can do is go from here."

Briony opened her mouth to protest. But what Ruby said made sense. It's not like she'd been *trying* to hurt Caleb. Or cost her parents all that money. But that still left one big question.

What did going from here mean?

Nate stepped out into the warm July night, eyes streaming, nose and throat and lungs burning. He yanked off the surgical mask and pulled in a long, slow breath. His brain was already clicking. The carpets, drapes, and furniture of the library and TV room would need to be fumigated. Replaced if that didn't work. He also—

Amelia joined him on the front steps of the community center and handed him a bottle of water. He drained half of it, then tried to speak but started coughing instead. "Keep drinking. I couldn't stop coughing, either, when I first came out. And you were in there a lot longer than I was," she said.

He finished the bottle, then tried again. "I couldn't find anything that could be making that smell. We need to get the Scentsations people over here."

"Already called them. I told them an enormous, lactose-intolerant giant drank a few dozen bean-and-Brussels-sprouts milk shakes in the place, then farted. A lot." Amelia shook her head. "Not even a chuckle. I was trying to cheer you up, boss."

"Sorry. There is nothing funny about that reek."

"True that. The Scentsations techs aren't going to be able to get over here until tomorrow morning. I told them it was an emergency, but no go."

"Okay." Nate took a few moments to organize his thoughts. "I want to get temporary replacements for the rooms set up before anyone shows up to use them tomorrow. I'm thinking the bungalow next to Gertie's since it's empty. And we need to get signs up. I don't want anyone even going in that hallway."

"On it."

"Let's also get the furniture and drapes hauled out to the back patio. We may as well not let them soak in any more of the stench, even though they probably can't smell any worse. We'll deal with the carpets later."

"Close the patio, right?" Amelia asked.

"Definitely. Get it roped off. There's the gazebo, and the benches in the garden will work for anyone who wants to gather outside." He raked his hair away from his face. "I don't think there's anything else we can do tonight."

"You want me to get Bob in here?"

Nate shook his head. He didn't see any reason to drag the head of maintenance away from home tonight. "I'll have him check the rooms over in the morning. See if there's anything I missed."

"I'll stop by Aldine in the morning and grab

74

some of the books from the sale racks on the sidewalk and see what else I can get for cheap," Amelia offered.

"You're off," Nate reminded her.

"So?"

"Put in for overtime."

"Will do, Captain, my captain. And I won't even make you give me hazard pay for the giant, giant farts."

This time, he did laugh. Amelia had been at The Gardens for more than twenty-five years. She'd played hide-and-seek with him and Nathalie on the grounds when they were kids. He'd thought it might be hard transitioning into being her boss, but she'd made it easy. A few people had left when he'd taken over, thinking he wouldn't be able to handle it. Not that he blamed them. He'd barely been out of high school. But most had stuck with him.

Mac stretched out on Diogee's pillow. It smelled like the bonehead, and his own pillow was more comfortable and smelled a lot better. But it had been fun to make Diogee let him have it. All he'd had to do was stare at him. Diogee had tried to stare back. Mistake. Mac had never lost a staring contest. Diogee'd given up almost as soon as he started and lumbered away.

He considered finding another game to play with the dog, but Diogee wasn't enough of a challenge. Mac decided to go out. This time he used the bathroom window. The latch was easy to whap open, and once it was, Mac took the tree down to the yard. He hesitated, whiskers twitching. A foul stench was keeping him from gathering as much intel from the air as he usually did. He felt the fur on his back rise. It was the odor of something dead, but more than that. The scent of death was mixed with a sweet, rotten smell, something that didn't come from the dead thing. It was too recently dead for that.

Whatever the source, Mac knew it was nothing he couldn't handle. But the scent was coming from the direction of the Sardine Man. He didn't have the same skills Mac did, so Mac decided to check on him.

He set off, loping across the complex. As he got closer, he was able to find the scent trail of the Sardine Man. There was no fear in it. He wasn't in need of a rescue. But he might need a new present. He'd barely looked at the one Mac brought him last time.

Mac made a stop at the house next to the Sardine Man's. He could hear running water inside. The human was in the shower. Humans, would they ever learn that their tongue was designed to keep them clean?

He slipped inside using the tear he'd made in the screen. The stench wasn't as strong in the house, but it still filled Mac's nose with every breath as he prowled through the house, searching for something . . . But what exactly?

He spotted something fuzzy on the dresser and leapt up. He loved fuzzy things. His Mousie was very fuzzy. This thing was smaller than Mousie, but it felt a little like his toy. He gave it a whack with his paw. It flew all the way across the dresser and onto the floor. *Nice.*

Mac retrieved the fuzzy and brought it to the Sardine Man's house. There was no sound of movement inside. Just the sound some humans made when they were sleeping. And some dogs, like Diogee. He decided to use the chimney entrance so he wouldn't wake his friend. He left the fuzzy near the coffee machine. Jamie always went straight for it—after she fed him.

Satisfied, Mac started for home. He hoped Diogee had decided to reclaim his pillow. It would be fun to make him give it up again.

The next morning, Nate got to the community dining room as soon as it opened for breakfast. For the next few hours, he made a point of stopping by the tables to update the residents on the situation.

"Here's the deal," he said when he stopped beside Peggy and the usual group. Eliza was sitting next to Archie, and Gib's usual chair was empty again. "The library and the TV lounge will probably be closed all day."

"We heard. And smelled. But it did give me a blast of inspiration." Rich cleared his throat and began to read from his notebook. " 'There once was a place called The Gardens/That smelled so sweet no heart would harden/Then it started to stink/Causing people to drink/And now we're all contemplating arson.' " He shut the notebook. "Still needs work."

"Good one," Nate said. "Bob brought in a few industrial fans first thing this morning, and a tech from Scentsations, the company that we use to pump aromatic oils through the vents, is here checking for defects in the system."

"Do you have any idea what's causing the smell?" Eliza asked, a tiny furrow forming between her eyebrows. "I'm worried that it might be some kind of toxin."

Archie patted her hand. "Don't worry, honeybuns. I haven't been in either of those rooms since that stench started up."

"Honeybuns?" Janet raised her eyebrows. "Is that what you call your granddaughter?" Nate had been wondering that himself.

"Not honeybuns, *honeybun*," Eliza told her.

"Ooops. I misheard." Janet smiled at Archie. "That's so cute."

"We haven't figured out the source of the smell yet. But I'll give everyone an update as soon as we do," Nate told Eliza. "In the mean-time, we're going to use the empty bungalow next door to Gertie's place as a temporary library and TV room."

"I wonder if something like 'making nose hair kink' would be a better line than the one about drinking," Rich mumbled, gnawing on his pencil.

"The situation is nothing to joke about," Regina snapped.

"All those beautiful books." Peggy sighed. She was in all of The Gardens' book groups. "I don't think it will be easy to get the smell out of them."

"I'm working on finding a place to get them fumigated," Nate reassured her. Well, he was about to work on it. "In the meantime, Amelia's going to a used bookstore to get us some replacements."

"I wasn't joking," Rich said to Regina. "I was commenting on the situation through my art."

"Art. That's being a little too generous, isn't it?" Regina asked. "It's like calling that, that *sweat suit* proper attire for a grown man." She smoothed her honey-blond bob. Not that it needed it. Nate didn't think he'd ever seen Regina with a hair out of place or wearing anything that wasn't expertly tailored and tasteful.

"I like color. I like pizazz," Rich said. He held

out one leg so he could admire the green-and-teal stripe running down the leg of his yellow track pants. "I consider this the kind of outfit Picasso would design."

"Picasso gives me a headache," Regina answered. "If I was going to wear something designed by a painter it would be Monet."

"Boring," Rich shot back. "But it would be an upgrade on the beige on beige on beige you usually wear."

"This is *not* beige." Regina fingered one of the pearl buttons of her sweater set. "It's champagne pink."

It actually looked beige to Nate, too, but he wasn't going there. "Looks like you've all finished," he said to the group. "Why don't we take a walk over to the bungalow and you can see the setup? We have tea and coffee, and the daily papers are there."

"I'm more worried about health risks than beverages and reading materials," Eliza said.

"Before we reopen the rooms, I'll have the air quality tested." He hadn't been planning to, but it would make extra sure everyone at The Gardens was safe.

Eliza toyed with the chain of the silver heart locket studded with diamonds she always wore, then gave a reluctant nod. "I suppose that will be all right."

"She's always looking out for me, and she's

no Dumb Dora," Archie said, giving his grand-daughter's waist a squeeze.

Nate's cell buzzed, and he glanced at the text that had come in. "That was from Amelia. She's already rounded up some books. Shall we go over to the bungalow? I know you two are going to be needing your crossword fix," he told Rich and Regina.

"Do you do crosswords, Archie?" Janet asked, fluffing her extremely bright red hair. "Those two"—she nodded toward Rich and Regina—"have a competition every morning to see who can do the one from the *New York Times* the fastest. In pen. Maybe you and I could try it."

"If Archie wants competition, he should go against me," Regina said. "You should play against Rich. It'll give him the chance to win for once."

"Does this kind of thing happen often?" Eliza inquired, falling into step beside Nate as the group headed out. "You had a very good rating in *U.S. News and World Report*. Do you know how often the residences are reevaluated?"

"Every year," Nate answered. "And while we do have minor issues with maintenance once in a while, this kind of thing isn't at all common."

"Not at all," Peggy chimed in. "I've been here for three years, and Nate keeps everything in wonderful condition. I love it."

"And I already love it, too," Archie told her, looking at her with such intensity Nate noticed that the tips of her ears had gone pink. Maybe it was a good thing Gib had skipped breakfast.

Nate appreciated Peggy jumping to defend The Gardens, but he didn't think Eliza was completely satisfied. She was definitely going to be a family member who needed a lot of attention. But he'd rather have someone like her, who was a micromanager, than have a resident whose family had almost no contact.

He opened the door to the bungalow. Amelia had pulled some furniture in from storage and had a bookcase halfway full. Multiple copies of several newspapers lay on the table in front of a sectional sofa. "Already looking good," he said. He started for the kitchen to check on the coffee and tea, but his cell started to play "Ghostbusters," his mom's ring, just because she had a lot of things she needed help with—and "who ya gonna call?"

"Hi, Mom. What's up?" he asked.

"There's someone lurking outside the house," she said, her voice tight.

Nate wasn't worried. His mom got lonely, and he understood that. He just wished instead of creating some kind of crisis, she'd simply invite him over for dinner. *No, she doesn't create them,* he reminded himself, trying to be fair. His mother truly believed it when she told him there were raccoons in the basement. She believed it when she told him she smelled something electrical burning. And now she believed there was someone outside her house.

"Lurking?" he repeated, already heading toward the closest exit.

"Yes!" she hissed. "I can see him right now. Under the jacaranda tree."

"Are you sure it's not just tree shadows?" he asked as he stepped outside.

"I'm sure! Are you coming?"

"Already on the way. We can stay on the phone until I get there." He should be at her place in less than two minutes. She lived on the grounds, in the house where he grew up, the house his great-grandfather built. "Is he still there?" Nate picked up his pace. Her fear was real, even if he was sure there was no reason for it.

"I . . . I think so," she replied. He could picture her rubbing the spot where her wedding ring used to be. She'd stopped wearing it when his dad took off, but even after all these years, she still fingered the place when she was feeling nervous.

"Don't worry. Almost there. I can see the house." He jogged straight over to the jacaranda tree. Nobody there.

But somebody had been. There were shoe

prints under the jacaranda between the low stone wall and the base of the tree.

"Well?" his mother called from the open front door.

"I don't see anything to worry about!" he called back. Then he used one foot to rub out the shoe prints he'd found. He wasn't going to terrify her by telling her the truth.

"I'm going to have security make some extra rounds around the place, just to be on the safe side," he added as he walked up the porch steps. "Make sure you turn on the security system, okay?" For someone as nervous as she was, she forgot to set the alarm as much as she remembered.

"Can you stay for a little while?" his mother asked. "I'll make hot chocolate."

"Great." He'd never been able to tell her that sometime when he was a teenager he started finding the drink way too sweet, especially with the gobs of marshmallows he'd loved as a kid. And it was never something he'd wanted in July.

She smiled at him. "They had the colored marshmallows at the store this week. I know they're your favorite. I bought the jumbo bag."

"Thanks, Mom." He was struck, as he often was, by how much younger she was than most of the residents at The Gardens. Not even sixty, but Peggy, Janet, and Regina were so much more active than she was, even though they were all seventy-something. They were always out and about. Still interested in everything. Still interested in romance. His mom went to the store once a week, and once a month she went with Nathalie to get their hair done. That was about it.

His cell played the ringtone he'd chosen for Bob, the head of the maintenance crew. "Got to take this," he told his mother. "I'll be right in." She nodded and headed for the kitchen. "Any news, Bob?" he asked when he picked up the call.

"Want good or bad?" Bob asked. He always acted like he had to pay for every word he used.

"Bad," Nate immediately answered. He always wanted the bad news first. Sometimes bad required immediate action.

"Scentsations guy found the problem."

"Great. And?"

"Parts of a dead skunk and some rotten food jammed in the boxes where we put the oil."

And then the system did its job and pumped the dead skunk smell into the library and TV lounge. Sabotage. It was the only possibility. "I'll be right over."

First evidence that someone had been watching his mother's house. Now this. What the hell was going on at The Gardens?

CHAPTER 5

B riony cracked open the front door and peered inside to make sure Mac wasn't poised to make an escape. The cat wasn't in sight, so she swung the door wide, and Diogee started yanking her toward the kitchen. Briony managed to shut the door with her foot, then trotted after the big dog. He stopped in front of his biscuit jar.

"I guess you worked up an appetite." Briony unhooked his leash and gave him a treat.

Okay, one thing off the to-do list she'd made yesterday when she got home from Ruby's. She'd walked the dog. More like he'd walked her, but it still counted. She pulled out her cell and scanned the list. She'd chosen the easiest first. Next up, her parents. She'd texted them to say she'd arrived safely, but she owed them a call. Well, a FaceTime. They liked to see her when they talked. And she looked absolutely presentable. She had on the black pants and striped shirt again, but she'd touched them up with an iron. Her hair was twisted into a chignon, and she had done the makeup basics, plus some extra concealer to cover the dark smudges under her eyes. She'd also doused her eyes with Visine, so she wouldn't look like she'd spent half the day yesterday crying. She was ready.

When the connection was made, her mother launched into a series of questions, without leaving any space for Briony to reply. "Are you all right? Are you okay being alone? Have you talked to Caleb? Have you talked to anyone from the wedding?" She sucked in a breath, then continued. "Should I come out there? I don't know what we were thinking sending you off someplace by yourself. If your cousin was home, that would be different. But I hate thinking of you all alone, after . . . what happened. I really think you need someone to look after you. What if you faint again? What if—"

"Mom, I'm fine," Briony interrupted. "Truly."

"That's impossible. No one would be fine after . . . what happened. I know we had the doctor look you over, but I wonder if you need to see someone else. Passing out like that . . . Maybe you need an MRI or a CAT scan. I can find out—"

"I'm fine," Briony repeated.

"Have you had any symptoms since you arrived?" her mother pressed.

"None," Briony told her. It was easier to lie when her mother was all the way across the country.

"Still, James, what do you think? Don't you

think a second opinion would be the smart thing to do?" Briony's mother asked.

Her dad looked back and forth between Briony and her mother, like he was deciding whose side to take. "It couldn't hurt," he finally said.

"I'll look into it," Briony replied, because otherwise they'd be discussing the possibility for the next hour. And actually, maybe it wasn't a bad idea. Maybe she'd passed out because of some kind of vitamin deficiency. Or maybe—

But in her gut, she knew the truth. Ruby was right. Her body had known what her brain wouldn't accept. Marrying Caleb wasn't the right decision for her, even though her parents and friends thought they were perfect together. Even though Caleb was, in fact, perfect.

"Let's talk about the gifts," Briony said. Dealing with the gifts was also on her to-do list. "I was thinking I could write notes to everyone and send the notes to you. If I do that, could you arrange for the presents to be returned?"

"Already taken care of," her father assured her. "Your mom wrote the notes, and the gifts are on their way back to the guests."

"Oh. Well, thanks. Thanks, both of you." She hesitated. "What did you say in the notes, Mom?"

"Just that you'd been doing so much before the wedding that you'd gotten run-down and dehydrated—which I still think could be true— and fainted. I said since we weren't sure when the wedding would be rescheduled, we'd decided to return the gifts."

"But I never said the wedding would be rescheduled," Briony protested. "I've already returned the ring to Caleb."

Briony could hear her mother's breath catch. "You can't possibly know what you want to do right now. You need time to rest and recover. And to make sure there isn't a medical issue we need to deal with, other than getting so run-down."

"I actually wasn't run-down. Caleb and the wedding planner, and both of you, did—"

"Don't make any decisions right now," her mother said. "And don't worry. Your father and I will take care of everything."

"Your mom's right." He leaned closer to the computer screen, as if that would bring him closer to her. "Right now, you just need to take care of yourself."

After giving several more reassurances that she would see a doctor, Briony ended the call. She wished her mother would have waited before she wrote notes to everyone, but at least the gift situation was handled.

Next up, she needed to get in touch with Vi. Her best friend since fourth grade and maid of honor had been bombarding her with texts and voice mails, but Briony hadn't been able to make herself read or listen to them.

Her heart began to palpitate a little as she

considered what to say about the whole wedding fiasco. Finally, she simply texted "Hi."

Vi replied almost instantly.

OMG. Where are you? Your parents wouldn't tell.

LA. Pet sitting at cousin's place.

Caleb's freaking out. Your parents didn't tell him, either. WHAT HAPPENED??

Panic attack. Mom insists I was dehydrated, run-down, possibly with a tumor. But actually total panic attack.

I need more info. Panic being in front of all those people???

I belatedly, extremely belatedly, realized I didn't want to get married.

Oh no! You kept asking everyone at your bachelorette party if they thought you should get married. But I thought that was just you being you.

What? I did? What do you mean, me being me?

You know. You always ask for advice. You ask if you should bring an umbrella, what shoes to wear, if you should ask for a raise. You asked the waiter at Olive Garden what college to go to.

No, I didn't!

Yeah, you did. You do it so much, you probably don't even realize you do it. That's why you and Caleb are so perfect together. He never gets tired of you asking his opinion. But he's not all controlling. So, you don't want to be with Caleb? Mind blown.

Mine too. He's perfect. I'm crazy for not wanting to be with him. But I don't. Even thinking about him? My heart is going boom, boom, boom. And not in a good way.

Have you talked to him?

No.

Briony!

I know! But I couldn't. What was I supposed to say? I sent the ring back. I said I was sorry. In a note. Just those words. "I'm so sorry." I know I have to do something else.

Ya think?

I just don't know how to explain.

Yeah. Noticed.

What should I say?

See! That's what I mean. You never do anything without asking a committee.

You're not a committee. And it's hard.

Sigh. Yeah. Tell him you've decided to become a nun.

I might. Actually, maybe I should join a convent. After what I did to Caleb, I shouldn't inflict myself on anyone.

Awww. No. You didn't hurt him on purpose. But you do have to talk to him.

I know. I will. Sometime . . .

I gotta get to work. To be continued.
Thanks. Sorry. I'll pay for your dress.
You will not. Laters, baby.
For that you get the eye roll.

Vi didn't respond. Briony would have to talk to her more later.

Had Briony really asked everyone at the bachelorette party if she should be getting married? She couldn't remember. There'd been Nutella shots at the party. And she'd had maybe a couple too many. She wasn't a big drinker.

She remembered Caleb making her a disgusting but surprisingly effective hangover cure the next day, but the details of the party were fuzzy-wuzzy. The bachelorette party was a week before the wedding. And if Vi was right, Briony was already having doubts. She let out a long sigh. It would have been helpful if she'd been conscious of that sometime before she started down the aisle.

"Okay, I know I need to call Caleb." Her heart gave a hiccup. "But at least I've started on my to-do list. I'm doing better, right, guys?" Briony asked.

Diogee thumped his tail from his spot by her feet. Briony scratched his head, which made the tail thump harder.

"What about you, kitty? What do you think?" Briony asked.

Oh, my god. I just asked a cat and dog their

opinion. Is Vi right? Do I really ask advice before I do anything? "Do I?" she asked aloud.

Diogee gave her more wags. Briony looked around for Mac. Where was he? She jumped up. "Mac? Mac, Mac, Mac? MacGyver?" She turned in a circle, searching the room. "Kitty want a snack?"

There was no answering mew, although at the word *snack,* Diogee ran to the kitchen and positioned himself underneath his treat jar. Briony gave him a biscuit, then began searching the house.

After she'd searched every room twice, she had to admit that the cat was gone. Again! "What do I do?" she asked Diogee, then slapped herself on the forehead. She was doing it again. Asking an animal his opinion.

She realized she was still holding her cell. That was it. She'd call that guy from the retirement place. She didn't remember his name, but his number was in the phone from when he'd called her.

Briony pulled up her call history. Yeah, okay, there it was. She punched the little phone receiver icon, and a few seconds later the guy picked up. "This is Nate."

"Hello. This is Briony Kleeman. I'm the person who is pet sitting for MacGyver, the cat you called me about yesterday." She forced herself to speak slowly and clearly, and not like an insane person, because he had every reason to think she was an insane person after the way she'd shown up yesterday. "The cat is missing again, and I wondered if perhaps you'd seen him."

"I haven't," Nate said. "But I'll keep an eye out, and let you know if I spot him."

"That would be terribly wonderful," Briony answered. Had she just started speaking with a British accent? That wasn't going to help her appear less insane! "Thank you awfully," she added. Yes, she was definitely using an accent.

"I think you should be human sitting me," she told Diogee after she hung up. "You have more sense. Where do you think MacGyver is?" And she was asking the dog for advice again.

Nate decided to stop by Gib's on the off chance that the crazy woman's cat was over there. Although she hadn't seemed especially crazy on the phone just now. Except for the part where it sounded like she started speaking with a British accent.

Whatever. He wanted to check on Gib in any case. Today, he was getting the man out of his bungalow, even if it took a crowbar. As he walked, he scanned his surroundings, trying to take in every detail. He'd checked in with security, and there'd been no reports of anything unusual spotted around his mother's place or anywhere else in The Gardens.

When he got to Gib's, he knocked, then called out, "I know you're home, Gibson!" before Gib could yell his usual greeting.

"I'm home. What about it?" the man asked when he swung open the door to let Nate in.

"Our friend MacGyver has gone missing again. Thought he might have stopped by."

Gib shook his head. "Haven't seen him since he went up the chimney." He shut the door behind them.

"Did I wake you up?" Nate asked. Gib was dressed in pajama pants and an old Angels jersey, his feet bare, his hair mussed.

Gib snapped his jaws open and closed a few times. "My teeth are in. That means no. You want coffee?"

"Sure," Nate answered, and followed Gib into the kitchen. "You better get dressed. Art class in less than half an hour." Gib was a regular at the class and had real talent. He'd given Nate a painting of the peperomia plant for Christmas, and Nate had it up in his office.

"Not on my calendar." Gib popped a K-Cup in his Keurig, stuck a coffee mug in place, and pushed the button.

"Your calendar pretty full for the day, is it?" Nate asked. "Ten thirty, putter. Eleven, clip toenails. Twelve thirty, open up a can of beans for lunch. One—"

"You can stop, funny guy," Gib said. "Just so

96

you know, I may be old, but I don't need a keeper."

Nate needed a new approach. "Actually, I was hoping you were going to the class, because I wouldn't mind having another pair of eyes right now. Can you keep something to yourself?"

Gib didn't bother answering. He just handed Nate his coffee and sat down at the kitchen table. Nate sat across from him and quickly filled him in on the ventilation system sabotage. "If you could just spend some time in the community center and let me know if you see anything that looks off, I'd appreciate it."

For a moment, Gib didn't answer. He just narrowed his eyes and studied Nate, probably trying to decide if he was being played. He was, but he wasn't. Gib was sharp. Who knew what he might come up with? "All right." He glanced at the black cat clock with the swinging tail. "I can still make the class. I'll get dressed. You finish that coffee."

Nate felt a burst of satisfaction. It hadn't even taken a crowbar. What should he take on next? He needed to find someone to check the air. He still needed to find a place that could fumigate books. And furniture. And rugs. Maybe he should get the locks to his mom's place changed. Nate took a swig of the coffee. As he started to set the mug back down, something caught his attention. What was that? Something gray and hairy lay on the counter by the sink. It looked like some kind of mutant caterpillar. Nate walked over to investigate. Whatever it was, it wasn't alive. He gave it a poke with one finger. It felt a little sticky.

"Ready," Gib said, returning to the kitchen. "What you got there?"

"I don't know," Nate admitted. "I just noticed it."

Gib frowned. "Nothing I've ever seen." He took the furry thing and rolled it between his fingers, then tossed it back on the counter. "If we're going, let's get a move on."

They headed out of the bungalow and walked over to the community center in silence, both in vigilance mode. When they started into the Manzanita Room, where art class was held, Gib froze. Nate immediately got what the problem was. Archie was seated in the chair used for models, and several ladies, including Peggy, were clustered around him.

"Gib, want to hear my latest?" Richard called from behind one of the easels.

Gib shot a look over at Peggy—and Archie— then straightened his shoulders. "Sure thing." He sauntered with extreme casualness over to the easel next to Richard's.

"I want to hear it, too." Nate followed Gib, figuring he owed the guy a little moral support, since he'd talked him into coming to the class.

"There once was a man called Archie/When he spoke he was full of malarkey/He loved his granddaughter/Maybe more than he oughter/And I wouldn't want to meet him at a party." He frowned. "Just a rough draft."

"Sam!" Peggy called as the volunteer art teacher came in. "We want to do live drawing today, and we found the perfect model." She gave Archie's shoulder a squeeze.

Gib got very interested in rearranging his charcoals. "All right," Sam answered. "Not what I had planned, but I'm flexible. Remember, start by planning your composition, then draw the whole figure in fast."

"Sam, don't you think it would be interesting for us to draw a couple?" Janet asked. She pulled a chair over next to Archie's. "I think trying to capture our expressions as we gaze at each other would be an interesting artistic challenge." She took his chin in her hand and turned his face toward hers. "Oooh. You did some manscaping on your brows. I love a man who takes care of himself."

"Now you're on the trolley!" Archie exclaimed. Nate wondered if Archie'd grown up in California. He didn't recognize half the expressions Archie came up with. Maybe they were regional.

"Oh, but, Janet, if you pose, that would mean you wouldn't be able to draw," Regina protested. "And you always do such beautiful work."

Janet's work was . . . interesting. Nate didn't think anyone other than Regina, who had ulterior motives, would call it beautiful.

"Let me pose with Archie instead," Regina continued. "I draw so badly anyway. I don't mind skipping for today." She tried to ease Janet off the chair.

Janet didn't budge. "Nonsense, just last week Sam said he loved all the detail you included in your sketch."

"How about if Archie and I pose?" Peggy suggested. "It could be an *American Gothic* for the new century. Instead of a pitchfork, Archie could hold a cell phone."

"I don't have one of those dang phones. Don't trust them." He smiled at Peggy, Janet, and Regina in turn. "But I'd be happy to pose with any or all of you dolls."

Gib snatched up a charcoal and began to sketch furiously. Sam came over to watch. "Such passion," he commented.

Nate took a look and had to bite back a laugh. Archie's thinning hair had been reduced to a few scraggly strands, while the hair in his ears and nostrils was flourishing.

Mac followed the scent of the Sardine Man. Gib was his name. And Nate was the other one Mac was keeping an eye on. He'd learned that from their blah-blah. Gib wasn't home, but it

100

was easy to track him. He was close by. Mac found him in a room with a bunch of other humans, including Nate.

Gib smelled the way Jamie did when Mac explored what had been hidden in the trash can. Mac wondered if Gib had found the pressie he'd left for him last night while he was sleeping. He didn't smell like he'd been having any fun. Neither did Nate. They would both require more work. Mac rubbed his cheek against first Nate's pant leg, then Gib's, to make sure everyone knew they were under his protection.

"What a gorgeous kitty!" a female exclaimed. She hurried over and knelt down in front of Mac. Gib's scent immediately changed. Now he smelled the way Jamie did when David came home. The female gently stroked Mac's head. But at the same time, the tang of loneliness Gib always had grew stronger.

"He's a friend of mine," Gib blah-blahed. "His name's MacGyver."

"I better call his sitter," Nate said. "Maybe MacGyver's the one who should pose with Archie," he added, to neutralize the tension that had started building between the ladies.

"Excellent idea!" Sam agreed. "We've never had an animal as a live drawing subject."

The female picked Mac up and deposited him in the lap of a man sitting at the front of the room. Mac breathed in, assessing. The man smelled happy enough, but Mac could tell the man didn't like him. And that was just wrong.

Game on. Mac curled up on the man's lap and began sliding his claws in and out of the man's thin pants.

"I don't know about this," Archie said. He pinched a piece of Mac's fur off his vest and let it drop to the floor.

"An adorable cat and adorable man. What could be better?" the female said.

"I'm never a wurp. You want it, you've got it," Archie answered.

The man's legs were hard under Mac's belly. He let his claws dig a little deeper, just enough to leave thin scratches in the skin. The man gave a little yelp. MacGyver began to purr.

CHAPTER 6

*C*alm, cool, collected, Briony told herself when she located The Gardens' community center. *I will be calm, cool, and collected. Then I will put MacGyver into the cat carrier and leave in a calm, cool, and collected way.*

She didn't know why she was so worried about making a better impression on Nate. She'd only be around for a few more weeks, and she'd probably never have to see him again. Unless Mac kept finding a way over here.

Briony remembered what Ruby had told her about MacGyver being a matchmaker. If that was what he was up to—which he couldn't be, because, come on, he was a cat—she'd already ruined his plans. No matter how perfectly she was dressed or how perfectly she behaved today, she was sure whenever Nate saw her he'd always think crazy-faced, crazy-haired crazy woman. Not that it mattered.

The pleasant scent of citrus and something she couldn't identify, possibly bergamot, greeted her when she opened the door. The large room felt more like the lobby of an elegant old hotel with its Persian carpets and comfy overstuffed sofas. Well, a mix of that and a greenhouse. There were plants everywhere. She paused to admire what she thought was a boxwood that had been trimmed into a spiral on her way to the Manzanita Room, where Nate had told her he—and MacGyver—would be.

She spotted Nate the moment she stepped inside. Her eyes just went *zoop* right over to him. Those pheromones were already slamming into her. It was so damn wrong for him to be so attractive without even trying. And a second later, she was overcome with guilt by how damn wrong it was of her to be thinking about how damn attractive a guy was when she'd been about to get married a few damn days ago.

Nate was standing by an easel where the older man whose bungalow she'd barged into the other night was working. Good. She could show him her calm, cool, collected self, too. His opinion was just as important as Nate's. Not that Nate's really mattered, she reminded herself.

She glanced around the room and quickly found Mac. She couldn't stop herself from smiling at the naughty thing. He was the center of attention, being sketched while sitting on the lap of a spiffy gentleman wearing a bow tie.

Mr. MacGyver wasn't going to get away from her this time. Firmly grasping the cat carrier she'd found in Jamie's closet, she started across the room. She paused next to Nate. "Thank you for calling me again," she said, calm, cool, and collected.

"Any chance you'd be willing to let MacGyver hang for about another half an hour? I didn't know he was going to be one of the models," Nate said.

"That would be fine," she answered, because that was the calm, cool, collected response.

"Great. We could go have coffee in the kitchen." Nate turned to the older man at the easel. "Gib, can you make sure our buddy doesn't get out of the room?"

Gib glanced away from his drawing. He'd captured Mac perfectly. The stripes of his fluffy fur, the *M* marking on his forehead, the intelligence in his gold eyes. The spiffy gentleman looked more like a troll in a bow tie. "You clean up pretty nice," he told Briony. "Since there are no chimneys in here, I think I can keep your cat corralled."

"I appreciate that." There. She'd calmed, cooled, and collected all over the place, and not just in front of Nate, in front of *both* witnesses to her madness. "I love what I've seen of the place," she commented as Nate escorted her to the kitchen. "It has such a wonderful feeling. You're the manager, is that right?"

"He owns the place," a woman with purple ombre hair answered. She and a younger woman, probably early twenties, stood at the kitchen island with an array of vegetables in front of them.

"Well, my family does," Nate said, running his hand through his longish dark brown hair. "My mom, and sister, and me."

"But they don't have anything to do with it," Ombre told Briony. "Nate runs everything. I mean everything."

"Everything," the younger woman agreed.

"Let me introduce my cheering section," Nate said. "This is LeeAnne." He gestured toward Ombre. "She's our chef. And this"—he nodded to the younger woman—"is Hope. She's—"

LeeAnne jumped in before he could finish. "The person who right now is going to get me through the gruesome task of pantry inventory."

"Didn't you do that the other—" Nate began.

LeeAnne pointed at him. "When you hired me, you promised me no micromanaging. Now I say it's inventory time, so inventory time it is." She pulled Hope out of the room.

"Have a seat." Nate waved toward a round table.

"Big," Briony commented. The table could probably seat fifteen.

"Staff is welcome to come in for any meal," Nate explained. He filled two cups from a big urn on the counter. "How do you take it?"

"Just milk." He added a spoon to her saucer, set the cup and a small silver pitcher in front of her, and sat down himself. Briony turned the spoon over in her fingers, suddenly at a loss for what to say. Should she apologize again for her behavior the other night? Or was it better not to remind him of it? Should she go back to talking about The Gardens? Would it be intrusive to ask about why he was the only one in the family who was directly involved in running it?

What was wrong with her? Did she always dither like this? Vi might really be right. Maybe Briony really couldn't make even a simple decision without help. How had she never noticed that about herself?

"I'm sorry I was all *bullurgh* the other day." She waved her hands wildly in the air. Oh, nice. Very calm, cool, and collected. And she'd been doing so well. "I'm pet sitting for my cousin. I would have felt terrible if I'd let something happen to MacGyver."

"MacGyver," Nate repeated. "Suits him."

"I never actually watched that show," Briony said. There. She sounded, if not calm, cool, and collected, at least rational.

"My grandpa and I used to watch reruns with some of the residents," Nate said. "His father was the one started the place. Bought the property and turned it into a retirement community." He pulled the potted plant in the center of the table over in front of him and began checking the under-sides of the leaves, his fingers sure and nimble.

"The people I saw today seemed like they'd be independent." Briony took a sip of her coffee, watching him tend to the plant. To her shock, her mind briefly skipped to a vision of those fingers moving over her. She shoved the thought away.

"They are. We have other residents who need more help. Instead of living in the bungalows, they stay in one of three larger houses with round-the-clock nursing," he explained as he continued inspecting the plant. "If they're able, they also come over here to the community center for meals and activities."

"What's it like being part of a family business? Did you grow up assuming you'd take over at some point?"

He hesitated. Looked like she'd touched something sensitive. Briony decided to fill the silence. "My family doesn't have anything like your place, but my dad is an accountant, and from when I was a little kid, my parents acted like of course I'd be one, too. They said no matter what, people will always need accountants. I actually got a financial calculator for my seventh birthday."

"Seriously?" Nate widened his eyes with exaggerated awe, then moved the plant back in place. "That's what I wanted when I was seven. But I got a Talkboy instead, just like the one from *Home Alone*." He deepened his voice and said, "This is the father. I'd like one of those little refrigerators you open with a key." Briony laughed. "Did you really become an accountant?" he asked.

"I did. I—" She suddenly felt unsure about something she'd always accepted as a given. "There wasn't something else I had this big desire to do. And I like the, hmmm, the neatness of it. Everything adding up." That was true. She knew she was good at what she did, and she liked going to work every day, something that wasn't true for everyone.

Suddenly, *wham!* It hit her that she didn't have a job anymore. Caleb had gotten an amazing job offer at a law firm in Portland. They'd decided he should take it. They were going to move after the honeymoon. Caleb had already found a place. The firm was paying all the relocation expenses. When they'd gotten settled, Briony had been planning to look for another accounting job. Like her parents said, people always need accountants.

But she wasn't going to be moving to Portland now. Could she get her old job back?

"Are you okay?" Nate asked.

Briony nodded. "Just remembered something I need to do when I get back from my, uh, vacation." Something like get a whole new life.

"How long are you here?"

"About three and a half more weeks. My cousin is on her honeymoon in Morocco."

"Morocco. Wow." Nate gave a low whistle.

"I know. I've never even thought of going someplace so exotic. So much to figure out and navigate."

"I'd go in a heartbeat. They have a rose festival in the spring. It would be awesome to see the M'Goun roses in the wild. And to smell them." Nate sounded like an excited little kid.

"Are you responsible for the jungle in the lobby?"

He smiled, and *whomp,* another pheromone bomb. It made Briony go to jelly, and not in that walking-down-the-aisle-toward-Caleb way. The man was seriously dangerous. What was wrong with her? She ignored her body's reaction to Nate and focused on his words. "I set it up. The grounds crew keeps it going. I wish I could, but too much else to do. There's always something." His brow creased, worry flashing across his face.

"You do an amazing job."

"I do, huh?" He raised one dark eyebrow. "You've been here for probably a total of twenty minutes, most of it in the kitchen."

"I know I don't really know. But I just met two of your staff, and they adore you. And you were over visiting Gib the other night. I bet all managers—owners, I mean—don't do that. Both things tell me a lot. I stand by what I said. You do an amazing job."

"Now, maybe. But when I started? I was only nineteen."

"No way."

"My dad had taken over from my grandpa.

He'd only been running the place on his own for about four years; then he hit his fiftieth and bought himself a Mustang convertible. Red. And a leather bomber jacket to go with it. Classic mid-life crisis cliché. A few months later, he was gone. Just, gone. I had to step up. My mom was useless." He grimaced. "That's not fair. My mom was heartbroken. I'd spent all this time here with my grandfather and later my dad. I'd picked up a lot, so I stepped in. Didn't think it would necessarily be permanent. But here I am almost ten years later."

"LeeAnne said you had a sister."

"A twin. Nathalie," Nate said. "But she had no interest in the place. She had this thing when she was a teenager where she didn't want to be around old people. Like it was contagious. When she was little she'd come over—our family house is on the edge of the grounds—but later, no way."

"Nate and Nathalie. Cute, cute."

"It's worse than that. Nathaniel and Nathalie."

Briony playfully narrowed her eyes. "Did you get dressed alike?"

Nate laughed, which was her intention. "I have this picture of us when we were about three, me in a little sailor suit, her in a sailor dress. That was the last time we twin dressed. I somehow managed to rip or otherwise destroy my half of any other matching outfits."

"And you go by 'Nate,' not 'Nathaniel.' "

"I tried to get people to call me Parka when I was kid, but it never stuck."

"Parka? Like a coat?" Briony found herself twirling a curl that had come loose from her chignon around one finger. She jerked her hand down. Hair twirling was a classic flirting move. And she was not trying to flirt.

"Like a coat? No. *Parka*. Like La Parka. Wrestler. Dressed like a skeleton."

"No idea what you're talking about." She realized she'd just been talking talking. Like she did with Vi or Ruby. With Caleb, she was more careful. He was so perfect, she wanted to be perfect, too. And with her parents, she didn't like to say anything that would make them worry, so nothing that would make them think she was unhappy in any way.

"Did you wrestle in school?" Briony tried not to picture him in one of those unitard things.

"I want to say yes. But I don't want to lie to you. I was—"

Nate was interrupted by Gib shoving through the door into the kitchen. "He's gone. I don't know how he did it. The door was closed. The windows were closed. There's no chimney. Is that cat's middle name Houdini?"

It was dark when Nate finished visiting with Iris. She'd had hip-replacement surgery a few days before, and he'd gotten word that she was resistant to working with her physical therapist. He'd stopped by to give her some flowers and a pep talk.

As he walked toward his office, he decided to ask Janet to stop by and see her the next day. Janet had had a hip replacement about four years ago and was doing great. She was one of the gym regulars.

He hesitated when his office came in sight. Even though he knew security would keep a close eye on his mom's place, he'd feel better if he swung by himself.

Maybe he'd even talk to her about his dad. He never really had. It was like it was easier for her to act like he'd never existed, and Nate had gone along with it. Talking to Briony earlier had made Nate think maybe it was finally time to have a real conversation with his mom and maybe with Nathalie, too.

A text popped up from LeeAnne as he changed direction. He read it as he headed toward his mother's.

You should ask her out for a drink.
What?
She doesn't know anyone.
What?
She's at her cousin's place for a few weeks.
Were you eavesdropping? Never mind. Obviously, you were.

Well, I did inventory two days ago.
Why are you still here?
Not. I don't live at work like you do.
Not at work. Going to my mom's.
Oooh. Exciting.
Shut up.
Call her. She's cute.
Hanging up.
You can't hang up on a text.
Putting phone away.

Nate stuck the cell in his pocket. Maybe he *should* see if Briony wanted to hang out. He could show her around LA a little. LeeAnne was probably right about her not knowing—

The shadows shifted under the jacaranda tree in his mom's yard. But there was no wind. The branches were motionless.

Someone was there.

Nate took off. He vaulted over the low wall—just as someone scrambled over it to the sidewalk. Nate launched himself back over. He spotted the side gate of the bungalow across the street shutting. He raced over and into the backyard.

"Get him, Peanut!"

Clang! The metal dog door flipped open. Light suddenly filled the windows overlooking the yard. One of the windows opened. "Who's out there?" Martin Ridley yelled.

"It's Nate!" Carrie Ridley exclaimed.

Peanut, their rotund dachshund, gave a high yelp. He'd only made it halfway through the dog door and had become wedged in place.

"My Peanut!" Carrie cried.

"I'll get the treats," Martin announced.

Nate looked around the yard. Whoever he'd been chasing was gone.

"Here. Hold one of these in front of him." Martin leaned out the window and shook a box of dog treats at Nate. Nate thought that might only add to the problem, but he obediently went over and took a biscuit, then held it about a foot from Peanut's nose. Peanut gave a wriggle, another yelp, and he was through. He snatched the treat, downed it, then latched his teeth onto Nate's ankle.

Nate reached down to pry the dog off him. "No!" Carrie screeched. "Peanut's teeth are bad."

"Peanut, treat!" Martin opened the door and waved a biscuit.

Peanut instantly released Nate and started waddling toward Martin. "Sorry to bother you," Nate said. He tried to think of something he could say that wouldn't alarm them. "I saw that your back gate was open and wanted to latch it so Peanut wouldn't get out. You must have heard me. Sorry to cause all the commotion."

"No worries," Martin answered.

"Will I see you two at Wii bowling tomorrow?" Nate asked.

"We wouldn't miss it."

"We have to put the Scared Splitless team in their place," Carrie added from behind the open window.

Nate told them good-bye, then walked back over to his mother's house, texting the head of security as he went to let him know what had happened. He tried the door. Locked. Well, that was something. He gave a knock, and when his mom answered she was beaming.

"You're going to be so proud of me," she announced. "My computer got locked up, but I called the number, and talked to a technician. He took control of the computer from where he was, remotely. I didn't even know they could do that. Then he—"

"Mom," Nate interrupted. "That was a scam." He managed to keep the exasperation out of his voice. He'd talked to her about computer security.

"He didn't ask for any money. He was from Microsoft," his mom explained.

"Here's the thing. Once someone gets into your computer, which is what happened, they can get your credit card numbers, they can—"

"Oh no!" his mother cried. "What am I going to do? I don't know what to do!"

"It's going to be all right," Nate said. He put his arm around her shoulders. "I'll run a check on your computer to see if anything was installed, and we'll call your bank and let them know what happened. The homeowner's insurance covers identity theft, just in case we need it, which I don't think we will."

He abandoned the idea of starting a conver--sation about his dad that night. She was already too upset.

His mother leaned into him. "You take such good care of me and Nathalie. What would we do without you?"

"You're not going to have to find out," Nate promised.

Mac eyed the dangerous fluffy thing as it slowly wiggled across the floor. He waggled his hips back and forth, making sure he had his balance right, then—pounce!

The fluffy jerked out of the way just before he landed. Mac gave a little growl as his nemesis began whipping around him in circles. Taunting him.

Mac did his hip waggle again. This time his pounce was right on target. He pinned the fluffy to the ground with his body, then dug his teeth into it, refusing to let go even when it tickled his nose so badly he sneezed three times in a row.

Peggy—he'd heard other humans blah-blah her name—laughed. "You win, you win!" She dropped down in an armchair, breathless. "My boa is never going to be the same. But it was worth it. I was going to get something new for this year's talent show anyway. You should have seen me last year, with that boa wrapped around my neck. I did 'These Boots Were Made for Walking' and got a standing O."

She started making a kind of purring sound. It didn't sound exactly right, the tone going up and down too much. It was to be expected. She wasn't a cat after all. But Mac appreciated the effort. He abandoned the dead fluffy. That's right. He killed it. He ruled. He jumped up on Peggy's lap and settled down for a rest.

Peggy rubbed the side of Mac's face, and he began to purr. Let her see how it was done. He could easily have stayed there for hours, but it was getting late. He'd been gone from home for longer than he ever had. He was sure the bonehead had peed all over Mac's yard. Mac would have to deal with that. And he needed to check up on Briony. She'd smelled better that afternoon, but who knew how long that would last. Humans were so unpredictable.

Mac enjoyed a few more scratches, then stood and stretched. He jumped down, trotted over to Peggy's door, and gave a single mew. Peggy came over and opened the door right away.

"Thanks for the visit!" she called as he slipped outside.

Mac could see why Gib liked the smell of her. Mac did, too. But Peggy hadn't seemed to notice Gib's scent. Oh, well. He could find a way to fix that.

CHAPTER 7

I have a craving for chicken and waffles," Ruby announced when Briony answered the door the next morning. "Not any chicken and waffles. Roscoe's. And since you're new in town, and haven't experienced the mighty Roscoe's, I came over to get you. Have you eaten?"

Briony looked around for Mac. He'd been there for *his* breakfast, so she was pretty sure he was still in the house, and she didn't want to give him the chance to make a break for it. "I had some toast."

"Toast. Pfft. So are you coming? My treat." Ruby grinned. "If I'm being annoying, just make up a polite excuse and send me on my way."

"Sounds great. I'm in," Briony told her. She did another Mac check, ran over to the coffee table to get her purse, then rushed out, slamming the door behind her.

"Isn't cat sitting Mac fun?" Ruby teased.

"He got out again!" Briony exclaimed. "He came back again, but still."

"Roscoe's is only a few blocks away. We can walk," Ruby said. "Where'd he go this time, do you know?"

"Back to The Gardens. I went after him with a cat carrier and found him posing for some art students." Ruby laughed so hard she snorted. "Yeah, you can think it's funny. You're not in charge of him," Briony told her. "I gave permission for him to stay until the end of the class, but when it was over, he vanished."

"Good. The line's not too long." Ruby nodded to a few people sitting on a bench in front of a long building with horizontal wooden siding, and narrow rectangular windows set too high for anyone to see inside.

"I walked right by here on the way to FedEx and didn't even notice it," Briony said. "Of course, I did have other things on my mind. Like returning my jilted fiancé's wedding ring." Her breath started coming a little fast.

Ruby let the jilted fiancé comment slide, probably to prevent Briony from starting to full-on hyperventilate. "It's low on ambience, but the food is insane," she said as they joined the line.

"Have you ever felt an overwhelming attraction to someone you don't even know?" Briony asked. "Truly overwhelming, not just an, oh, he's good-looking kind of thing."

"Holy non sequitur, Batman." Ruby stared at her. "Or maybe not. I think there might be some logic here. You were talking about The Gardens. And that got you thinking about the owner. The cute owner. Which led to your question. Am I right?"

Briony groaned. "You should not know me so well already. And I should not feel so comfortable with you already. I really wasn't planning to say that. I just—blurt." She'd wanted to say something that didn't have anything to do with Caleb, and that's what had come out.

"So, I'm right."

"Yeah, I was asking because I saw Nate, the owner, yesterday. And *blam*. That's never happened to me before. Not like that. I notice if someone's cute or whatever, but this was—" Briony shook her head. "I kept it together, though. I'm sure he didn't know. My goal was to show him I wasn't always a hysterical mess of a person. I don't think I even told you what a freak I was the first time I saw him. I was too busy being a freak the first time I met you."

Ruby patted her arm. "You weren't being a freak. You were having a panic attack, which was completely understandable after what you'd been through."

"Well, I wasn't having a panic attack the first time I saw Nate, not quite, but I was horrified that Mac had gotten out on my watch. When he called I went running over to The Gardens without even thinking about what I looked like. When I got home, I realized I had mascara smeared halfway down my face, and, please, let's not even speak of my hair or the streetwalker rip in my dress that went up to my thigh. Also, I'd lost a shoe."

"Like Cinderella."

"Oh, right. I forgot about how Cinderella went to the ball and screeched at the prince for letting her cat escape," Briony answered. "Seriously, Ruby, I was a maniac. But yesterday, I had it together. I may have briefly spoken in a British accent, but other than that I was calm, cool, and collected. We actually ended up having a nice chat."

"A nice chat?" Ruby repeated. At least she hadn't asked about the accent, which Briony had no idea how to explain.

"Yes, a nice chat about how he took over running The Gardens after his dad had a mid-life meltdown and bought a red convertible and basically drove away in it, never to be seen again."

"That sounds more like a heart-to-heart than a chat." The group ahead of them went into the restaurant and Briony and Ruby moved up.

"I guess it was kind of personal, for basically our first conversation," Briony admitted.

"What about you? Did you spill your guts, too?" Ruby asked.

"My guts stayed right where they belonged. I told him I was an accountant, like my dad. That's as personal as it got." Another question popped up in her mind. Another one she shouldn't ask. One she shouldn't even be thinking about. "Did Mac really get my cousin and David together somehow?"

"Yep. Mac kept stealing things from David. Nothing valuable. Little things like socks. Then he'd leave them on Jamie's doorstep. He brought her stuff from other guys in the complex, too, but David was clearly his top pick. He brought more of David's things than anyone else's," Ruby explained. "And they weren't the only couple he got together. There were two others. He also reunited twin sisters who'd been feuding for years."

"Nate has a twin, a sister who isn't interested in The Gardens. I didn't find out why," Briony volunteered. Like she was a teenager who'd use any excuse to talk about her crush. *You're a victim of pheromones,* she reminded herself. *With some instability mixed in. You don't really know the guy.*

"We're up." Ruby led the way inside the dimly lit restaurant that had lots more wood—wood walls, wood planks on the floor. The hostess showed them to a small table next to a curving wooden half wall. "Low ambience, insane food," Ruby reminded Briony softly after the hostess left them.

"The smells already have my mouth watering," Briony answered.

Before they could get back into their conversation, their waiter, friendly and face tattooed, came up, introduced himself, and asked for their drink order. "I always get the Sunset," Ruby said.

"I have no idea what that is, but I'll have one, too," Briony told their waiter, and he was off.

"It's fruit punch and lemonade. The fruit punch floats on top. That's partly why I order it. It's so pretty, all yellow and pink," Ruby told her.

"Can we go back to Mac?" Briony asked. "I'm having trouble wrapping my head around how he did all this matchmaking. And fence-mending with sisters."

"None of us understands how he does it. We just know he does. He even did it for me." Ruby brushed her bangs off her forehead. "Not matchmaking exactly, but sort of. I don't have kids, but I always wanted them."

"Okay." Briony had no idea where this was going. It's not like Mac could have left a baby on Ruby's doorstep. At least she hoped not.

"There's a single mom who lives in Storybook Court. She has two daughters, a teenager, Addison, and a little girl, Riley. Addison had to take care of Riley a lot, because of their mom's work schedule, and, being a teenager, she wasn't always that happy about it," Ruby began. "I don't know how Mac knew any of his, if he did, but he took Riley's favorite toy, I mean the toy she couldn't live without, and left it on my porch. Long story short, I'm now Riley's honorary aunt, and pretty much a part of the whole family."

Briony noticed Ruby's eyes had become bright with unshed tears. "It's like that cat knew I had a hole in my heart and he knew what it would take to fill it." She choked out a laugh. "I can't believe I'm talking like a Hallmark movie. But it's how I feel."

Briony was finding the whole thing hard to buy. It was like some kind of urban legend everyone had decided to believe. "And you don't think it would have happened without MacGyver? You don't think you would have become close to Riley and her family some other way? They live nearby, you said."

Ruby shrugged. "Maybe. But they'd lived nearby since before Riley was born, and it didn't happen until Mac stole that pony and left it for me."

"Okay, I'm not saying I believe in Mac's magic, but if it's real, maybe Mac led me to Nate for some other reason. Or maybe it wasn't Nate he was taking me to! Maybe it was Gib. He's one of the residents. Mac was at his house the first day and in his art class the second. Maybe Gib and I are supposed to connect." *I sound crazy,* Briony thought. *This whole thing is ridiculous.*

"Maybe. Except for the part about the over-whelming attraction, which I'm assuming you didn't feel for Gib," Ruby answered. "And the conversation that got way beyond chitchat."

The waiter brought over their drinks. "Beautiful." Briony took a sip. "And yummy. Thanks for suggesting it. Now tell me what food I should order."

"Obama's favorite order is on the menu. Three chicken wings and a waffle," the waiter volunteered.

"I always do a chicken breast and a waffle. And a side of mac and cheese," Ruby said. "Which is what I'll have today." The waiter made a note on his pad and looked over at Briony.

"Make it two. I'm putting myself in her hands," Briony told him. It wasn't until he was heading for the kitchen to put the order in that she realized what she'd done. She'd let Ruby make her decisions for her. It was like Vi said. Like how Briony couldn't even decide whether she needed an umbrella.

"What?" Ruby asked. "You went pale, and you're on the pale side to begin with."

"It's . . . It's that I was talking to my best friend the other day, my maid of honor, and she was saying that at my bachelorette party I was asking everyone if I should get married. I guess I was really drunk. I couldn't believe Vi hadn't told me, but she said she thought it was just me being me. That I never do anything without asking for someone else's opinion." Briony turned her glass back and forth, watching the pink and yellow begin to blend. "When I thought about it, really thought about it, I realized it was true. And I just did it again. I didn't even look at the menu. I just was all 'I'll have what she's having.'"

"You're being a little hard on yourself, don't you think?" Ruby put her hand over Briony's to stop her from nervously playing with the glass. "It's a local place. You've never been here before; I have. Don't you think most people would ask the California native what was good?"

"Ask, yes. Then think if it's what they wanted. I didn't even think!" Briony exclaimed. "Vi thinks that's why Caleb was so perfect for me. Because he's the kind of guy who likes taking care of people. He was happy to give me advice. But never in a bossy way. Because he's perfect."

"Here we go with the perfect again."

"I told you, it's not just me who thinks he's perfect. Everybody thinks he's perfect."

"I have another story where the point will become apparent, like the one about being a biology major," Ruby told her. "Once when I was in high school, I found this dress that was

127

perfect. I loved it. Loved, loved, loved it. I still remember exactly what it looked like. Black-and-white check, belted waist, with a little red rose at the throat. So classy. And so not me. I never wore it, not even once, even though I begged my mom to buy it for me. When I put it on, even though it was a perfect dress, it didn't look right on me."

"Didn't you try it on at the store?"

"Of course. But I loved it so much I convinced myself it looked great. But it didn't. And I didn't have the shoes for it. Or the jewelry. Or the hair. Or the body type. It just wasn't me."

"So, you think Caleb was my perfect slash not perfect dress," Briony said.

"It's a possibility," Ruby answered; then she exclaimed, "Oh no! Did I just give advice? I shouldn't be giving you advice after what you told me. In fact, I promise right now, no, I will not give you advice, even on breakfast foods, ever again."

"It's okay. I—" Briony was interrupted by her phone ringing. She glanced at it, and her heart gave a *bam!* "It's Nate." She answered, "Hi, Nate. Is Mac there again?"

"Not that I know of. Is he missing again?" Nate asked.

"I'm not sure. I'm not home. But it's definitely possible," Briony said.

"I was actually calling because I wondered if

you'd like to go out for a drink tonight, see a little of LA."

Her heart gave a double *bam*. "One sec," she managed to say. "I have to, um, do something." She muted the phone and turned to Ruby. "He just asked me out. What should I do?"

Ruby smiled. "Don't ask me."

Briony pressed her lips together. Should she? She was a woman who had been about to get married less than a week ago. But it was just a drink. It wasn't going to lead to anything, even if he made her body weak. She was going home soon.

Ruby started to hum the *Jeopardy!* theme.

Briony unmuted the phone. "Thanks for asking, Nate. I'd love to."

"Get ready, LeeAnne. You're gonna love this," Nate told her when he swung by the kitchen. "I'm about to head over to Briony's to take her out for drinks." LeeAnne gave a whoop and slapped Hope a high five. "Where do you think we should go? The bars around here change every thirty seconds, it seems like."

LeeAnne snorted. "Oh, please. I bet you haven't stepped inside a bar for at least a year."

Nate thought about it. She was right. The last time was about a year and a half ago, when Nathalie had dragged him to a place in Echo Park where one of her boyfriends was doing stand-up in the backroom. He was pathetic. But with The Gardens, and his mom, and his sister, it was almost impossible to find . . . Yeah, he was pathetic. "So where do you think would be good?"

"She's visiting. She'll want something really LA. But which LA?" LeeAnne murmured, staring up at the ceiling as if there were a list of bars up there. "Got it. Mama Shelter. Rooftop, not restaurant."

"Never been there," Nate admitted.

"Really? You?" LeeAnne asked with mock amazement. "Relaxed vibe, amazing views, great cocktails." She looked over at Hope for backup.

"I don't go anywhere. My life is study, work, study, work, sleep, repeat," Hope reminded her, with a smile. "And anyway, I'm sure it's out of my league."

"Will you stop saying things like that! I don't want to hear anything like that from you again." LeeAnne used such a sharp tone that she surprised Nate.

"Sorry," Hope muttered. "I'm going to see if there are any new dietary restrictions." She hurried out of the kitchen.

LeeAnne sighed. "Well, I handled that beautifully. I just hate that she doesn't think she's as good as anyone else. She acts like she goes to school wearing a sandwich-board sign saying 'I

Live with My Parents in Public Housing.' And that she really believes that makes her out of anyone's league. She's so great. I just want to strangle her."

"It's good she has you around to tell her that. Just maybe say it softer next time," Nate said. "And avoid strangling. A murder at The Gardens would affect our ratings."

She shook her head. "Get out of here. And make sure you stay until sunset, dude. There's nothing more romantic."

"This isn't a romantic thing. It's a friendly thing," Nate protested. "She doesn't know anyone. She's new in town. That's why you said I should call her, remember?"

"Stay until sunset anyway. It's the best tourist attraction around." LeeAnne took him by the shoulders and turned him toward the door. "Now get out of here."

Nate could tell LeeAnne had made the right pick as soon as he and Briony stepped out onto the rooftop bar. She turned around slowly, taking in the entire view. "Gorgeous."

"You can even see the ocean. Way down there." Nate pointed.

"I feel like we're on a beach with all the bright colors and lounge chairs," Briony commented.

"Shall we sit or lounge?" he asked.

"Um." Briony looked from the little tables to

the extra-wide loungers. He wondered if she was thinking the loungers might be a bit too intimate. They didn't have to be. There was plenty of room for two people. Although it would be easy to get close, too. "What do you—" she started. Then she gave her head a shake. "Lounge. Definitely lounge."

Nate led the way to a spot where they'd be facing the sunset, if they ended up staying that long. Briony stretched out, crossing her ankles. "Ahhh." He started to sit down when he felt his phone start up. He'd put it on vibrate, but he hadn't been able to bring himself to turn it off entirely. Not with someone prowling around his mom's place and someone—most likely the same person—sabotaging The Gardens.

"We need drinks. I'll go up to the bar." Which would give him a chance to check his messages. "What would you like?"

She hesitated a moment, considering. "Something . . . beachy."

"Are we talking little umbrella?" he asked.

"Absolutely," she answered, grinning up at him. The first time they'd met, all he could see was a mess of a woman. Okay, a mess of a woman with fantastic legs, from what he could see through the tear in her dress. The second time, he was struck by how different she looked, with her auburn hair pulled back, all sleek, and her face free of makeup streaks. This time, he took in how truly pretty she was, with her deep blue eyes and smooth skin sprinkled with freckles. He had the sudden crazy impulse to play connect the dots with the ones near the base of her throat. They'd make a perfect star.

He realized he was staring, and that possibly it seemed like he'd been staring at her breasts instead of those five freckles. He *had* taken a quick look, and her breasts were worth staring at. But he hadn't, because he wasn't fifteen.

His phone vibrated again. "Right back," he told Briony, then headed to the bar. He paused briefly and checked his messages. Both from work. Both nothing Amelia couldn't deal with. He shot messages back saying so.

A few minutes later, he returned to Briony and handed her a drink. "This is the beachiest one I could find. No umbrella, but it does have a Life Saver, also lemon, and cherry bitters."

She took a sip. "Yum. What'd you get?" she asked as he stretched out next to her.

"Something with tequila and jalapeño and lime. I like a little kick." He took a swallow. "It's good. Want to try it?"

"Sure. If you try mine."

They traded. He found his gaze going to her mouth as she brought the glass to her lips. He looked away, not wanting to stare, and tried her cocktail. "Better than I thought it would be," he said.

"Yours is amazing." She took another taste.

"You want to keep it?"

"Let's share both." Briony took one more sip; then they traded back. "You want to hear something stupid?" she asked.

"Sure." He was intrigued.

"It wasn't until about a year ago that I realized why Life Savers are called Life Savers. I took one out of the roll, and it was like I actually looked at it. I couldn't believe I'd never noticed it looked like—"

"A lifesaver," they both said together.

"It's like when I was looking at a picture of the Sistine Chapel," Nate said, "and I realized in the part where God's reaching out his finger toward Adam, the part around God kind of looks like a brain."

"Oh, now that's unfair!" Briony exclaimed. "I tell you I noticed something completely obvious about a piece of candy and you throw back something not at all obvious about a masterpiece."

Nate gave a snort of laughter. "I'm obviously just a lot more intelligent than you are." She surprised him by giving him a light sock on the arm.

He was feeling really comfortable with her. He wouldn't have teased her if he didn't. Weird for a first date, where he was usually choosing what to say fairly carefully. Except this wasn't a date. Maybe that was the difference. He'd never hung out with a woman as a friend. Back in high school, as part of a group, yeah, but not like this.

"We're almost exactly as high as the palm trees," she commented.

"Now that I think about it, I might have been high as the palm trees when I had that realization about the Sistine Chapel," Nate said.

"You're goofy. You had me fooled. I thought you were completely responsible and logical, but you're goofy," Briony informed him.

Goofy. No one had ever called Nate goofy. Maybe it was a reaction to having a night off.

"Just so you know, that getting high comment? Joke. Although when I was fifteen, sixteen, different story. Back then, I walked around in my Electric Wizard T-shirt acting like a badass, which I in no way was."

"Um." She lightly bit her bottom lip. "Can we still share drinks if I admit I have no idea who that is?"

"Oh, man. Only the best doom metal band ever. Their music sounded like it was playing backward even when it was playing forward." He shook his head at his younger self. That kid would never have imagined himself taking on the responsibility of The Gardens and the family almost as soon as he graduated from high school.

"A later version of being Parka?"

"Exactly!"

"And I was thinking you were such a nice boy, watching TV with your grandpa and the residents at The Gardens," Briony teased.

"I did that, too. I just changed my shirt first. It's not like I was high all the time. And, anyway, have you ever watched *Home Improvement* while stoned? Genius."

"I never smoked weed." She looked embarrassed. "I was a ridiculously good girl. I didn't even cut school on Senior Cut Day. If there was a rule I followed it. I did watch *Home Improvement*, though," she added quickly. And looked even more embarrassed.

"Did you have any fun at all?"

"Did I have any fun?" she repeated, clearly not able to come up with an answer right away. "I guess so. Sometimes." A small smile tugged at the corners of her mouth. "I got good grades. Does that count?"

Instead of answering her, he handed over his cocktail. "You finish it. You deserve it."

Briony drained the glass. "I know I already said it, but this place is gorgeous. Do you come here a lot?"

"I've actually never been here. I had to ask for advice on where to take you," he told her.

"Really?" She sounded surprised. "I'm trying to give that up."

"Give what up?"

"Asking for advice. I've been told I do that too much."

"I've been told I don't get out enough. Which is probably true, since I needed to ask advice on where to go tonight. It's hard to find a good time to get away from The Gardens."

"You had to grow up fast," she commented. "Well, we're at the beach now. We don't have to think about work. We don't have to think about anything." She closed her eyes, tilting her face up toward the sun. Nate watched her for a moment, then did the same. He felt his muscles begin to relax. Muscles he hadn't even realized were tight. Muscles he hadn't even realized he *had*.

After a few minutes, he felt the lounge shift underneath him. He opened his eyes and saw Briony sitting up, looking at him. "Unless you want to talk about work. Because that—"

Nate held up one hand, stopping her. "Not at the beach." She lay back, took a couple sips of her drink, then held it out to him. He took a swallow and started to hand it back.

Then his cell vibrated.

Damn it. He had to check it. He finished off the glass. "We need more drinks. Same again? Or something different."

She opened her mouth, then shut it, and rubbed her fingers over her lips. "Something different. Two something differents so we can try more.

Cal—People always say you shouldn't mix types of alcohol, but I say, what the hell." She threw both arms over her head.

"That's a myth. It's the amount of alcohol you drink and how fast you drink it that are important. Turns out mixing doesn't really make such a difference."

"Now you're back to reasonable and logical. The respectable owner of a retirement home. I like goofy better," Briony said.

"I'll work on it when I get back." Nate took a quick look at his phone as he walked to the bar. Text from Amelia asking something that wasn't at all important. He shot a message back telling her to make the decision. Then he sent her another text telling her that she should make all the decisions until he got back.

When he reached the bar, he couldn't stop himself from sending a third text that said: "Unless it's an emergency. Then definitely call!"

He ordered drinks from the bartender in the "Mama Loves You" T-shirt. Seeing it made him send a fourth text: "If security sees anything out of the ordinary at my mom's place, then call. Anything." His mom would definitely call him if she noticed someone outside her place again, but it was possible security would spot something she hadn't.

"I have a How I Met Your Mother and a

Throw Mama from the Train. Which do you want first?" Nate asked when he returned to Briony.

"Throw Mama."

He handed her the drink. "I also got us two bottles of water. We should stay hydrated while we drink," he said. "I'll try to make that my last responsible act of the night."

"Good."

He returned to his spot beside her on the lounger, and they started trading drinks again, talking about absolutely nothing important. They fell into silence as the sun began to set behind the Hollywood sign, the clouds turning deep pink, then orange as the sky darkened.

"I didn't think the view could get any better," Briony said. "But that was something I'll remember forever."

Nate thought he'd remember a lot of this night. He didn't want it to end, not yet. He'd been planning to head back to The Gardens after drinks. He had a lot of work to do. But he always had a lot of work to do. It would be there tomorrow. "Want to go downstairs and get something to eat?"

"Should I? I don't know. Should I?" Briony asked, laughing.

"Are you buzzed off two drinks?"

"Possibly," she answered. "And I would like to go downstairs and get dinner with you."

There must have been some magic going on, because they didn't have to wait for a table. Although it would have been okay if they had. The ceiling would have kept them entertained. It was covered with chalk drawings of mothers.

Briony read a sentence from the ceiling. " 'One time my mom told me, *Be a mango, not a coconut.*' " She looked over at Nate. "I don't know what that means, but I love it. And I hope you're not going to tell me you know what it means, smarty-pants, because not knowing is part of the enjoyment. I will try to be a mango from now on."

"I have no idea what it means. Maybe it's about not having a hard shell," Nate suggested.

"A hard, hairy shell," Briony added.

"Exactly. Maybe it's about how you shouldn't have a hard, hairy shell. You should be more . . . accessible. That's not the word I want."

"Vulnerable? Open? Unguarded?" Briony frowned. "Weak. Defenseless. Exposed."

"Whoa, whoa, whoa," Nate protested. "That took quite the dark turn. We're still at the beach. We're under the boardwalk."

"Right. Yikes. Sorry," Briony said. "My parents raised me to be cautious. My cousin Jamie was joking that they probably didn't let me cross the street until I was in college, and it's practically true. It made me feel—" She shook her head. "Not beach talk."

"No, I want to hear," Nate told her.

"Somehow it made me feel bad about myself. Like they thought I wasn't capable." She blinked a few times. "I never thought about it quite like that, but that's it. I know they were just taking care of me, but they were so protective it seemed as if they didn't think I could handle things." She picked up the menu. "Therapy session over."

"You don't have to stop."

"Oh, they have avocado toast as an appetizer!" she exclaimed. Clearly, she wanted to stop, and Nate wasn't going to push. "I've heard how everyone in California eats avocado toast, but I've never had it. We need to order some. Oh, and you have to let me pay half. You shouldn't go into debt just because you decided to be friendly to an out-of-towner."

Ice bath. Nate reminded himself that this wasn't a date, even though it had sure started to feel like one.

Briony reached out and put her hand over his. "Did I say the wrong thing? I heard myself talking about appetizers and I realized I was being thoughtless."

"No worries. And you weren't," Nate told her. "You can have all the avocado toast you like, and I hope you'll let me treat you."

"Thank you." Briony slowly slid her hand away, but he could still feel the warmth of it.

His cell vibrated. He couldn't make a bar run to check it. "I need to quickly get this," he told her. "There've been some things going on at The Gardens. I told them not to call if it wasn't an emergency."

"Take it. Of course you should take it," Briony said.

Nate almost groaned when he saw that the text was from his sister: *Need you now.*

"Is everything okay?"

"It's from my sister. Let me just see what's going on with her. I'll be right back. Order the toast if the waiter comes back before me."

Nate strode outside and hit the speed dial for Nathalie. "What?" he demanded.

"I'm desperate for a babysitter!" she cried. "I need you over here right now."

Nate almost hung up. "I'm about to have dinner. I'm out with a friend."

"Well, bag it up. You can bring Mike or whoever it is," Nathalie said. Mike was one of his high school friends he saw once in a while.

"No. I'm not coming," Nate told her.

"Abel is picking me up in fifteen minutes. He just texted." Nate had no idea who Abel was. "I guess the kids are old enough to stay by themselves for a few hours."

"Are you crazy? No, they aren't." His niece and nephew were ten and seven. "You can't expect Lyla—" He realized his sister was gone. He immediately called her back. She didn't pick up. He texted. She didn't answer. *Damn it.* Would she really leave the kids alone? He didn't think so. But if you got Nathalie in a particular mood, anything was possible.

He returned to the restaurant and hurried over to Briony. "I have a situation. It's possible that my sister has decided to leave her kids alone since I told her I couldn't come watch them. It's also possible she's trying to make me think that's what she's going to do to get me over there. But I—"

"Can't risk it," she said along with him. She stood up. "I'll come with you."

He started to refuse. He didn't want to drag Briony into his problems, and he knew he could handle it alone. But she'd offered. . . . "Thanks," he told her. "That would be great."

CHAPTER 8

As Briony and Nate headed up the front walk of his sister's place, the door flew open. A boy charged out and rammed Nate in the stomach with his head. Briony assumed it was a typical greeting, because Nate only laughed as he grabbed the boy under the armpits and swung him around and around. "Where's your mom?" he asked when he finally put the boy down.

"In the bathroom," the boy answered.

"Good," Nate said. Briony could tell Nate was trying to hide his annoyance, and she thought he was doing an excellent job. "Okay, Lyle, Lyle, Crocodile, meet my friend Briony. Briony, my nephew, Lyle."

"Hello, Lyle." Briony felt a little self-conscious. She hadn't spent much time around kids, and she didn't know quite how to act. *Just don't put on the British accent,* she told herself. *You are* so *not Mary Poppins.*

"When you meet someone, you say 'hello' or 'hi' and shake hands," Nate told Lyle.

Lyle immediately looked her in the eye, stuck out his hand, and told her "hi." They shook.

"Nice grip," Nate said. "He used to think

shaking was a test of strength," he added to Briony.

"Not too hard, not dead fish. That's how you do it," Lyle said. Nate had obviously been working with him on manners. Briony found that just so sweet. "Now can we play fort?"

"Sure. But I need to talk to your mom first. Why don't you show Briony the—"

Nate was interrupted by the double beep of a car horn. The front door flew open, then slammed shut, and a woman with dramatic cat-eye makeup and her hair in long messy waves—styled messy, not messy messy— flew toward the car. Briony didn't know it was possible to run that fast in barely there sandals. She was sure she couldn't do it.

"Nathalie, stop," Nate ordered. She didn't even toss him an over-the-shoulder wave. She vaulted into the waiting convertible and it was gone seconds later.

"Fort?" Lyle asked hopefully.

"Did you and your sister eat already?" Nate asked.

"Yep. Pizza," Lyle answered as they walked into the house. "Lyla picked all the pepperoni off hers. Last night she decided to be a raw foodist. So, I got double pepperoni."

"Lyla, come in here a minute. I want to introduce you to someone!" Nate called as he started picking up used napkins and paper

146

plates from the coffee table. Briony grabbed the empty pizza box.

"You don't have to—"

"Stop it," Briony told him. "I'm here, I'm helping." She didn't think she'd ever said anything like that to Caleb. Because Caleb never seemed to need help. He'd helped her with a ton of things, but it didn't go the other way.

A girl in jean shorts, a white T, and clunky black boots came into the room. She had the same long hair as her mother, topped with a black baseball cap that had small cat ears on top. "I want that hat," Briony told her. "I'm too old to wear it, but I want it. Not yours," she added quickly. "One like it."

The girl's eyebrows rose as she looked at Briony. "Thanks."

"Lyla, this is my friend Briony," Nate said.

"Hi." She took the pizza box out of Briony's hands. "I got this." She carried it out of the room, Nate behind her with the rest of the trash.

"I'm getting the pillows and stuff," Lyle announced, and disappeared.

Briony saw a T-shirt on the floor. Should she pick it up and fold it? Or would that kind of cleanup be somehow offensive? Only been away from the magical beach building for less than half an hour and she was feeling more like her usual dithery self. Somehow, hanging out with

Nate earlier, the constant questioning had begun to fall away. Maybe it was the alcohol, although she should still have some in her system.

Nate and Lyla returned to the living room, just as Lyle came running back in with a stack of pillows in his arms. A stack of pillows higher than his head. Nate had to grab him to stop him from running into the side of the sofa.

"I guess it's fort night." Lyla sounded bored, but Briony thought she could see a spark of enthusiasm in the girl's eyes. "I'll get the blankets."

"What should I do?" Briony asked.

"Help me move the sofa," Nate said. "After much trial and error, we've figured out that the best blanket fort has the sofa facing that corner over there." They each grabbed an end of the sofa and dragged it into place, Lyle yanking off the sofa cushions as they went.

"I've never made a blanket fort," Briony admitted when Lyla joined the group with a bunch of comforters, quilts, and sheets.

"You have clearly missed out on some of life's main pleasures." He smiled at her, a slow, sexy smile.

No, not sexy. This was not a night for sexy. They were just hanging out. With his niece and nephew. Having fun. Good, clean fun. It was a warm smile, she decided. A nice, warm smile. "What do we do next?"

"You never made a blanket fort? Seriously?" Lyle sounded horrified.

"Seriously," Briony answered. "So, are you going to teach me?"

"Okay. First we need the painter's tape." He ran out of the room again. Lyla started to drag a recliner over to the sofa, and Briony hurried over to give her an assist.

Nate and his niece and nephew were expert fort builders. With speed and efficiency, Nate taped a sheet to the wall, then Lyla draped it over the back of the sofa. "Now we anchor it with books," Lyle told Briony. She followed his lead and put a few big books on the bottom of the sheet to hold it in place.

Lyla draped a sheet over the chair, and Nate taped it to the sheet running from the wall to the sofa. Briony got another book to keep the other end of the sheet pinned to the chair. She was getting the hang of this.

"Can we do the kitchen table, too?" Lyle asked Nate. "There are more of us. We need to bust out the super-size tent."

"Briony and I will get the table. You two get chairs," Nate answered, and Lyle gave a happy whoop.

Once the table and chairs were in place and draped with sheets, they all started moving the pillows and cushions inside. Lyle ran to his bedroom and returned with an armload of stuffed animals. "Want one to hold while we watch the movie?" he asked.

Warmth spread through her chest. "That would be great. Which one do you think?" She didn't feel bad for asking advice, because he took the decision seriously, studying each animal.

"Panda." He handed the big, cuddly toy to her. "He's the friendliest."

"Perfect." Briony gave Panda a hug.

"You two get the laptop and pick a movie," Nate told the kids. "Briony and I will make popcorn."

"They're so great," Briony said when they reached the kitchen. "And you're great with them."

"Thanks." Nate took a box of popcorn out of the cupboard and stuck a package in the microwave. "I get a kick out of hanging out with them. But I hate it when Nathalie manipulates me the way she did tonight. She knows if she makes it sound like the kids might be in danger I'm there. Tonight, I was ninety-nine percent sure she wasn't going to leave them alone."

"But that one percent . . ."

"Yeah. Although Lyla could probably handle anything. She's only ten, but she's really responsible."

"Lyle and Lyla. The family tradition continues," Briony commented.

Nate grinned. "Lyla is even spelled with a *y*.

Neither of them seems to mind it the way I did, maybe because they aren't twins." He took out the popcorn and put in another bag. "We need some actual food." He opened the fridge and started pulling out things—hummus, olives, mini mozzarella balls, grape tomatoes. "My sister knows how to shop. You want to grab some plates?"

Briony found the right cupboard on the second try and took out four little plates; then she and Nate headed back to the kids. "You first," she said to Nate, gesturing toward the tent. Her blue-and-white paisley skirt, bought for the Paris honeymoon, wasn't designed for crawling. It wasn't tight, but it *was* short. Still, she managed to enter the tent while keeping her modesty intact and took a seat on a large pillow. "Oooh, pretty. Love the fairy lights."

Lyla smiled at her. Lyle said, "Forts aren't supposed to be pretty."

"I got the lights. You got to pick the movie," Lyla reminded him.

"What are we watching?" Nate asked, handing out the popcorn, then starting to fill the plates.

"*LEGO Batman*," Lyle said and started it up.

Her parents probably would have been afraid she'd suffocate under the sheets if she'd ever tried this as a child. Or get crushed by a falling piece of furniture.

She popped an olive in her mouth and glanced over at Nate. The laptop was casting a faint glow on his face. He was already laughing at the movie, and his laughter made Briony laugh, too. She'd never done anything like this with Caleb. They'd hung out with his niece together several times, but they'd done things like apple picking or the ballet. Enriching activities.

Diogee was lying on his pillow, slobbering and snoring. Mac could never walk past Diogee when he was asleep. There was just too much fun to be had.

He watched the dog for a moment, considering. Time to play wrestle! He launched himself into the air, landed on top of Diogee's head, and wrapped his front legs around Diogee's neck.

The bonebreath jerked to his feet. Mac kept his hold but let his body slide around, so he was hanging underneath Diogee's jaws. He pulled back both legs, then smacked both paws into Diogee's chest at the same time. Whap! Whap! Whap! The dreaded upside-down double-paw maneuver.

Now what? Maybe he could get Diogee to wedge his head under the sofa again. The meatbrain had never figured out how big he was. He had whiskers, but he didn't seem to know how to use them. Big surprise.

Mac dropped to the floor, then took off. He

could hear Diogee lumbering after him. Then he heard the front door open. He stopped so suddenly that the bonehead ran right past him and bopped his nose on the wall. Bonus! The dog turned around and returned to his pillow.

Mac trotted down the stairs. Briony and Nate were standing by the front door, smelling happy, a little like how Jamie and David smelled when they were together.

The scent of night air grew stronger. Nate had opened the door again. He was leaving! Mac was tempted to slip outside, but he was needed here. He could go on an adventure later. It's not as if he needed a door.

Mac streaked across the living room into the front hall and slammed his body into the tall table. It toppled with a crash! The vase on top of it shattered. Now the front door was blocked. Mac raced back up the stairs.

Mission accomplished.

Nate stared down at the wooden pedestal table lying across the doorway, surrounded by pieces of glass. "Did that really happen?" He looked over his shoulder. Mac was nowhere in sight.

"I think that's what's called a catapult. I'll get a broom," Briony said. She took one step and let out a cry of pain.

"Did you cut yourself?"

She nodded. "I stepped backward and my

heel came out of my shoe, my stupid, pretty, backless shoe."

"Do you know if there's a first-aid kit any-where?"

"I saw one under the sink in the bathroom off the upstairs hall."

"Right back." Nate started for the stairs, then turned around and caught Briony up in his arms. He carried her into the living room and set her down on the sofa. "Now, I'll be right back." He took the steps two at a time, found the kit, and returned to her.

"It's fine." She studied her bare foot. "Only a tiny piece of glass. It's too small to get a grip on it."

"Which is why every first-aid kit has tweezers." Nate sat on the coffee table and took her foot in one hand. "I see it." Carefully, he tried to grasp the tiny shard with the tweezers. He heard the metal click on the glass, but the tweezers slipped off before he could pull the piece free. He tried again, same thing. "Once more." Her foot twitched, and he tightened his hold a little, noticing the sparkly blue polish on her toenails. Not relevant. He made another attempt to grab the glass. Couldn't do it. "I think you need to soak it in some warm water; then I can try again."

He lowered her foot to the coffee table and stood up. "I'll find something."

"No! You don't have to. I can do it." Briony started to struggle to her feet, wobbling.

Nate caught her by the shoulders. "You'll grind it in more if you try to walk on it," he told her. "Just wait here."

Nate went into the kitchen and rummaged around until he found a bucket under the sink. He rinsed it and filled it with warm water and a little white vinegar, a home remedy Peggy had told him about. "Here you go," he told Briony when he returned to her.

She gingerly slid her foot into the water.

"You spent hours helping me babysit my niece and nephew. How come I can't help with your foot?"

"You helped. You're helping."

"If I hurt my foot, I'd be having you fetch the remote, snacks, a pillow, beverages—"

Briony laughed. "I just don't like to feel helpless." Unlike his mom and his sister, who seemed to thrive on it.

"Well, try to endure it long enough for me to sweep up the glass," Nate told her.

"I can do that later," she protested.

He ignored her. "Hanging out with you and the kids in the fort?" she said as he swept. "That was more fun than I've had in months. More than months."

"I had fun, too." Although sitting so close to her, breathing in the subtle scent of her perfume,

155

all he'd wanted was to touch her. It was almost all he'd been able to think about as he pretended he was all into *LEGO Batman.*

He sat down next to her and immediately started getting those thoughts again. This wasn't a date, he reminded himself. It was being neighborly to someone from out of town. Neighborly. Suddenly, Mr. Rogers appeared in his mind, putting on his sweater. No, not neighborly exactly. Friendly, maybe.

"Do you have any volunteers at The Gardens?" Briony asked. "Because I was thinking I need to do some volunteer work. Put some good out into the world. I know I'm only going to be here for a few weeks, but is there something?"

"Sure. Tomorrow is Family Night. The residents' families are welcome for meals anytime, but once a month we do a special event. If you could spend a little time with the people who don't have family coming, that would be great." He reached out and brushed a loose lock of her hair away from her face. Shouldn't have done that. Friendly. He was supposed to be friendly. Although she didn't seem to mind . . . "And there you are helping me again. You are definitely not a helpless kind of person."

Her dark blue eyes were serious as she looked back at him. He couldn't read her expression. What was she thinking about? He leaned a little closer. *Friendly,* he reminded himself. "I know Gib won't have family tomorrow. Most of them live in the Bay Area, and it's too far for them to drive every month. Although I might not be able to get him to Family Night at all." There. That was a nice, safe topic. You didn't start kissing in the middle of a conversation about senior citizens. Not that he would start kissing her in the middle of some other conversation.

"Why not?"

For a crazy second, Nate thought he'd said that thing about kissing out loud. Then he realized she was asking why Gib might not be at Family Night. "He's been avoiding all the group activities, even meals, since a new resident moved in, Archie. You saw him the other day, the one posing with MacGyver."

"With the bow tie and the Paul Newman eyes."

"Definitely don't say that around Gib. All the ladies are half in love with Archie," Nate said. "He flirts with them all, including Peggy, who Gib has a thing for. He's been into her since they were in high school, but I'm pretty sure he never talked to her back in the day."

"What does Peggy think of him?"

"I think she enjoys his company. I also think that she probably hasn't thought about him as a potential—I don't know what to call it. Can you call a septuagenarian a boyfriend?"

"He seemed like a guy who says what he

thinks." Briony swished her foot around in the water. "Has he let her know how he feels at all?"

"Nope. I try to lecture him about it. But he always throws it in my face that I'm not going out with anyone right now." *Yeah, go ahead, make it sound like you're a loser,* Nate thought.

"I could write you a recommendation. You're a fun date." Their eyes locked for a moment, then they both looked away.

"I think you can take it out now. Let me get a towel." He went back into the kitchen, found a dish towel, and returned to her. He sat on the coffee table again. She took her foot out of the water, and he dried it off for her. He really did need to get out more. Drying off a woman's foot so he could do some first aid was the most sensual experience he'd had in way too long.

He studied the spot where the glass was dug in, then gently squeezed it. "It's starting to work its way out. I think I can get it now." This time he got the shard on the first try. "And now a Band-Aid." He found one in the kit and put it on. "You're all set." He gave her foot a friendly pat. "You have cute feet."

Had he actually just said she had cute feet?

"My toes are all pruney," she protested.

"My grandmother always bragged that a stream of water could run under her foot and that was the sign of a lady. You have high arches like that." Since he still held her foot, he ran his hand along the curve of the arch.

Briony gave a sharp intake of breath. And with that sound all his intentions to be *friendly* shattered. Slowly, he ran his hand higher, exploring the curve of her calf. Her lips parted.

And they were kissing, her mouth so sweet and slick and warm. He heard a groan, and it took him a few seconds to realize he had made the sound.

CHAPTER 9

The sunlight was coming from the wrong direction, and Nate was on the wrong side of the bed. It took him a moment to realize why. He wasn't home. He'd stayed at Briony's last night. After they had sex.

What the hell happened to friendly? Had he gone without sex for so long that he'd lost all self-control?

He cautiously turned his head so he could look at her—and found her looking back at him.

"Um, hi," she said.

"Hi," he answered, feeling like he should have said more.

They stared at each other.

"So," she said.

"So," he said. "How's your foot?"

How's your foot? That's what he came up with?

"Good." She smiled at him.

And that smile made him realize it wasn't that he hadn't had sex in a long time. Or it wasn't *just* that he hadn't had sex in a long time. They'd had fun last night. Not just here in her bed or drinking on the rooftop, but hanging out with Lyle and Lyla in the fort.

"Maybe we should check it." Nate rubbed his hand over his chin, smiling back at her. "How does this feel?" He ran one of his feet over hers.

She giggled, her cheeks turning pink. "Really good."

"Maybe you should stay off it, just in case." Nate grabbed her around the waist and rolled her on top of him.

"That's probably wise," Briony whispered, her mouth a breath away from his.

Then his cell rang.

"Dancing Queen" started to play. Amelia's ringtone. If he tried to change it, she always managed to change it back. Nate groaned. "I'm sorry. I have to get it. It's my night manager. There might be a problem."

"Absolutely. You have to answer." Briony eased herself off him. It took him a moment to find his cell, because first he had to find his pants. "Amelia, what's going on?" he said, instead of "hello."

"Archie's not really hurt," she began, and Nate went into crisis management mode.

"What happened?" He managed to keep his voice calm.

"Archie was on the treadmill. He said the machine went crazy, that the speed kicked up all of a sudden," she began to explain, fast and a little breathless. "He fell off. I got Young

162

Doc over there." Amelia refused to use the names of coworkers until they'd been at The Gardens for five years. "He says it's just a sprained ankle."

"Where is Archie now?"

"We got him home. I already called his granddaughter."

Nate wished he'd been there to make the call to Eliza himself. She'd gotten in knots over the possibility of toxins after the ventilation system was hacked. Now that her grandfather had actually been injured, he was sure she'd need a lot of reassurance. "I'll be there in ten."

He ended the call and pulled on his pants. "Is there anything I can do?" Briony asked. She was sitting up in bed, holding the comforter around her.

"Nothing. But thanks," Nate told her. "I have to get over there." He jammed his feet into his shoes without bothering to find his socks, then looked around for his shirt.

"Be safe." Briony leaned down, grabbed the shirt from the floor by the bed, and tossed it to him. He put it on as he rushed to the front door. His oxfords weren't great to run in, but running was faster than getting his car.

When he got close to Archie's street, he forced himself to stop. He buttoned his shirt and tucked it in, combed his hair with his fingers. Walking in looking like he was panic-stricken wouldn't help him get the situation under control. He pulled in a deep breath, squared his shoulders, and continued on.

Amelia opened the door as he was coming up the front walk. "Eliza's already here," she said softly.

Nate nodded. "How's the patient?" he called out as he stepped inside.

"If you could convince my granddaughter to give me some giggle water, I'd be fine," Archie answered from the sofa. The foot with the bandaged ankle was resting on a pillow on top of the coffee table. For a second, Nate couldn't keep his thoughts from going to Briony. Without her injury, he doubted they'd have ended up in bed last night. But once he was touching her, even only enough to deal with the glass, it was hard to stop.

Eliza came in with a glass of water. "This and some aspirin will have to do," she told Archie. She handed him the water and pills and watched until he swallowed them; then she turned to Nate. "I should have taken my grand-father out of here when your ventilation system contaminated the air in the community center. If I had, he'd never have been injured. He got very lucky. He could have broken a hip when he fell. He could have hit his head and be in a coma right now."

"Don't be such a Mrs. Grundy," Archie told

her. "I'm fine. I'd be even finer if I could have a drink. That's how my father treated everything from a toothache to an ingrown toenail."

"I'm not being a Mrs. Grundy, whatever that is, just because I want you in a place where the safety of the residents is a priority." Eliza's usual soft, sweet tone was gone.

"The residents—"

Eliza didn't let him finish. "Don't bother," she told him. "I believed the excellent ratings I found for this place, but in the short time my grandfather has been here he's been put in danger several times by your mismanagement. I want his contract voided, and I want a refund of what we've already paid. I'm moving him out as soon as possible."

"Now, Eliza," Archie protested. "You're getting ahead of yourself."

At least Archie was willing to let Nate find out what was going on. "I'd like to have the chance to get the gym equipment—" he began.

Eliza interrupted him again. "Checking the equipment is something you should do routinely," she snapped. "Not in response to an injury."

"I agree, which is why we have regularly scheduled maintenance and inspections."

"Done by incompetents," Eliza shot back.

"I understand why you feel that way." Nate could tell reasoning with her wasn't going to work, at least not until she had time to recover and take in the fact that her grandfather was really fine.

"This place is berries," Archie said. "Great food, great company. I'm staying."

Eliza sat down next to her grandfather and put her hand on his knee and squeezed. "I understand you like it here, Grandpa, but your safety is what's most important to me."

"Why don't you and Archie talk, and let me know your decision about staying," Nate suggested. "The contract and the refund won't be a problem if that's the way you want to go."

Eliza sighed. "All right. Obviously, my grandfather and I have things to discuss."

It was clear he was dismissed. He left the bungalow, Amelia right behind him. "Did Henry see what happened in the gym?" Nate asked.

"He was wiping up some water in the women's changing room," she answered.

"Water? Where did it come from?" The last thing he needed right now was a leak.

"I don't know," Amelia admitted. "I thought just from one of the ladies coming in from the pool. Henry heard Archie cry out and got there pretty much immediately. No one else was using the gym, but Archie insists the treadmill jumped from a walking pace to a full-out run." She scrubbed her face with her fingers. "Eliza's right about Archie's injury. It could have been so much worse."

Nate nodded. He couldn't remember the last time Amelia went that many words without making one of her terrible jokes. She knew what they were dealing with—another act of sabotage. The equipment was only about a year and a half old, and Henry, the trainer at The Gardens, was great with upkeep.

The sabotage was escalating. Rigging the ventilation system to make it spew dead skunk smell was a practical joke compared to what had happened this morning. The person who had tampered with the treadmill obviously didn't care about hurting one of the residents. What were they planning next? Somehow, he had to get a step ahead of whoever it was, because he had no reason to believe they were through.

When Briony heard the door close behind Nate, the sense of euphoria slowly drained out of her. It was Thursday. She'd left her fiancé at the altar on Saturday. Yes, maybe he wasn't really the right person for her. Maybe her body had been trying to tell her that by erupting into a panic attack. But still. She'd had a fiancé six days ago, and she'd just slept with someone else, someone she barely knew.

She needed to talk to Vi. Except it was way too early in Wisconsin. Besides, Vi knew Caleb. Vi liked Caleb. Could Briony really admit, even to her best friend, what she'd done now?

Ruby! Briony could talk to Ruby. It was almost seven forty. Too early to call her, except in an emergency, and even though this felt like an emergency to Briony, she knew it wasn't one. She was pulled away from her thoughts by the sound of Mac giving a long, demanding meow from downstairs. He'd be in the kitchen, stationed by his food bowl. He was off his schedule this morning. He must have slept in. Or maybe the matchmaking kitty decided to let her enjoy a few more minutes with Nate. She shook her head at the goofy idea.

"I'm coming, Mac."

Once she had His Highness fed—wild salmon and venison, along with bits of organic fruits and veggies—she decided to take Diogee for a walk. Maybe a walk that took them past Ruby's. And if her light happened to be on . . .

About four minutes later, assisted by some yanking by Diogee, Briony was in front of Ruby's. The light was on. Now that she knew Ruby was up, probably, maybe she should go back home and call. No one wanted to be barged in on first thing in the a.m. Although Ruby had come by to get Briony for breakfast yesterday. That was later, though.

Her thoughts were driving her insane. This was why she needed someone to tell her what to do. She couldn't make up her mind—about anything.

No. Not true. That was the old me, the me that was going to marry Caleb, Briony told herself. *The new me is changing, maybe not fast, but it's happening. I'm going to make my own decisions, and—*

Diogee started barking like a maniac. "Shhh! Please, shhh!" Briony hissed at him. He kept on barking. The dog clearly made his own decisions.

The front door of the witch's cottage swung open, and Ruby poked her head out. Diogee's barks got faster and higher as he dragged Briony up the front walk. When they reached Ruby, the dog flung himself at her feet and rolled onto his back, tail wagging like crazy.

"He wants his belly rubbed," Ruby explained to Briony as she crouched down next to Diogee and began the rub he'd asked for.

"You feel like going out for coffee? Or breakfast?" Briony asked. "My treat!"

"Actually, I have company," Ruby answered.

"Oh, too bad." Then Briony got it. "Oh! Sorry! Go back." She was surprised Ruby was wearing My Little Pony pj's when she'd had an overnight guest. Caleb liked what Briony thought of as classy lingerie.

"No, no, no! It's Riley. The little girl I told you about, the one Mac arranged for me to meet. I'm taking her to a dentist appointment later, and since she's skipping preschool, her mom said she could sleep over. We're about to have

169

pancakes shaped like ponies," Ruby explained, switching from rubbing Diogee's belly to scratching it. "You're welcome to join us."

"Uh, actually I wanted to talk to you about something not rated G," Briony confessed.

"Well, then you *have* to come in." Ruby straightened up, said, "Diogee, treat!" and walked inside. Briony had no choice. Diogee hauled her after Ruby into the kitchen.

"DiDi! My huckleberry." A little girl in pony pajamas that matched Ruby's flung herself at Diogee, and he began licking her face.

"Riley, this is my friend Briony. She's going to eat breakfast with us," Ruby told her.

"Pleased to meet ya," Riley drawled, before Briony could say hello. Then she clambered onto Diogee's back, grabbing one of his ears in each little hand. He didn't seem to mind, not if his thrashing tail was any indication, but Briony tightened her grip on his leash.

"Is that safe?" she asked Ruby. Riley's toes were barely scraping the floor. "It doesn't look safe."

"She does it all the time," Ruby reassured her as she turned on the stove.

"DiDi's my horse, and I have a pony named Paula. Also, ones named Patricia, Paisley, and Elvis. Do you like ponies?"

"I love ponies." She'd begged her parents for riding lessons for about a solid year. They'd responded by giving her piano lessons and painting lessons that they'd insisted were just as fun. It was one of the few times Briony had whined and begged. Until her mother explained if she fell off a horse she could be badly injured, paralyzed even.

"All right, buckaroo," Ruby said to Riley. "I'm about to get the flapjacks started. That means you need to get off that there animal and get those hands washed lickety-split."

"You got it, cookie." Riley climbed off Diogee and ran out of the kitchen.

"In case you didn't notice, Riley's gotten really into cowboy slang. I found a list online." Ruby grabbed a rawhide out of a cupboard and handed it to Diogee. He dropped down to the floor with a contented sigh and started to gnaw on it. "Talk fast. We've got about five seconds before the one with the underage ears is back." She added butter to the pan.

Briony let go of Diogee's leash. "So, Nate and I went out for drinks last night. He took me to the most—"

"No time. Skip to the good part," Ruby interrupted.

"Weslepttogether." Briony's words came out smashed together, partly because she was trying to talk fast and partly because she was so embarrassed.

"Mac, Mac, Mac." Ruby shook her head. "If I

171

didn't love my job, I'd become a matchmaker with that cat as my secret weapon." She looked over her shoulder, checking for Riley. "How was it?"

"Ruby! I didn't come over here to give you salacious details!" Briony exclaimed. "I came over here because—what did I do?"

"I'd guess you had some pretty hot sex." A huge smile appeared on Ruby's face. "Didn't you, ya old coot?" she added in a loud, overly enthusiastic voice.

"She just called you a ninny," Riley told Briony as she galloped back into the room, having traded Diogee for an imaginary horse.

"I might be a ninny," Briony admitted. Except she felt so good. Her body felt like it was filled with warm honey, her limbs so relaxed she was surprised her legs had been able to carry her over there. It's like she was a completely different person than she'd been the last time she sat at Ruby's kitchen table.

Riley dragged a little stool over to the stove and climbed up on it. "I like to watch the squirts," she told Briony.

Briony was about to ask if it was safe for her to be up on a stool so close to the stove but stopped herself. The two of them clearly had a routine, and Ruby had to know what Riley could handle. "What does 'squirts' mean in cowboy talk?" she asked instead.

"By gum! 'Squirts' ain't cowboy," Riley told her. Ruby held up a squirt bottle and waved it at Briony, then squeezed a thin stream of pancake batter, *purple* pancake batter, into the pan. Riley gave an "oooh" of appreciation. "I do the mane."

"In one second." Ruby continued adding more batter to the pan, then she put down her squirt bottle, picked up another one, and gave it to Riley. "You want help?" she asked. Riley shook her head. Holding the bottle with both hands, her brow furrowed with concentration, she began squirting pink batter into the pan.

"Beautiful," Ruby told her when Riley handed the squirt bottle back. She added some more batter. "Now we wait—"

"Until it gets bubbles," Riley finished.

Briony was impatient to talk to Ruby about what happened with Nate, but she couldn't help enjoying the interaction between Ruby and Riley. When she was Riley's age, her parents spent lots of time with her, but there was always this, this overlay of caution. "Stay within sight. Let us do that. Be careful." Thinking back, she understood some of the fun had been sucked out.

"Look!" While Briony had been caught up in her memories, the pancake, make that flapjack, had been finished, and Riley was holding her plate out for Briony to see.

"Awesome!" Briony exclaimed. The pink-and-purple pony was adorable. "You did a great job on the mane."

Riley sat down in the chair next to Briony. "I did the eye, too."

"Fabulous eye," Briony said as Ruby put a plate down in front of her.

"You know what would be good on this? Some cow slobber," Riley announced.

"Okay, I got this. 'Cow slobber' is cowboy for syrup, right?" Briony asked. The little girl was covering every inch of her pony in the stuff.

Riley giggled and shook her head.

"Butter?"

Riley shook her head, giggling harder.

"Chocolate chips, bananas, strawberries," Briony continued, enjoying Riley's reaction. "Oh, I know! Whipped cream. That one actually looks kind of like cow slobber."

"She's kind of close, isn't she, chickabiddy?" Ruby joined them at the table.

"It's morandgee," Riley said.

"Meringue," Ruby translated. "And I'm not sure it would taste good on pancakes, but I'm willing to try next time you come for breakfast," she told Riley.

Ruby had to be the coolest babysitter ever, Briony thought. Although Nate gave her a run for her money. She wondered what he was doing right now. Did he have that warm-honey feeling in his body, too? He was so cute that morning, asking her about her injury. That look he gave her right before he ran his foot over hers . . . It was almost like he was touching her with his eyes.

"Briony?" Ruby's tone made Briony think Ruby had said her name more than once.

"Uh-huh?"

"I don't even want to know what you were thinking about just now. Or maybe I do, but later," Ruby said. Briony felt her face get hot. She was never, ever going to tell Ruby that when Nate looked at her it was like he was touching her with his eyes. That belonged in a high school diary. Not Briony's high school diary. Briony hadn't gone out with anyone in high school. But somebody's. It didn't belong in the head of a twenty-seven-year-old woman.

"What were you asking me before?"

"If you wanted another pancake."

"I didn't—" Briony looked at her plate. The pancake was gone. She must have eaten it on autopilot while she was daydreaming about Nate. "No thanks," she told Ruby.

Diogee finished his rawhide and came over. His muzzle was way too close to tabletop level. Before she could react, he swiped his tongue across her plate. "Back, back, back!" Briony ordered. He took a step closer and managed to get another lick. "I don't know how to control him!" she cried.

"Neither do his owners," Ruby answered. She got up and grabbed another rawhide for Diogee. "That's my method." She picked up Briony's shiny plate. "All ready for the dishwasher. No rinsing required."

"Can he do my plate?" Riley begged.

"No. All that syrup isn't good for him," Ruby answered. "If you're done, why don't you go get dressed. I made you something. It's in your room." That's all it took. Riley ran out of the kitchen.

"Her room?" Briony asked.

"The guest room. She uses it more than any-body," Ruby answered. "I get such a kick out of that kid. I owe Mac big-time. Now back to you. And *him*. Full disclosure, I looked him up online. He's fine as cream gravy, to continue in the cowboy vein."

Briony groaned. "I'm so confused. Last night was amazing, all of it. But I was engaged not even a week ago. Which Nate doesn't know. Because I wasn't expecting to sleep with him, so I didn't think I had to tell him. And now I don't know what to do. What should I do?"

"Oh no. I'm not falling for that. I promised I wasn't giving you any advice."

"Can you tell me if you think I'm a horrible person? That's not advice." Briony felt like there was a battle going on inside her. Bad Person vs. Honey Body.

Ruby shook her head, then relented. "I don't think you're a horrible person. Which isn't going to help if *you* think you're a horrible person. Do you?"

"If somebody told me they did what I did, I might not think they were horrible, but I would think they did the wrong thing," Briony admitted.

"Okay." Ruby slapped her palms on the table. "This isn't advice. This is just another question. Say you came out here for vacation, no ex-fiancé, just a fun trip to California. And you meet Nate. And you're attracted to each other. And you have sex. And you both know you're not from here and it's just a fling. How do you feel?"

"That's so not me that it's hard to imagine it," Briony said. "I'm not a fling kind of person. I mean, I've never been a fling kind of person. I've had two long-term relationships. That's it." She thought for a moment. "If we both knew I was on vacation and it was just a fun kind of thing . . . I don't think that's horrible. But that's not exactly the situation."

"More questions. Are you hurting Nate?"

Briony considered. "No."

"Are you hurting what's-his-name, Caleb?"

"Not more than I already did," Briony admitted. "I get your point. Last night, it was a blast of attraction. I didn't stop to think. Well, only long enough to deal with precautions. Now, though, I'm thinking." She rubbed her forehead, as if that would help her figure things out. "I'm supposed to go help Nate at this Family Night they have at The Gardens. But maybe it's better not to even see him again. Except he's such a good guy. I have to at least say something."

Briony let out a silent scream of frustration. She didn't want to scare Riley. "You've just been given the view of what it's like inside my head all the time. I can't decide anything."

"Until you pass out in the church." Ruby smiled, taking the sting out of the words.

"Right. Until that."

Mac returned home just in time for Briony to open the door for him. He'd decided to do a little morning shopping for Gib. So far he hadn't found something that gave Gib the happies, but Mac would keep trying until he did.

"Out again?" Briony exclaimed as he trotted inside. He went directly to his water dish. One of the presents had left his tongue coated with something thick. There was plenty of water, but he could smell that it had been standing since breakfast. He gave a meow to put in an order for fresh.

"It's not anywhere near time for dinner,"

Briony told him. "That's hours and hours away." She fetched him a treat from his jar and leaned down to give it to him. He batted it out of her hand. Diogee appeared and caught it in mid-air. Mac wished he'd eaten it himself, even though he didn't want it. The bonehead should not be allowed cat treats. He wasn't worthy.

Mac gave Briony another meow. She still needed training. She didn't understand him the way Jamie did.

"Mac! What did you do to your mouth? Your tongue is all brown." She knelt down next to him and tried to pry his mouth open. He had to give her a nip, just a little one.

"Ouch!" Briony exclaimed. She picked up his water dish, emptied it, and refilled it. *Good human.* She set it on the floor and watched intently as he began to drink, the gunk coating his tongue washing away. "Whatever it is, it's coming off," Briony said. "At least I won't have to tell Jamie you've contracted some strange disease in addition to escaping over and over and over again."

CHAPTER 10

Nate felt itchy. He'd been trying to get some paperwork done, but he couldn't focus. Instead, he kept running over everything he'd done to address the sabotage. He'd had Bob go over the treadmill and all the other equipment in the gym. Henry too. They'd found nothing. Nate had tried out the treadmill himself and found nothing. The machine had stayed steady at every setting. Still, to be on the safe side, he was having it replaced.

He'd texted Eliza with an update, because he hadn't thought another conversation could possibly be productive. She hadn't answered. Later, he'd sent a second text, asking if she'd like for him to arrange for Archie to get an X-ray on his ankle, just to be sure it wasn't broken. He'd gotten a terse reply saying she'd already had that done.

He'd had security cameras added to the community center and the gym that afternoon, and he personally checked that they were working. He'd talked to every member of the staff to find out if they'd noticed anything, no matter how small, out of the ordinary, but got nothing. For once, Nathalie and his mom weren't calling or texting with a crisis, although right now he'd almost welcome one, one he could do something about. He had no idea what his next step should be.

It was more than an hour before he needed to be over at the dining room for Family Night. He stood up from his desk, finally accepting that he wasn't going to get anything done in the office right then. Instead, he decided to walk over to his mom's. She'd have called if she'd seen that man again, but it would make her feel better if Nate dropped by. It would make him feel better, too.

When he arrived, he found her in her pajamas. "Aren't you feeling well, Mom?" he asked.

"No, no. I'm fine."

He nodded. He'd have heard about it if she were sick. "Do you want to get dressed and come to Family Night with me?" he asked as they headed into the living room. He hadn't invited her in a while, not that she needed a special invitation, because she almost always said no. "There's always great food, and we're showing *Hairspray* afterwards."

"No, no. I'm fine." She sat down and stared into space.

Nate sat down next to her, worry skittering through him. The TV was off. There wasn't a book facedown on the coffee table. None of her crafting stuff was out. "What have you been up to all day?"

She didn't answer for a long moment, then said, "I got up this morning, and I smelled oranges. I don't have an orange in the house."

His stomach tightened. Phantom smells could be a sign of a brain tumor, Parkinson's too, he thought. And Ed Ramos, one of the residents who required more care, had complained of smelling wet dog for days before his stroke, even though no dog, wet or dry, had been anywhere near him.

"Mom, I'm trying to remember. When are you due to see Dr. Thurston? You're about due to check in with her, aren't you?" he asked, trying to keep his tone casual.

She ignored his questions. "Then I realized it wasn't actually oranges. It was that cologne your father wore, Creed Orange Spice," his mother said, still staring out at nothing. "It was like he'd just walked out of the room."

"Is today the first time you've smelled it? Since he left, I mean."

She nodded. "I still have the bottle that was in the bathroom cabinet when he left, but I never open it. I don't want to. . . . I don't know why I haven't thrown it away."

"I didn't think you had anything left of his." He couldn't say "Dad's." It wouldn't come out of his mouth, not in front of her. She'd never told Nate or Nathalie they couldn't talk to her about their father, but she'd gotten almost hysterical any time they had. It didn't take either of them long to realize it was better to say nothing. He and his sister stopped mentioning him even between themselves, like they could erase the pain if they acted like he'd never existed.

"There were a few things I somehow couldn't get rid of, even though I wanted to."

"Could the bottle have broken? Maybe that's why you're smelling it." Nate wanted a logical, non-medical explanation.

"I put the things in a garbage bag in the crawl space back when . . . That was as close to throwing them out as I could get." His mother finally looked at him, and he saw unshed tears shining in her eyes. "I haven't even looked at them since that day, but I can't let them go."

She's never gotten over him, Nate realized. *After all this time.* He'd thought her life had gotten so small because his father had left her, not because she still somehow loved him. "Mom, I'm so sorry." He put his arm around her shoulders.

"I know you are." She leaned into him. "You're a good boy, Nate."

The itchy feeling was returning. He wanted to wipe away her sadness. He wanted to fix this, the way he wanted to fix what was happening at The Gardens. But he didn't know how.

"Are you sure you won't come to Family Night with me?" he finally asked. "I don't want to leave you by yourself."

"No, I'm not in the mood for all those people. You go on."

Nate stood. "I'll check on you later."

"I'm sure I'll be asleep."

"Tomorrow morning then." He stood, promising himself that he'd get her to her doctor as soon as he could make her an appointment, just to rule out any physical causes for his mother smelling the cologne. "Make sure you lock the door after me," he added.

As he walked out, it hit him that it was only a few days until the anniversary of the day his father left. That was probably the explanation for what his mother experienced. She didn't want to think about him, but the memories were there, right under the surface, the same way that old cologne bottle was stuffed down in the crawl space.

Maybe when he visited her in the morning it would be time for them to really talk about his dad. He'd pulled back so many times, including tonight, because he didn't want to upset her. But whether they talked about it or not, the feelings were there.

Tonight, though, he had other things to focus

on. He wanted Family Night to be perfect. At least some of the residents' families might have heard about the problem with the ventilation system or the treadmill or both, and he wanted to be able to reassure them. He picked up his pace. Would Eliza be there? If she was, he had to figure out the best way to approach her. Nate didn't blame her for wanting to move Archie out. He'd only been at The Gardens a few weeks and there'd been two catastrophes.

Nate rounded the corner, and the community center came into sight, lights shining in every window. Clusters of people stood in the huge lobby, laughing and talking, as the waitstaff circulated with appetizers. It looked like a place you'd want someone you loved to be. And it was. It still was. He'd get to the bottom of the sabotage. Maybe he needed to hire a—

All Nate's attention snapped to one person, to Briony, as she stepped into view, smiling at Rich and his grandson. Her auburn hair was loose tonight, falling down her back in waves. Looking at it, he could almost feel its silkiness as she'd leaned over him last night, her hair forming a curtain around them. He took the long, wide steps two at a time. When he walked inside, he had to force himself to give greetings and smiles to the people he passed. All he wanted was to get to her, feel her against him again. He had to settle for kissing her cheek—

and for watching her face pinken when he did.

"Ah, romance in the air." Rich pulled his notebook out of the pocket of his sweatpants, those ones with a swirling purple pattern and the name of a cough medicine down one leg.

"I have to know where you got those sweats," Nate said.

"L.A. ROAD Thrift Store. It's pretty much the only place he shops," his grandson, Max, answered.

Rich was probably one of the fifty wealthiest people in California and that's where he bought his clothes. Gotta love the guy. "Did you know those pants are—"

"Something a nineties rapper would wear?" Max finished for him. He shook his head. "I tried to explain the concept of purple drank, but whoosh." He flew one hand over his head.

"What's purple drank?" Briony asked.

She'd clearly spent her formative years inside a G-rated bubble. "You're adorable," Nate told her. He hadn't planned to actually say that, but it slipped out, and it got her blushing again.

Rich looked from Briony to Nate. "I feel a poem coming on." He began to scribble.

"You're a poet?" Briony asked, letting the purple drank thing go.

"I am. My form is the limerick." Rich began to scribble with one of the little golf pencils he always had on him.

"The lowest form of poetry," Regina commented as she joined the group.

"Salman Rushdie wrote limericks. So did Auden and Shakespeare and Thomas Aquinas. Shall I go on, my lady?"

"We'll talk when you've written a novel that wins the Booker, a poem that brings one to tears—and not because of its crudeness—a play that will still be read in a hundred years, or a piece of philosophy that will still be discussed in that time." With that, Regina turned to Briony. "I'm Regina Towner."

"I should have introduced you. Regina, this is Briony. She's cat sitting for the cat you used as a model in art class yesterday."

Rich interrupted with a recitation. " 'The moon's my constant mistress,/And the lovely owl my marrow;/The flaming drake/and the night crow make/Me music to my sorrow.' " He looked Regina in the eye. "*That* is a limerick."

Regina blinked. Nate didn't think he'd ever seen her at a loss for words before that moment.

Finally, she said, "A limerick by definition is humorous. That was a limerick in meter only."

"Touché." Rich bowed his head toward her. That was a first, too. Rich conceding a point.

Regina returned to her conversation with Briony. "That certainly was a gorgeous kitty cat."

"He's a gorgeous escape artist. Every time he comes out, it's straight to The Gardens. He loves it over here. I don't blame him." She briefly touched Nate's arm. "It's a beautiful place."

"I agree."

"Are Bethany and Philip going to be able to make it tonight?" Nate asked Regina.

"Not this time, but next week definitely. You see, Nate is what makes The Gardens truly special," she told Briony. "He knows the names of my niece and her husband, and every other person who's ever visited a relative here. The grounds and facilities are first-rate, but it's Nate who makes this place home."

"Thank you." Her words, especially today, after dealing with Eliza, reminded him that the work he did was important. Regina feeling like The Gardens was home, that's what he wanted for Archie and every other person who lived there.

"Agreed." Richard put his pencil away and clapped Nate on the shoulder.

"Wow. They finally agreed on something," Max said. He came around a lot and knew all Richard's friends. Or whatever Richard and Regina were. Sparring partners, maybe.

"Because Regina finally said something that made sense," Rich answered. He flipped a few pages back in his notebook. "Now who wants to hear my latest?"

Regina glanced at her dainty watch. "More than a minute before he tried to read one of his poems. A record."

"I'd like to hear it," Briony told Rich.

Rich shot a grin at Regina. "I'd be honored." He cleared his throat and began to read. " 'There once was a man in a bow tie/Who reminded all of a coyote/He—' "

"Now's not the appropriate time to poke fun at Archie, so soon after his injury," Regina said.

"Injury? What happened?" Rich asked Nate.

Nate had been expecting to get asked this question. Still, it was tricky to answer. He didn't want to completely leave out the possibility that the treadmill malfunctioned. They'd hear it soon enough. Gossip traveled fast at The Gardens. Still, he didn't want to frighten them. "He took a spill off one of the treadmills and sprained his ankle. He said the machine jumped up a few speeds when he was walking. I had it checked, and there didn't seem to be a problem, but I'm having it replaced, just to be on the safe side."

"Poor man," Regina cooed. "I need to make him a poultice. I learned one from my grandmother."

"The poor man looks like he's getting everything he needs from his granddaughter." Rich jerked his chin toward the door—where Eliza was rolling Archie inside in a wheelchair, a knitted blanket draped over his legs.

Regina didn't bother replying. She hurried off, heading toward Archie. Peggy and Janet were already rushing toward him, too. Nate wanted to go straight over there but decided to hold back. He had to handle the situation carefully. He needed to appear concerned, but not overly anxious.

Rich stared over at the women clustered around Archie, his lips pressed together. Then he took out his notebook and pencil and began to write again.

"Before you got here, Rich was telling me Max goes to UCLA." Briony turned to Max and smiled. "What are you studying?"

"M-marketing." Max hadn't stuttered when he was talking about his grandfather's shopping habits to Nate. From what Rich had told him, it was something Max struggled with as a child, but it had mostly disappeared unless he was particularly anxious. Maybe it was having the attention of a beautiful "older" woman focused on him. Nate probably would have felt the same way when he was that age.

"Have you had to take Principles of Accounting yet?" Briony asked.

"I'm taking it right now. It's a lot more l-law than I thought."

"Exactly! People who haven't studied it think it's boring."

"Or that it's easy. Just adding up rows of numbers." No stutter that time. She'd already gotten him feeling more comfortable.

"But it's more like solving a—" Briony began.

"Puzzle," she and Max finished together.

"Anyone for a phyllo-wrapped asparagus with prosciutto? I also have LeeAnne's famous spinach brownies," Hope asked briskly. One of the waitstaff must be out. That's the only time Hope served. Usually, Nate would have been up on the situation, but today had been full of distractions. "They're yummy," she added, but the words sounded stiff and she wasn't engaging with the residents the way she usually did. Was she upset about something? Nate made a mental note to ask LeeAnne.

Max opened his mouth, shut it. He hummed, then shook his head. Rich kept writing. "I'd love one," Briony said, and selected an asparagus appetizer. As she took a dainty bite, Nate found himself staring at her mouth. He had to force himself to look away.

"Nate?" Hope held the tray out to him, and he took a spinach brownie and put it on a napkin. He wasn't hungry, but he didn't want LeeAnne finding out he'd refused one of her specialties. It would take a bunch of compliments to make it up to her. He decided he'd try one more time to get her to change the name. Calling something with no chocolate in it a brownie was wrong, no matter how good it was.

"You sure you don't want one of the wrapped asparagus, Max?" he asked. "I know you love prosciutto." Nate made a point of knowing more than names.

When Max didn't answer right away, Hope turned and walked off in a way that was borderline rude. Max stared after her. Nate recognized the expression on his face. It's probably exactly the way Nate had just been looking at Briony.

Mac ding-donged Gib's bell. The man blah-blahed something, and Mac heard him walking toward the door. There was no smell of sardinsies tonight. But he wasn't there for sardinsies, he reminded himself. He was there to deliver the present he'd just found. *This* one should work.

When Gib opened the door, Mac dropped the smelly on his foot. Gib picked it up, rubbed it between his fingers, then raised it to his nose. It really didn't deserve to be called a nose. Gib had to press his face blob into it just to get the scent, and the scent was strong.

But Mac could smell Gib getting happier. Just the way Mac knew he would.

"You got out again? Bad kitty." Gib said "bad" the way Jamie did, like he didn't really mean it. Not that Mac minded being bad. Bad was fun. "Well, this time, I'm returning you." He reached down, like he just wanted to give Mac a scratch. But Mac knew better. He knew Gib was going to make a grab for him.

He turned around, trotted a few steps away, then paused. He put his tail straight up, which everyone knew meant "follow me." At least everyone who knew what was what. That, sadly, probably didn't include humansies. Mac took a few more steps, looked over his shoulder, and gave a loud meow, then started toward the sidewalk.

"Dang it, cat." Gib stepped outside and locked the door.

Mac moved slowly, keeping just ahead of the human. The present had made Gib happy, and Mac knew how to make him even happier. He led him straight over to the source of the smell.

"There's my boy." The human called Peggy made little tongue-clicking sounds at Mac, and Mac accepted her invitation, jumping into her lap. She immediately began scratching the sweet spot under his chin. Here was a human who understood at least a few things.

"I need to get him back to his owner," Gib said.

"She's here. She's going to watch the movie with Nate. So, he can stay until then," Peggy answered.

"I suppose I'll have to stay, too. I want to keep an eye on him." Gib sat down next to her. "He's a wily one."

Now that his people were behaving themselves, Mac could have a little playtime. He stood and leapt from Peggy's lap into the lap of the man on her other side. The man who didn't like him. You disliked Mac, you paid the price. Mac reached up one paw and patted the man's face. Mac could smell how much he hated that, so he did it again.

"Good night, nurse!" the man blah-blahed. "Who invited you? If I wanted someone to sit on my lap I would have asked." He looked over at Peggy. "Maybe I still will."

Mac's nostrils itched. Gib's smell was changing. He smelled the way Jamie had that time Mac refused to walk on a leash. He'd probably smelled like that, too. He was *not* happy with her that day.

Gib stood up. "Tell Briony where the cat is. I'm leaving."

Mac stared at him as he headed for the door. What was wrong with humans? Mac had led Gib to the exact spot that would make him happiest. And what did he do? He scatted. Now Mac would have to start all over again. But not tonight. He needed a nap. It was exhausting trying to teach humans how to behave.

"I need to go over and say hello to Archie and his granddaughter before the movie starts," Nate told Briony. As they'd walked from the dining hall to the screening room, he'd given her a fast rundown on Archie's accident and Eliza's reaction.

Briony wanted to go with him, give him some moral support. "Is it okay if I come? Or—"

"It'd be good. I want to keep it casual tonight." Nate led the way over. Archie had on another spiffy bow tie. And the same gold-and-tan-striped cat he'd posed with in art class sat in his lap.

"Mac! Again?" Briony cried. "What am I going to do with you?" The cat responded by purring.

"He can stay until the movie's over, since you're here, too, can't he?" a striking woman with a thick gray braid asked from a chair next to Archie.

Briony threw up her hands. "I clearly have no control over him. He can do what he wants. Make that he *will* do what he wants." Mac kicked his purr up another notch, sounding like an outboard motor.

Nate made the introductions, and Briony studied Eliza, wondering how much trouble she was going to bring Nate. She dressed in a way that hid her figure, with a skirt that hit her at mid-calf and a flowered blouse that was probably a size too large. She wore a pearl collar necklace, with a single pair of matching earrings, but had several more ear piercings.

Briony decided to make a little conversation.

196

Help Nate keep things casual. "Did that hurt? The piercing right above your ear canal?" Briony still only had one piercing in each ear. Basic. Or whatever a level below basic was.

"The tragus?" Eliza asked, brushing a finger across one of the tiny holes in her left ear. "Not really. The cartilage is thicker, so there's more pressure. This one was worse." She moved her finger to a spot almost across from the first one. "But probably just because the piercer sucked. If you're thinking of getting one done, I could—"

Archie shifted in his wheelchair and gave a grunt of pain. Eliza jerked her head toward him, whatever she'd been about to say to Briony forgotten. "Grandpa?"

"The ankle giving you trouble, Archie?" Nate asked.

"Isn't it obvious?" Eliza shot him a disdainful look. "I didn't want him to come. He should be home with me with his leg up."

"My leg is up." Archie gestured toward the chair's raised footrest. "And it's feeling swell. It just gave me a little tingle when I moved."

Eliza shook her head. "He's only saying that because he wants to convince me it was only a minor injury. He's insisting that he doesn't want to leave. He refuses to accept that using that faulty equipment could have left him with a broken hip. Or worse."

"Leave? You weren't thinking of leaving, I hope." Peggy gave Archie's arm a squeeze.

"Of course I'm staying," Archie insisted. "This place is the elephant's manicure. Eliza's being a Mrs. Grundy again."

He used as much crazy slang as Ruby and Riley did in their cowboy game. Briony guessed the expressions must be from when Archie was younger. She'd never heard any of them.

"I'm happy to hear it," Nate said. "I'll send the doctor around in the morning to check on you."

"No, thank you. I have an appointment to take him to a specialist." Eliza adjusted the blanket covering Archie's legs, her hand lingering. "His G.P. gave me a referral."

"Let me know what they say. And let me know if you need anything, Archie," Nate said. "We can have someone wheel you over for meals when Eliza's not here to bring you. Or we can have meals sent over if you'd rather."

"I'd be happy to bring Archie meals!" a woman cried from the sofa behind them just as Regina called, "I'll bring them!" from farther down the row.

"Looks like your grandfather will have as much help as he can handle," Briony said to Eliza. Eliza ignored her. The friendly woman who'd started to give her piercing advice had disappeared. It seemed weird that she had so many ear piercings, now that Briony thought about it. Eliza's style of dress was so conservative. But maybe that was because she was visiting her grandpa. Who knew what she wore when she went out for fun.

"You know I'll do anything you need while you're recovering," Peggy added.

Archie was clearly popular. Briony glanced around the room. The ratio of residents looked to be about seven women to one man. Maybe that was part of the reason, although Archie was a good-looking older guy. Those bright blue eyes of his were gorgeous.

The lights blinked. "Movie's about to start. We need to grab seats," Nate said. "Just let me or any of the staff know if you need anything, Arch."

"I'm still very concerned about the conditions here," Eliza told Nate. "If I see one more thing that makes me worried for my grandpa's well-being, I'm going to have to move him."

"Now hold on there, honeybuns," Archie protested. "It's my life we're talking about."

Eliza put her hand on his knee and gave it a squeeze. "This is one time you'll have to let me have my way."

At least she sounded willing to give The Gardens another chance, even though she wasn't happy about it. That would give Nate time to figure out who was sabotaging the place. The lights blinked again. "Enjoy the movie," Briony told the little group, then she and Nate found an open love seat on the other side of the room.

"Saved it for you two," Rich said from the row behind where he sat with his grandson. "A love seat for the lovebirds. There might be something there." He began to mumble to himself as the lights went off.

Briony couldn't help smiling as the opening number began. "Good Morning Baltimore" was such a joyous song. She hadn't seen *Hairspray* when it came out. Caleb thought musicals were silly, and he had a low tolerance for silliness. But even though the movie was delightful, it couldn't hold her full attention. She was distracted by Nate. All he was doing was sitting next to her, but that was enough. Their thighs were only a few inches apart, and she could feel the heat of his body through that short space, through his clothes and hers.

And the smell of him . . . He didn't wear cologne, but the scent of soap and *him* was better than anything artificial. It filled her with every breath, taking her back to lying in bed with him. She completely forgot about the movie as she relived every moment, every touch. It was making her crazy.

How long until she could have him again? She thought the movie was wrapping up. Once it ended, Nate would have to stay and be social for, what, another half an hour? An hour? Then would he take her home and take her to bed? Or was last night a one-time thing? It was so hard to sit there, waiting. She shifted slightly, bringing her thigh against his, although that hadn't been her plan. Probably hadn't been her plan.

Nate leaned close. "How's your foot?" he whispered in her ear. His breath was warm against her skin, but it sent shivers through her.

"Maybe you should take a look," she whispered back.

He grabbed her hand, stood up fast, and tugged her out the side door into the hall. He must have been feeling as impatient as she had, because the instant they were alone he pressed her against the wall, the length of his body tight against hers. She wrapped her fingers in his hair, pulling his head down to hers for a kiss. Her breathing started coming hard and fast. But this was nothing like a panic attack. It was the opposite. A lust attack.

Briony gave herself over to the sensations Nate was creating in her body, glad she had the wall to support her, because her knees didn't feel like they could. She'd gone all warm-honey again.

"Where did you get that?"

The voice was loud. Nate jerked away from her. Briony looked up and down the hall, buttoning her blouse as fast as she could. It was empty. They hadn't been seen.

"I asked, where did you get that?" The voice came from the screening room.

"I need to see what's going on in there." Nate buckled his belt and started for the door.

"Zipper!" Briony hissed, smoothing her hair with her fingers.

He zipped. "Thanks." He reached for the doorknob.

"Lipstick." She hurried to him and wiped her lipstick off the side of his mouth.

He grabbed her and gave her a fast, hard kiss. "Lipstick again?" he asked. When she shook her head, he opened the door. The lights were on. Briony wasn't sure how long they'd been gone, but the movie was over.

"That necklace is mine," Eliza told Peggy. "Did you take it from my grandpa's?"

Briony and Nate hurried toward the group where the argument had broken out. "Have you been over to his place?" a short woman with crimson hair demanded, eyes narrowed at Peggy. She was the one sitting behind Regina who'd offered to bring Archie meals.

"No. I found this. In my bedroom," Peggy answered as Briony and Nate reached them.

"Has Archie been in your bedroom?" Regina exclaimed.

"None of your business," Peggy shot back, one hand clasping the sparkling silver heart locket she wore.

"That's a yes, then," Gib muttered.

Peggy turned on him. "I thought you left."

"I wanted to check on the cat. Looks like he's gone again," Gib commented.

"Oh no." Briony sighed. "I admit defeat. He'll probably be back home when I get there."

"I thought maybe the locket was left by a previous tenant. The cleaning lady came in yesterday. I assumed she'd found it under my dresser or something like that," Peggy told Eliza. "I can't imagine how something of yours would have gotten inside my home, but if you say it's yours, here." She yanked the necklace over her head, the catch on its side nicking her lip.

"You're bleeding." Gib pulled a handkerchief out of his pocket and started to bring it up to Peggy's mouth, then handed it to her instead.

Peggy stared at it, fingering a rose embroidered on the corner. "This is mine. How did you get it?"

"The cat brought it to me," Gib answered.

"MacGyver?" Briony asked. What was that wicked kitty up to?

CHAPTER 11

Briony couldn't help laughing when she went inside the house with Nate. Mac was curled up in the center of a gigantic pillow on one side of the living room, while Diogee was scrunched up on a small pillow that didn't come close to supporting his whole body.

"Look who's back," she said. Diogee leapt up and rushed over. He planted both paws on Nate's chest. "I think he's asking for protection from Mac."

"I don't know if I can help you there, buddy," Nate said to the big dog. "That cat is too crafty for me." Mac opened one golden eye for a moment, looked at Nate, then closed it and returned to his nap.

"You want to go outside?" Briony swung the door open wider, and Diogee galloped out into the fenced-in front yard. He immediately began dousing the trees and bushes with pee. Briony left the door open for him. There was no point in keeping it shut. Mac got out whenever he wanted to.

"Want a drink?" she asked Nate. "I have some wine." *And after that you can take me to bed,* she silently added. After the hall, there was no question that he wanted her as much as she wanted him.

He gave a huge stretch. "Sure."

"Long day for you, huh?" Briony led the way into the kitchen and got a bottle of fumé blanc out of the fridge. She'd bought it that afternoon, hoping Nate would be over again. Then she'd spent a couple hours deciding what to wear—without asking anyone's advice. Nate seemed to approve of the cute little short-sleeved wrap dress. The one she'd bought for her honeymoon because it was reversible and she'd wanted to pack light. She shoved the thought away. Her honeymoon was the last thing she wanted to think about when she was with Nate.

"Long, good, bad, hard, strange," Nate said, leaning against the counter. When she grabbed a corkscrew from a drawer, he took it from her and opened the bottle. She found two glasses, and he poured.

"I get the long part, because I know what time you went to work. And the bad part, with Archie's accident. What about the rest?"

"I think you can figure out the good part, too." Nate ran his eyes up and down her body, and her skin flushed everywhere his gaze touched.

She swallowed. "Watching *Hairspray*? It's definitely a feel-good movie."

"No, not that part." He put his wine down, cupped her face in his hands, and kissed her, soft and sweet. "That part."

"Was that the hard part, too?" she teased, something she'd never say to Caleb. He didn't like anything crude, even just a little innuendo.

Nate laughed, swatted her lightly on the butt, then kissed her again, not so soft and sweet.

"The *other* hard part was dealing with the Archie situation," he said when he pulled away.

"Eliza is definitely unhappy. But he doesn't seem to blame you for his accident. He said he wants to stay."

"He settled in fast. No problems," Nate answered. "The family has to be happy, too, though. That's one of the first things I learned."

"You'll bring her around. You have a gift," Briony reassured him. "So, we've covered the good, the bad, and the hard. What about the strange?"

Nate took a swallow of his wine, then sat down at the table. Briony sat down next to him. "The strange has to do with my mom. A little of the bad, too, I guess. I went over there to check up on her before Family Night. I told you how there's been somebody hanging around her place." Briony nodded. He hadn't told her much, just mentioned it when he was filling her in on the sabotage. "She wasn't even dressed, which isn't like her, and she seemed distracted, almost vague," Nate continued. "She said she'd been smelling my dad's cologne in the house, even though she'd put the only bottle of the stuff in the crawl space back when he left."

He shoved one hand through his hair. "I didn't know that until today. I thought she'd thrown out everything a few weeks after he left. We'd been desperate to figure out what happened to him, calling everyone we could think of, checking hospitals. It never occurred to us that he just . . . left us. Then we got the postcard."

"The postcard," Briony prompted when he seemed to have become caught by memories of the past.

"I only read it once. But it's not like I'll ever forget it," he answered. "It said, 'I'm fine. I needed to get away. I was smothering. I'll send money.' Which he did. Not often, and not enough to support my mom, but something. Anyway, the next day I came home and everything of his was gone. Everything, including the post-card. Even the barbecue. Barbecuing was his thing. I didn't know she'd kept anything. Then yesterday, she tells me she couldn't let every-thing go."

"You haven't really had time to process this, have you?"

Nate shook his head. "I guess not. I had to go straight from her place to Family Night. It was important to make things normal. To get out there and make contact with everyone, reassure anyone who was upset about Archie's accident, especially coming so close after the ventilation system issue."

"You were great. Wonderful, actually. Watching you, it felt like you were friends with every person you came into contact with. You showed everyone you were interested in them, that you cared about them. You even knew Rich's grandson's favorite food."

"It's part of the job," Nate told her.

"Come on. It's not just part of the job. You weren't going through the motions. I could see that. That lady said you made The Gardens a home. You, Nate."

"Regina," Nate told her.

"Right, Regina. And the poet, Rich. He thought so, too. I could tell everyone feels the same way. When I saw you with LeeAnne and Hope the other day, it was obvious they adore you."

"You don't have to—" Nate began. "I wasn't asking for a pep talk."

"It's not a pep talk. It's just my observations. You should be proud of yourself, of what you've created."

"My grandfather's the one who—"

"You're the one who's kept the place going for how many years now?" she interrupted.

"Nine years and four months." He didn't give her the number of days, although he knew it.

"That's not just your grandfather. That's you. Be proud, Nate."

"I am," he said, although he hadn't ever thought of it in terms of an accomplishment. He'd just done what needed to be done. He'd done what he thought his grandfather would do, until he got enough experience that he could make the decisions on his own.

"How involved was your dad when he was running The Gardens?" Briony asked.

Twice in one day he was having a conversation about his father. Definitely strange. After the postcard, it was like his father never existed. All his stuff disappeared, or so he thought. Every picture of him, although maybe there was one or two in the crawl space?

"When my grandfather was seventy-three, he had a stroke. Totally unexpected. He wasn't even close to thinking about retiring, and it seemed like he never would. He was so vital. But overnight, he went from running the place to being a resident who needed full-time nursing care."

"Oh, Nate. I'm so sorry." Her deep blue eyes were full of sympathy. He pressed on, wanting to get through it all. "My dad was never really into The Gardens. Which, fine. Not everyone wants to be in the family business. I get that.

He should have hired a manager, but he took over in a half-assed way. I was still in high school, but I knew more about it than he did, just from hanging around with my grandfather."

"You really loved him. I can tell," Briony said.

"Yeah. He spent a lot of time with me, me and Nathalie. He really got into the whole grandpa thing. Maybe because my grandma died a few years after we were born," Nate said. "My dad sometimes made these comments, like that Grandpa was a lot better grandfather than he was a father. I never got the story, not from either of them."

"Was your mom really upset when you saw her tonight?"

Nate thought about it. "Not the way I thought she'd be if she ever brought up my dad. Right after he left, she'd get completely hysterical if I tried to talk about him, so I stopped trying. Most of the time, we all basically pretend he never existed. Today was the first time I really saw any sadness from her since back then. I've seen her cry at movies, even TV commercials. I've seen her upset over a billion tiny things, like a bad haircut. Maybe all that was about my dad, at least partially."

"Hey, a bad haircut is devastating to a woman," Briony gently teased, then added, "Do you think now that she brought him up, with the cologne, that she'll keep talking about him?"

"I'm not sure. Maybe it'll go back to the way it's always been. I don't know." He suddenly felt exhausted. "What about your family? What are they like?" He wanted a break from his own family crap.

"My family. Well, my family is just me and my parents. No brothers or sisters," Briony answered. "We, my parents and I, spent a lot of time together when I was growing up. Lots of trips—D.C., the Grand Canyon, Disneyland, even Europe a few times."

"Sounds great."

"It was," she said, but he could see there was something more there.

"But?" he prompted.

"But. Hmm. It sounds ungrateful to have any complaints. But I never went to a slumber party. I never went trick-or-treating. Well, no, that's not true. I went trick-or-treating when I was little enough to go with them and they could take me right up to the door. Then we'd go home and they'd inspect all my candy and dole it out to me a piece a day until it was gone."

"A piece a day? Mine was gone before the week was up."

"Which sounds so fun," she answered. "When other kids started going trick-or-treating by themselves, my parents still wanted to go with me. So, I told them I wasn't into it anymore. I was embarrassed to be seen walking around the neighborhood with Mom and Dad waiting for me on the sidewalk in front of every house, like I was a toddler."

"How old are we talking?" Nate asked.

"I think when I got to be twelve I made one last attempt to convince them nothing would happen to me if I went with some friends with no adults," she answered. "No go."

"That's excessive," Nate said.

"It's crazy. It made me feel . . ." She didn't finish.

"What?"

She sighed. "It made me feel like, kind of like, there was something wrong with me. Like they could see I was incapable. That I wasn't as smart or whatever as other kids."

"When they just wanted to protect you."

"Yeah. Protected me right into being helpless."

"So that's why you got so bent when I tried to help with your foot. You said you didn't want to be helpless. Just so you know, you don't seem helpless to me."

She gave a bark of laughter. "You should see inside my head."

"You're out here. On vacation, a cat-sitting vacation, by yourself. A lot of people wouldn't do that. A lot of people can't even go out to dinner by themselves. My sister, for example."

Before Briony could reply, the dog barreled in, way too fast. He tried to stop but slid across the floor, only stopping when he bashed into Nate's legs. He gave one loud woof. "He likes to have a treat when he comes in."

When she said "treat," Diogee began to wag his tail so hard he almost lost his balance. Briony stood up and opened a ceramic jar with "Feed Me" written on the side. She pulled out a biscuit, but before she could hand it to the dog, Mac appeared and gave a long yowl.

"Okay, okay, you first." She opened a smaller jar and flipped a cat treat to Mac, then gave Diogee his biscuit. "You're forgetting the other strange part of your day; at least I think it was strange."

"What?" Nate asked.

"The part where Peggy somehow ended up with Eliza's necklace and Gib somehow ended up with Peggy's handkerchief."

"Which he said Mac brought him. And the other night, he said Mac brought him this pair of very skimpy pink panties." They both looked at the cat.

"My cousin did say he likes to steal things," Briony replied. "He's also supposed to be kind of a matchmaker. Supposedly, Mac got my cousin and her husband, David, together. He stole things from David and left them on Jamie's doorstep."

"If Mac got Gib and Peggy together, Gib would buy him a case of sardines," Nate answered.

"It would be so romantic if he'd always had a thing for her and they got together after all these years." She looked at Mac. "Is that your plan, Mr. Kitty?" His only response was a flick of the tail. "He's not telling."

Nate reached out and grabbed Briony by the waist. He pulled her up between his legs and sat her on his lap. "Mac's how we met. You think he was playing matchmaker then?"

She smiled. "I'm sure he knew you wouldn't be able to resist me, seeing me in that torn dress, my hair in knots, and mascara smeared down almost to my chin. Plus, I think I yelled at you."

"You did. But the next day—"

"The next day, I promised myself I'd be calm, cool, and collected, and show you that I wasn't really a madwoman. And it worked, because you asked me out for drinks."

"And then you managed to cut your foot, so I had to take care of you."

"And then you pounced on me."

"No, you pounced on me. Like this."

And they were kissing. Again.

"Nate. Nate, Nate."

Nate awoke to find Briony, naked and warm, half lying across his chest, calling his name. He grinned. "Something I can do for you?" He ran his hand down the length of her spine.

"I can think of a couple things. But I woke you up because your phone was ringing."

Nate muttered a curse. "What song? The ringtone, what song?"

"The *eee-ee-eee* from *Psycho*."

He cursed again, fumbled around the floor for his pants, and took out his cell. "My sister," he told Briony as he pulled up his voice mail. He didn't bother listening to the whole thing. "She's having a breakdown. Again. A guy broke up with her by text. Again. I need to get over there. If I don't she'll make Lyla listen to her, and she's only ten. She doesn't need that."

Briony sat up. "Want me to come? I could hang with the kids."

He was tempted. It would be great to have her there. But Nathalie would be pissed if he brought her, and she was already in a crap mood. "How about this instead? We didn't even get appetizers last time we attempted to go to dinner. You didn't even get to try avocado toast. How about if I take you out tonight?"

"I would love, love, love that."

He smiled at her enthusiasm, then kissed her, quickly. If he kissed her slowly, he'd never get himself out of this bed.

She grabbed his wrist as he started to stand. "I have to keep reminding myself that I'm only here for a few more weeks."

He met her gaze. "Me too."

"It's been kind of fast," Briony said.

"Too fast?"

She shook her head. "Just unexpectedly fast. And fun."

"A lot of fun."

"And tonight, more fun."

"As much fun as you can stand until you go," Nate said. He dressed quickly. He wanted to get this situation with Nathalie resolved, check in on his mom, check in on Archie, do a walk-through inspection of all the grounds and public buildings, then get back over here. "I'll call you."

"I'll answer," Briony told him.

He let himself have one more fast kiss, then left, retrieved his car, and started for Nathalie's. Including a fast stop for donuts, it only took him about ten minutes to get to his sister's. She'd wanted to live close. As he pulled into the driveway, he saw Lyle and Lyla sitting on the front porch, probably so they wouldn't have to hear their mom crying. He promised himself he'd make plans to take them someplace awesome. Maybe while Briony was still here. She'd been great with them, and they'd liked her, he could tell.

"Donuts!" Lyle exclaimed, spotting the green-and-white box Nate held. He ran over, grabbed the box, and started looking at the possibilities.

Lyla approached more slowly, not as easily

cheered up as her brother. "Are there sprinkles?" she asked.

"Are you ever going to trust me again? It's been about two years since I got you plain strawberry instead of strawberry with sprinkles."

Lyla smiled at him. "In maybe another year."

"Two of the chocolate cakes are for your mom," he said as Lyla and Lyle started divvying up the donuts. "The rest are up for grabs."

"You don't want any?" Lyle asked, through a mouthful of an Oreo Cookies and Kreme. He'd never settled on a favorite.

"I'm smart. I had mine in the car. I didn't want someone grabbing my maple."

Lyla handed him a napkin with the two donuts for her mom, and Nate walked into the house without bothering to knock. Nathalie wouldn't want to drag herself over to the door.

"What took you so long?" she demanded from the sofa, where she lay stretched out, still in the clothes from the night before. Unless she'd started wearing Lycra pajamas. A half-empty glass of wine sat on the coffee table. He hoped that was from the night before, too. Probably was. Nathalie wasn't the best mom, but she had her limits.

"It wasn't long. But maybe I shouldn't have stopped for donuts."

"Chocolate?"

He pushed her feet off the edge of the sofa and sat down, then handed over the donuts. "I was thinking in the car that you should give Mom another chance to help you when you're in a dating crisis. It's a mom and daughter thing, not a brother and sister thing."

Nathalie raised her eyebrows, then winced. "I already told you that will never work. I had to pretend I never had a boyfriend in high school. The one time I didn't, she kept predicting that I'd get my heart broken. Which I did." Nathalie sat up and reached for the glass. "It's morning, isn't it?" She pulled her hand back.

"Ding, ding, ding. You win a brand-new car." Nathalie shook her head at him, then winced. "It would be nice if you knew what time it was before you called me," he added.

"It was an emergency."

"It wasn't an emergency. It's something that happens all the time. Actually, less than a week ago you got broken up with by text."

Tears sprang into his sister's eyes. Nate *had* been harsh. He hoped he hadn't just spurred a crying jag. She'd clearly had one before he arrived. "I shouldn't have said it like that. I just mean . . ." He tried to choose his words carefully. "Maybe you and the guys you go out with aren't communicating well enough. Maybe you think you're further along in your relationship than they do." What he really meant was maybe they didn't see two dates as a relationship, but he knew better than to say it. "Possibly they don't even think they're breaking up, as much as deciding it was good to get to meet you, but that they don't . . ." There was no way to say this in a good way. "That they aren't ready to take it further right now."

"You mean they got some and have no use for me anymore."

This was what he didn't want ten-year-old Lyla to have to listen to. "What I mean is, maybe you should be pickier."

"At least I get out there. I try. Unlike you."

Nate didn't protest. He wasn't going to talk to Nathalie about Briony. It would only make her feel worse.

"You're so afraid of getting hurt, you don't even give yourself the chance to get attached to anyone."

Except he was getting attached to Briony. He had to remember what they talked about that morning. She was leaving soon. They'd just been having fun. Although staying in touch wasn't an impossibility. Staying in touch, maybe getting together over on her side of the country at some point.

He hadn't met anyone he felt this way about in a long time. Maybe it was worth trying to hang on to.

• • •

Mac pulled in a deep breath, enjoying the smell of Briony's happiness. Happiness he had provided. If everyone would settle down and obey the paw, they'd all be feeling as good as Briony and Nate. And Jamie and David.

This would be the perfect time for a celebratory nap in the spot of early morning sunshine that fell on Jamie's pillow, except that the other people he was responsible for still needed help. Mac gave a huff of exasperation. He'd nap when he'd finished all his missions. It would be helpful if humans were a little smarter, but it wasn't their fault that they weren't cats.

CHAPTER 12

Briony checked herself in the full-length mirror inside the bathroom door. She spun from side to side to make her short skirt swirl around her legs. She'd decided to wear her hair down, and it bounced against her shoulders as she moved. She gave a full twirl, then laughed at herself. She felt giddy, like what she imagined a high school girl going on a first date with her crush would feel. Nate would be here in less than half an hour.

You shouldn't be so happy, a little voice whispered to her. She ignored it, or at least tried to ignore it. Being miserable wasn't going to make Caleb, or her parents, or his parents, or anyone else feel any better. And she only had two weeks and two days left in California; then she'd be back home, trying to put her life back together. For this little stretch of time, here in this beautiful place, with him, she wanted to soak in every bit of pleasure. It didn't come around that often.

She decided to write a quick e-mail to Vi. She'd had a couple texts from her friend and she owed her a response, but she didn't want to get into a live conversation. That involved questions, and the questions and answers could wait until after she got back.

Vi! Hello! Sorry I've taken days to get back to you. I've—

She'd what? Been having steaming sex with an almost stranger, not that Nate felt that way. No. Maybe at some point she'd tell Vi about her California fling—

Fling. That didn't seem like the right word. But that's what it was. By definition a fling was short and wild. It's just that with Nate it was also tender and fun and more than just a sex thing. She'd met the residents he cared so much about. She'd met his niece and nephew.

But even if it hadn't just been wild—although the wild was amazing—it was still short. It would still be over soon. And once it was she'd probably tell Vi about it, but not now, not when she was still *in* it. She wanted her time with Nate kept inside a shining bubble of happiness, just the two of them.

Okay, so . . .

been using the time out here to do a lot of thinking. And chasing after my cousin's cat, who could escape from Alcatraz. If Alcatraz was still a prison.

I've gotten messages from Savannah and Penelope (and a bunch of others). Please tell them (and anyone else who asks) that I'm fine. When I get home, I'll take you all out for drinks, and try to explain. . . .

Love you!

Briony

It wasn't great, but it would do. She should probably write one to her parents. They—

Skype blipped at her. She had an incoming call from her parents. It was like thinking about them had made them appear. Briony clicked "Answer with video," and her dad's face filled the screen. Up close, she could see every line in his face. He looked weary and worried, and she was sure she was the cause. Her stomach tensed.

"Hi, Dad!" She smiled, glad she had her going-out makeup on. Maybe seeing her without red eyes and pale—paler than her usual pale—skin would reassure him. Not that she could ever tell him or her mom what had her feeling so good. They'd never understand her going out with a guy so soon after she'd been moments away from getting married. She found it hard to understand, too, but it felt so good, so right, that she was going to try not to analyze it anymore. "Where's Mom?" Her parents almost always called together.

"At the grocery store. I'm sure she'll try you later, but I wanted to see how you are. Did you make an appointment for a CAT scan? Your mother thinks that's really important."

"I'm fine, Dad. Really. It was a panic attack, like Dr. Shah said." She almost asked him if that was okay. She didn't need permission anymore. Why did she still so often feel like she needed permission?

"You said last time that you'd sent Caleb back his ring."

"Yes." She hesitated, then went on. "Dad, I'm sure you and Mom are finding all this hard to understand. Actually, I am, too. I truly thought I wanted to marry Caleb." Except, apparently, at her bachelorette party when she was asking everyone whether or not she should. "But in that last minute, it's like my body told me no." That was actually Ruby's explanation, not her own, but it felt right.

Her father ran his thumbs over the bags beneath his eyes. "Maybe your mom and I pushed you too hard. Caleb had so much going for him—great job and all that. And it was obvious he adored you. We thought he was someone who'd take good care of you."

"And he would have." She was absolutely sure of that. Taking care of people was in Caleb's nature. If a friend needed something, Caleb was there. If a stranger needed something,

Caleb was there. Whenever she needed some-thing, he'd always been there. "He would have. But maybe that's not the most important thing. I'm twenty-seven. I should be able to take care of myself. Why don't you and Mom think I can take care of myself?" The question came out shrill, filled with so much emotion it surprised her.

"We do," her father reassured her. "Of course we do. We know how smart you are. You always got top grades."

"But you and Mom didn't trust me to ride my bike to the park with my friends. You guys convinced me to live at home during college. I swear Mom was still cutting my French toast when I was eleven," Briony burst out, releasing feelings she'd had all through her childhood. "Why didn't you think I could handle anything? I felt like there had to be something so wrong with me."

"Oh, sweetie, no. No." He sounded appalled. "We wanted to keep you safe, that's all. Not because we thought you couldn't handle things. Just because so many horrible things can happen that are no one's fault."

"I'm sorry. I shouldn't have said that."

"You should have. I want to know how you feel, what you think. You're my daughter. I don't want to be treated like some acquaintance you want to be polite to. I wish you'd told me earlier."

"Honestly, I don't think I knew earlier," Briony admitted. "What happened at the wedding, the panic attack, made me think about a lot of things, including how hard it is for me to make decisions. I could hardly dress myself without asking someone's opinion." She tilted her head back and sighed, then returned her gaze to the screen, to her father's face. "I guess that's why it was easy to convince myself I should marry Caleb. He was great at helping me decide stuff I should have been able to decide for myself."

Mac jumped into her lap, and she stroked his warm, soft fur. "I wish I'd realized all this earlier. I wish I hadn't hurt him. And you and Mom. And—"

Her father cut her off. "Don't worry about us." He looked over his shoulder, then turned back to face Briony. "Your mother had three miscarriages before we had you."

"What?" Briony exclaimed.

"It was devastating. To both of us, but to her even more so. We were so thrilled, and so relieved, when you were born. I guess we went too far, trying to make sure nothing bad happened to you. But something did anyway. I never thought you'd feel inadequate or—" He blinked rapidly, and Briony realized there were tears in his eyes.

"Oh, Dad. No. You and Mom were great. We went so many fun places. We had so many good times." Mac rubbed his cheek against her chin. "This is Jamie's cat," Briony added, wanting to get away from the subject that was causing her father so much pain. "He's a cutie, isn't he?"

Her father ignored the question. "I'm glad you have some good memories. I'm just sorry I didn't notice how you were being affected back them."

"Hey, I left Caleb at the altar." Briony tried to bring a jovial tone to her voice, but the words came out serious. "I made a decision. I trusted myself. Well, no. My body made a decision and I had to go with it. But my body is part of me, so it sort of counts. And now, out here, I'm deciding all kinds of things."

"Bri, there's a reason I called. I—"

The doorbell interrupted him. "Dad, that's . . . a friend at the door. Can we talk later?"

"It's—"

She didn't let him finish. "I'll call you back. I promise." She leaned close to the screen and kissed it. "I love you, Dad. Let's have more talks like this."

She closed the computer and almost skipped to the door. When she opened it, Nate took her in his arms, dipped her, and kissed her breathless. When he brought her back up, she told him, "I've never been dipped before!"

So he dipped her again.

• • •

Did those humans know what he'd done for them? No. If they did, they'd be feeding him sardine after sardine, along with turkey and ice cream. They'd be giving him a Mousie freshly filled with catnip every hour. They'd make Diogee live outside. They'd show Mac some real appreciation.

He couldn't blame them, though. Not really. They mostly just didn't have the intelligence to make the connection between how happy they were and Mac. They didn't know what they owed him. He stood and stretched, arching his back. Time to go assist some other ungrateful humans. He trotted into the kitchen and leapt up next to Diogee's treat jar. Once the dog had given him a boost up to the window, he slipped outside, dealt with the reek Diogee had left behind, then headed to The Gardens.

Before he got to Gib's house, a smell pulled at his attention. Nate. He took another sniff. No, not Nate, but a human who had some of the same odor. He followed the scent trail and found a man, not Nate, but with a smell that reminded Mac of Nate, although the smell was overlaid with a fruity smell, like what David drank at breakfast. The man stood behind a tree, his body pressed up against the trunk. Mac expected him to start to climb, but he didn't. He just stared.

Mac tried to decide what the man was looking at. A bird? A squirrel? No, it seemed like he was looking at a woman behind a glass window. Looking at her like she was prey. Mac had a lot to do, but he decided to stay there and watch the man. No one else was going to take care of it, so it was up to him. Mission accepted.

"Worth the wait?" Nate asked as Briony took her first bite of the Mama Shelter restaurant's avocado toast.

"Mmm. Yes. Want to try?" She held the toast out to him.

He shook his head. "I'm one of the rare native Californians who doesn't like avocado."

"But it's so creamy. And green," Briony said. She took another bite.

"What have you been up to all day?" he asked.

"I stayed in bed for a long time. Thought about you."

Her answer sent heat through him. He could see her there, in the tangled sheets. "What kind of thoughts?"

"I really wish Nate was here. . . ." Those dark blue eyes drifted halfway closed, grew dreamy, then she gave him a mischievous grin. "So he could fetch me a cup of coffee."

"That hurts. I'm wounded. You've wounded me."

"Aww, I'm sorry. I can't tell you what I was really thinking, not out in public. But later I will," she promised.

Another blast of that heat. "Did you manage to do anything other than lolling around, day-dreaming about all the things I'm going to do to you?"

"Actually, I talked to my dad."

Okay, that was like a splash of cold water. "Good conversation?" Nate asked.

"Good, but uncomfortable. I actually talked to him about how overprotective he and my mom were when I was a kid, and, like I told you, how it made me feel kind of inadequate. I even told him that I felt like they had to be so protective because they could see there was something wrong with me, something that kept me from being able to do things by myself."

"I'm sure it didn't have anything to do with you."

"Now I can see that. But back then . . . It's not like I ever thought it consciously. It's just something I felt."

"You know bryony is a plant, right? It's an especially strong climber. They chose a good name for you, a strong name," Nate added.

"I actually didn't know that. Thanks." She smiled. "It was amazing to actually talk to my dad about it. It was like throwing off a lead coat. I feel so light, like I could float away."

He put his hand over hers. "Don't. At least not yet."

"Not yet," she agreed. "I'm not ready yet."

He wondered if he should bring up the idea of staying in touch when she was back in Wisconsin, maybe even visiting. He decided to wait a little. They still had some time.

"What about you? How was your sister?"

"My sister was wrecked. But Nathalie's almost always wrecked over some guy. I told her she needed to be more picky. Which she does. She goes for guys who send very strong signals that they aren't going to be there, like a guy who says up front he doesn't want kids. Then when one of them breaks up with her she's shocked."

"She picks the wrong guys, and they're always leaving her. Like your dad left your mom. Maybe that's somehow the way she thinks relationships should be." Briony shook her head. "Sorry. That was way too psychobabble. How'd she react to what you said?"

"She got mad. That's typical. But if it helps her to vent, I can deal." He picked up a wing and dipped it in the Korean BBQ sauce. That was his idea of an appetizer.

"What about Eliza? Did anything new happen with her?" She stole one of his wings. "We haven't even been apart a whole day, but I have so many questions."

233

"Seems like everything's okay for now. Archie was at bingo this afternoon. There were no new incidents or anything. But I still have to figure out what's going on."

"You will." She sounded absolutely certain.

"Oh, and I got another offer on the place. Somebody must want the space for loft apartments or something. This one real estate company keeps coming, even though I've told them no so many times."

"Are you ever tempted?"

"No. There's no way. Selling would mean breaking up a family. That's what the residents are to each other. They might not always like each other, but if one of them needs something, they all come out," Nate answered.

"What if the people were out of the equation?"

He was surprised. He thought she got how special The Gardens was. "Can't separate it like that."

She nodded. "You're right. I guess I just wondered because you were kind of thrust into taking over running the place. Was that something you had in mind for yourself? Or did you have other things you wanted to do?"

"When I was a kid, I had the usual kid ideas. You know about my dreams of wrestling. I also wanted to be an astronaut. I wanted to be a firefighter. A forest ranger," he answered.

"Forest ranger. I can see that. You love plants.

A forest, that's a lot of plants clumped together." She smiled. "Do you like how scientific I made that sound?"

"I don't think we ever talked about plants."

"A little. You told me you put in the plants in the lobby. And that day we were hanging out in the community center kitchen, you were going over one of the plants, examining it for . . . something. Watching your hands, wow. I think right that second I knew I wanted them to be touching me."

Before he could reply, the waiter came over with their entrées. *Damn.* "How hungry are you?" he asked.

She stood up and reached for his hand. "Very, very hungry. Starving."

He pulled out his wallet and tossed enough cash to cover the meal and a big tip on the table, then he took her offered hand and they hurried out of the restaurant and down the few blocks to where he'd parked the car. And as soon as they were inside, they were on each other. They only pulled apart when a couple teenagers pounded on the windshield and hooted. "Maybe we should take this home," Nate said.

"Yeah." She was panting a little and that made him want to kiss her again right there, but he got the key in the ignition and got them on the road. At least they weren't too far away, and the LA parking gods were on his side. Someone was pulling out of a parking spot right across from the Storybook Court courtyard just as he was coming down the street. He figured he could have Briony on the bed in less than two minutes if they walked fast, which they did.

But when her bungalow came into sight, she froze. "You know what. I realized I am actually hungry." She grabbed his arm, hard, fingers digging in. "Hungry, hungry. My stomach is going *grrr.* Let's go get—"

A man in a blue-and-white-checked shirt and rolled-up chinos walked across the small front yard of her cousin's place. He looked like he'd just stepped off a yacht, with his short side-parted blond hair. Not that Nate would actually know. He'd never been on one. "Briony?" the man called.

Nate looked at her. Her face had gone slack with what looked like shock. "Who's that?" Nate asked. It was obviously someone she didn't want to see. He wrapped his arm around her and felt her trembling.

"That?" Briony repeated, as if she didn't understand English. "That's, that's . . ."

The man walked down the sidewalk toward them.

"What are you doing here?" Briony exclaimed.

"I needed to talk to you, face-to-face," he said.

"That's up to her," Nate told him.

The man kept coming. He didn't take his eyes off Briony. There was nothing threatening in his posture, but she was obviously scared.

When he reached them, Nate felt his body tense, preparing to move quickly if he needed to. "I'm so glad to see you, Bri. I've been worried. I hope you know how much I care about you," the man said.

What the hell?? Nate shot another glance at Briony. Her breathing was coming fast. "Do you want to talk to this guy?" he asked.

"I—I—" she stammered.

"I still love you, even after what happened. I know you love me, too," the man said. "Lots of people get cold feet before the wedding." He smiled gently. "I wish you'd talked to me, instead of leaving me standing at the altar." He shrugged. "But it's going to be okay. We'll work it out."

At the altar. Leaving him at the altar? "Who are you?" This time Nate asked the man directly, but it was Briony who answered.

"His name is Caleb Weber. He is—He used to be my fiancé."

CHAPTER 13

Mac stretched up on his back feet and dug his claws into the rough material of his scratching post. *Ahh. Yesss.* He scratched and scratched until the piece of claw that had been annoying him came off. He admired the sharp new tip that had been underneath. He flexed his paws. There was one other claw that needed work. He was about to return to scratching when he caught a fresh whiff of Briony's scent.

Something was wrong. She didn't have that wonderful happy smell anymore. There was something in her odor that made his muscles feel tight. He wasn't sure he'd be able to eat even a sardine, even though a few moments ago he'd have been able to gobble up a whole can and ask for more.

He ran down the stairs and into the living room. Briony was sitting on the couch next to someone Mac had never smelled before. He took a sniff. Briony's odor was so strong that it took him a moment to discover the man's. It was mild. Mac didn't pick up any anger or sadness. Nothing bad. Just the faint odor of coffee, the belts David wore, and the stuff Jamie put in her mouth and spat out every morning.

Mac kept waiting for her to figure out that if she had to keep spitting out the harsh-smelling liquid she shouldn't put it in her mouth in the first place. He'd tried to help her out by breaking the bottle, but as many times as he whacked it off the bathroom counter, it wouldn't even crack.

Did this man have anything to do with the change in Briony's smell? He wasn't sure. But he *was* sure Briony needed him. He leapt into her lap, and she immediately sank her fingers into his fur. Her body was vibrating, the way Mac's did when he purred. But even if she could purr, she wouldn't be purring now.

He gave a little hiss of frustration. He needed to figure out what was wrong. Then he was going to have to get back to work.

Briony ran her fingers through MacGyver's soft, soft fur, trying to calm herself. Everything felt wobbly, like in the church, like when she was walking down the aisle toward Caleb.

"Are you all right?" Caleb asked. His tone was soothing, like she was an animal he was trying to tame. He'd been talking since she brought him inside, but she hadn't been able to take in anything, still deeply shocked that he was there. "Do you need some water?"

She nodded. She didn't care about the water, but if she could have a few moments alone maybe she'd be able to pull herself together. What must Nate be thinking? He'd asked if she was okay, and she'd managed to tell him that she was. Then he walked away.

Mac gave her a little mew. It sounded like a question. She looked down and saw him staring up at her. He closed his golden eyes in a slow blink, then looked at her again. "What am I supposed to do, Mac?" she asked. "And there I am, asking advice from the cat again."

"What was that?" Caleb asked, bringing her a glass of water. He'd taken the time to put in ice, but not too much, just the way she liked it. How could he be acting like this? So, so . . . considerate. He wasn't angry, or upset, or anything. Just usual Caleb, even though nothing about this situation was usual.

When she took the glass from him, her hand spasmed. She would have sloshed water all over herself if Caleb hadn't thought to only fill the glass halfway. She carefully put it down on the coffee table. She'd never be able to bring it all the way to her mouth.

She had to give Caleb an explanation. He deserved it. And he'd come all this way, all the way across the country. As she tried to formulate the words, her heart, already racing, started slamming against her ribs, as if it wanted to escape from her chest. She swallowed, swallowed again. "I can't." The words came

241

out on a wheeze. She staggered to her feet, Mac leaping to the floor. Caleb stood, reached for her.

"No." She backed away from him. "Panic attack. You stay here, Caleb. Make—" She stopped for breath. "Yourself at home. Talk tomorrow." She rushed toward the door and heard Caleb coming after her. She whirled to face him. "No! Making it worse. Going to friend's." She had to stop for breath again. "Back tomorrow."

He held his hands up in surrender. "Okay. Okay," he said softly. "Are you going to be able to make it by yourself? Is it far?"

"No. S'okay." She felt a little better as soon as she was outside the house, with Caleb out of sight. She could make it to Ruby's, even though the sidewalk felt like it was rippling. *Not far, not far, not far,* she thought. *Step, step, step, step.* The journey to Ruby's door felt endless, but it probably took less than three minutes. She knocked, then let her palm rest against the smooth wood, bracing herself.

She stumbled a little when Ruby swung the door open. "You're here. Everything's okay. You're safe," her friend murmured as she led Briony to the kitchen, sat her down, then grabbed a dish towel. She wet it, wrung it out, and handed it over.

Briony's breathing started to slow as soon as she pressed the cloth to the back of her neck. "I'm sorry," she began.

"Don't talk," Ruby told her. "Not yet."

Ruby was right. Even though she wasn't panting anymore, she was still close to hyperventilating. She tried to keep her attention on the cold spot on her neck, the way she'd done the first time, and gradually the world became steady, her breathing became steady. She slid the cloth, now lukewarm, away from her neck and looked at Ruby. "I'm sorry I keep doing this to you."

"Don't," Ruby ordered. "What happened?"

"Nate knows. About what I did," Briony told her.

"The wedding?"

Briony nodded.

"You decided to tell him? I thought you were going to have a little vacation fun, leave it at that."

"I didn't tell him. I wasn't going to ever tell him," Briony answered. "But Caleb showed up on the doorstep."

Ruby's eyes widened. "Caleb? The fiancé?"

"Nate just walked off. No," Briony corrected herself. "He made sure it was okay to leave me alone with Caleb, then he walked off."

"Wait." Ruby's voice sharpened. "Why did he think it might not be okay to leave you alone with him? Was he acting threatening or something?"

"No! No. You'd realize that's impossible if you'd ever met Caleb. He just said we needed to talk face-to-face. And he's right. I owe him that. But I was too freaked out, and I basically bolted. I think I said 'make yourself at home.' " Briony laughed, and even to her ears it sounded borderline hysterical. "I did tell him I'd be back tomorrow and we'd talk then."

"Wow. Wow, wow, wow," Ruby said. "And again wow."

"I know." Briony dropped her head into her hands. "What am I going to do?" she mumbled through her fingers. "And don't say I told you not to give me advice. This is a desperate situation."

"You don't need advice." Briony moaned. "Just do what you said you were going to do," Ruby continued. "Tomorrow, go over there and talk to him."

Briony raised her head and looked at Ruby. "You're right. I just have to figure out what to say. I don't think I can go with 'you're perfect, just not perfect for me.' It's not enough. I have to really explain, and I'm still figuring it out myself. I'm actually not sure why he's not perfect for me. It's a gut feeling, not a brain feeling. Which is why I passed out instead of having a reasonable conversation weeks before the wedding."

"It's a lot to process. It's barely been any time."

"And yet I've managed to have sex with another man since then. Nate must think I'm a sociopath."

"Sounds like there's someone else you need to talk to," Ruby said.

"Yeah. I have to talk to Nate, too. No more running away for me," Briony answered. "Tomorrow will be a fun, fun day."

"I'll make pancakes for you in the morning. Any shape you want."

"I've only known you for a week and you already feel like such a good friend. Probably because you've helped me deal with a billion crises since I arrived. While I've done nothing for you." She'd really been taking advantage of Ruby's kindness.

"I can see you about to go into a guilt spiral. Don't. You're a little messed up, but I like you."

"Why?" Now that she was thinking about it, Ruby had to see her as a huge, sticky ball of neediness. A huge, wheezing, shaking, sticky ball of neediness.

"Can't explain it." Ruby smiled. "It's a gut thing, not a brain thing."

Briony found herself smiling back, then she gave a huge yawn.

"You've got to be exhausted. Let me get you a nightshirt. It'll be a lot shorter on you than me, but it'll work. I have one with ponies, of course, and one with cowgirls, and one with both ponies and cowgirls."

"Thanks." Briony stood up and found her legs—and the floor—were steady.

"I have a few spare toothbrushes, too. Kid sized, but one'll work. Riley is notorious for forgetting her toothbrush," Ruby said. "Come on." Briony followed her out of the kitchen. "You do know that you talked at least as much about how Nate was feeling as you did about Caleb."

"No, I didn't," Briony protested. She'd come over here completely thrown by the sight of Caleb.

"The first thing you said was that Nate found out, not that Caleb had shown up." Ruby stopped at the bathroom.

"I did?"

"You did." Ruby gathered a towel, washcloth, and toothbrush and put them on top of the hamper, then waved Briony on down the hall. "I wonder what that means?" she asked over her shoulder.

It means Nate somehow got under my skin way too fast, Briony thought.

Nate wandered around the grounds, unable to sit still, even though, as always, he had a mound of work waiting on his desk. Although he should be thinking about who was behind the sabotage at The Gardens or how to reassure Eliza about her grandfather's well-being, or how his mother was doing, or how his sister was doing, his brain refused. He couldn't think about anything but Briony.

She'd left that guy Caleb at the altar? And she'd been rolling around in the sheets with him how soon after? Not that long. It's not like Caleb would have waited months to come after her.

And Nate? After going out with her a few times, he'd been thinking about long-distance romance. He was an idiot. He obviously didn't even know her. He'd never have thought she was the kind of person who could be so heartless.

As he walked past the community center for the second time, he noticed the light was on in the kitchen. Had it been on the last time he went by? He wasn't sure. Because all he could think about was Briony. He had to stop. She wasn't worth it. Caleb could have her. Although why he'd want her after what she did was incomprehensible. Maybe he didn't. Maybe he just wanted to make her face up to what she'd done.

Nate veered over to the side door to the kitchen. He slid his key into the lock, then realized the door was already open. He briefly considered calling security to back him up, which was the logical thing to do with what had been happening, but he stepped inside without bothering.

And found LeeAnne pouring batter into one of five cake pans arranged on the kitchen island. "I thought you were out with Briony tonight.

Meaning tonight and tomorrow morning." She grinned at him. "I like her. She's actually managed to pry you away from here, and Hope told me she was great with the residents at Family Night. That says something about a person."

He'd thought so, too. *Wrong.* "Why are you here so late?" he asked, not wanting to get into a conversation about Briony. He'd wasted enough time thinking about her. He should have remembered bryony wasn't just an extremely strong plant. It was also poisonous.

"Making a cake for Hope's birthday."

"Big cake." LeeAnne always made cakes for staff birthdays, but this one looked especially elaborate.

"She has a lot of favorite flavors. This is going to have a layer of peach, a layer of strawberry, a layer of lemon, and two layers of chocolate, with whipped cream frosting. Actually, whipped cream might be Hope's favorite flavor. I'veseen her eat it straight."

"I'm sure she'll love it."

"She deserves it. She's a good kid. Works hard here, and at school. You should give her a raise."

"Already in the works," Nate answered.

"You're a good boss." LeeAnne gave him an approving nod. "So why are you lurking around here? Why aren't you out having fun?"

"Too much on my mind."

"The treadmill?"

"Among other things."

"Archie could have hit up instead of down," LeeAnne answered. "It's possible. I had a friend who fractured a shoulder falling off a treadmill that wasn't going all that fast. Maybe that's what happened to Archie and he made up the story about it speeding up because he was embarrassed."

"But there's still the ventilation system."

"It's really getting to you, huh? You look like hell. You better watch out. Lose your looks and Briony will kick you to the curb," she teased.

"She's only here for two more weeks," he answered. He'd be glad when she was back in Wisconsin. *Doesn't matter if she's here,* he thought. He wasn't going to see her again.

"You could always go visit her. You haven't been on a vacation in, let's see, ever. You may not think so, but we'll get along without you. Amelia is great, and you have a great staff." She reached around and patted herself on the back, then began loading the cake pans into the oven.

"It's pointless."

"I get that you haven't known each other very long, but it might be worth it to see where things lead. You seem pretty interested in her to me," LeeAnne commented.

"Look, I found out she was getting married

before she came out here. Left the guy at the altar. Nice, right? Then she starts up something with me. Doesn't bother to tell me anything."

LeeAnne raised her eyebrows. "Well, it's not like it's something you say as soon as you meet someone," she finally said.

"What about before you drag them into bed?"

"Drag?"

"Okay, we dragged each other. But don't you think that she should have said something when it looked like that was going to happen?" Not that there'd been a lot of time. It had been like a forest fire between them. A spark, then whoosh, an inferno.

"It's not like she was getting back together with him when she got home."

"That's not the point. What kind of person can get so close to marrying someone, then start something up practically right away? It's like she doesn't even have emotions."

LeeAnne studied him a moment, then picked up one of the mixing bowls. "Want to lick the spoons? Personally, I always go for chocolate when I get my heart broken."

"I didn't get my heart broken," Nate snapped.

In response, LeeAnne held out a spoon dripping with chocolate.

CHAPTER 14

Mac sat on the dresser, studying the man who lay in the bed where Briony had been sleeping. He smelled about the same as he had last night. He didn't seem to need any kind of help. But he was a human, so that meant he probably did. Mac just needed a little more time to figure out what kind of help. The man, Caleb, was in his house. That meant he was Mac's responsibility.

It was Diogee's house, too, but the bonehead wouldn't take any responsibility for Caleb. Even if he would, the bonehead was too much of a bonehead to be any help. And Mac preferred to work solo.

He felt something inside him go *click*. Breakfast time. Mac gave his wake-up meow, long and loud. He hoped this human was smart enough to operate a can opener.

Briony leaned toward the bathroom mirror, bracing both hands on the sink. She stared herself in the eye. "You can do this," she whispered. "You've *got* to do this."

There was a tap on the door. "You okay?" Ruby called.

"Yes." She gave herself a nod, then pushed herself away from the sink. "Yes." She opened the door. "Do I look okay?" she asked. Not that it mattered. What she found to say to Caleb was the important thing, not how she looked.

"You look great. I got every wrinkle out of your dress," Ruby answered. "Now, what shape do you want your pancakes in?" She rubbed her hands in exaggerated enthusiasm. "Anything. I love a challenge."

"I can't." Briony pressed her hands against her stomach. "All the space is filled with butterflies. Actually, more like giant mosquitos."

"You're going to be fine. And you're going to feel so much better once you've put the conversation behind you," Ruby promised.

"Which one?" Briony asked.

"Both." Ruby walked her to the door. "Let me know what happens. I'm around today. I just have a conference call with the director and the costumer in about an hour."

"I'll let you know for sure. Okay, here I go. . . ."

"You know you didn't move."

"I know." Briony pulled in a deep breath—at least she wasn't panting, at least not yet—and stepped outside. It was a gorgeous day, the sky a bright, clear blue. Someone was mowing, and the air had that wonderful freshly cut grass smell. But it could have been gray and raining as far as Briony was concerned. She wouldn't be able to enjoy anything until she did what she had to do.

She straightened her shoulders and raised her chin. She'd heard somewhere giving the impression of confidence could make you start to feel confidence. She strode toward home, as those mosquitos she'd been feeling dug their needle mouths into her stomach lining.

When she reached the front door, she wondered if she should knock. It was her place, well, her cousin's place, but it seemed rude to walk in without giving Caleb any notice. She settled for knocking, then letting herself in. "Caleb? It's me." Her voice came out with a tiny quaver, but not too bad.

"In the kitchen."

The smell of cat food hit her as soon as she entered the room. At a glance, it looked like there were at least five open cans on the counter. Mac was at his bowl, purring as he ate.

"You didn't give him all that, did you?" she exclaimed, startled out of starting the speech she'd prepared.

"He wouldn't eat the first two I tried," Caleb said, exasperated. "But then I found one he liked. It took a few cans to fill up the bowl."

"He's only supposed to get one."

"That's not what he told me." He shook his head at the cat, then turned to Briony. "How much is the dog supposed to get?"

"Never mind. You fed them. That's the important thing," Briony answered. "Do you want to go out and get some breakfast?" She'd done some strategizing and thought this discussion might go more smoothly in public. Not that Caleb would yell or anything. That was so not Caleb. But maybe she'd keep it together better if there were people around.

Or maybe she'd have a full-blown panic attack.

But ordering and eating would give them something to do besides look at each other. She didn't know if she could tell Caleb everything she needed to without a little distraction.

Like a full-blown panic attack.

Stop thinking about panic attacks, she ordered herself. *Not helping.*

"Actually, I made a frittata. It's been warming in the oven. I hope it's okay that I used things from the fridge."

She left him at the altar and he was worried about using her groceries. He was a much better person than she was. Although right now it felt like everyone, except maybe a few people in prison, was a much better person than she was.

Mac rose up on his back legs and gave a pathetic mew. "See. He's doing it again."

"No way, mister," she told the cat. "Kitchen's closed."

Mac lowered himself to the floor, then began grooming himself, pretending he hadn't just been begging.

"Of course it's fine that you used anything you found," she told Caleb, wishing Mac would act up a little more, giving her more reason to stall. "I hope you ate something last night."

"I had a protein bar."

Briony nodded. Caleb always had a protein bar on him in case his blood sugar dropped. He always had one for her, too, a chocolate walnut fudge LUNA bar, her favorite.

"Should I take out the frittata?" he asked.

Suddenly, Briony didn't want to stall anymore. She wanted to get this over with. She could feel her heart starting to rev up. She sat down at the table. "Let's wait a little. I owe you an explanation for what happened."

Caleb sat down across from her, and as much as she wanted to get through this, the words she'd planned evaporated from her head. "Whatever it is, you know I'll understand," he prompted.

His words shook something loose. "That's the problem. You always understand. It's so one-sided. You always support me in everything. You don't care if I ask you every single day what shoes to wear or what to order when we go to the same place we always go. But you never need anything from *me*." None of that had been what she'd planned to tell him, but she realized it was how she felt.

"I wouldn't be here if I didn't need you."

That made her stop and think. He *was* here. He didn't have to be. She raised one finger to her mouth and started nibbling on her cuticle.

He tugged her hand away. "Hey, I thought we stopped that with the self-hypnosis app I found."

It was true. He'd helped her break that habit. "Maybe you do need me," she answered, her thoughts slowly coalescing. "The thing is, I think maybe what you need is for me to need you."

"You think I want you to be weak?" He sounded appalled.

"No!" she said quickly. "No. You're not that kind of man. At all." She struggled to find a way to explain it. "What you are is a knight in shining armor. But to be a knight, you need a damsel in distress. And you know me, I am in all kinds of distress most of the time."

"You shouldn't feel that way about yourself," he protested.

"It's true, though. I've been doing a lot of thinking since I got out here, and I realized that I never make decisions by myself. I'm always looking for reassurance that I'm making the right choice. Somehow, I don't feel like I can handle much of anything by myself." She didn't bring up her parents. No matter how they'd made her feel as a kid, how she behaved as an adult was her responsibility. "But I don't want to be that way anymore," she added.

"You're saying that you don't think I'd want to be with you if you were more confident?" Caleb asked.

It sounded horrible. Suddenly, she felt confused. She'd felt so sure she didn't want to be with him. She'd felt so sure he was perfect, but not perfect for her, like Ruby's dress. What if she'd had a panic attack because getting married was the hugest decision of her life and she couldn't deal with it, even with Caleb? She'd been with him for a little more than three years. What was she thinking?

"Is that what you're saying?" Caleb pressed.

"No. I don't know." She felt herself falling into what she always called her dithering. She made a conscious effort to stop. "I guess it's hard for me to imagine what we'd be like if I was different."

"Why don't we see? Don't you think we deserve that?" he asked.

She didn't answer. She didn't know what to say. It seemed reasonable, but the thought was making things go a little wobbly around her.

"How about this?" he continued. "I still have some time off." He didn't say "for our honeymoon," but they both knew that was why. "Let's have a vacation together out here."

Something inside her pushed back against the suggestion. She wanted him to go home. She wanted to spend the time she had left here with Nate.

But that was impossible. And even if it wasn't, Caleb was making a reasonable request. She did owe him something. Maybe she was wrong. Maybe things would be so much better for them as a couple if she didn't expect him to make all the decisions. "Okay."

Caleb smiled, the crinkles at the sides of his eyes deepening. She loved those crinkles. But it still felt like there was something hard inside her, resisting the idea. "I don't want to jump right back into where we were before, though. I can't. I need to take it slow. You can stay here, but we have separate rooms."

"That feels like we're moving backward."

"It isn't. I left you at the altar, remember?"

"I'm not going to ever forget that."

She'd hurt him. She had to remember that. This wasn't all about her.

"What I mean is that we're moving forward from that. I broke it off, so spending time together is moving forward. I need time to figure things out, Caleb."

"All right. Agreed," he answered.

"First I need to do something. Alone."

He raised his eyebrows but didn't ask what it was. This wasn't the way to start. If they were going to do this, she couldn't start with a lie, even an unspoken one, between them. "I need to talk to Nate, the man you saw me with last night. And you need to know that the two of us have . . . been together. Which might change how you feel."

And now she'd hurt him again. She could see it in the way the muscles in his jaw tightened.

"People do strange things when they're under stress," Caleb said. "You were still planning to go back to Wisconsin when your cousin came home, weren't you?" Briony nodded. "So, this wasn't a serious thing. It was a, let's call it a fling. A distraction after what happened."

A fling. Something short. Something wild. Maybe that's all it had been. Something that never could have held together.

Relief flooded her. She'd needed to tell him the truth. "I feel so bad about what happened at the church. And about the other night. I'm sorry I hurt you. I'm so, so sorry. That's the first thing I should have told you," she said in a rush.

"Let's put it behind us. Go do what you need to do," Caleb told her. "Maybe I'll take the dog for a walk."

Diogee galloped into the room. He spun around, ran back out, then returned with his leash in his mouth. "Make that I'll definitely take the dog for a walk."

"I'll be back as soon as I can."

He'd been so understanding. He really was perfect.

Except if you really loved someone, should you understand her sleeping with someone else? Without even a day or two of completely hating her?

The sound of his cell playing "Coconut" woke Nate. He sat up, his stomach slowly turning over. He grabbed the phone and checked the time. Almost one. In the afternoon. He never slept this late. He'd slept through his alarm. He never slept through his alarm. He also never drank seven—Was it seven? Or had he stopped counting at seven?—beers in one night.

"Coconut" continued to play. And Nate's sluggish brain made the connection. "Coconut." That ring belonged to Yesenia, one of the nurse practitioners. What now? What had happened while he'd been sleeping it off?

"Where have you been?" Yesenia demanded before he even said hello. Something had to be very wrong or she'd never use that tone. "I think we have an outbreak of food poisoning. I've had eight people coming to me with abdominal cramps, vomiting, and diarrhea in the last hour. All of them ate brunch in the dining room."

Nate's tongue felt like it had been glued to the roof of his mouth. "On it," he managed to say. Then he hung up and jammed his fingers into his forehead, trying to force his brain to function. He needed to check on all the residents. He also needed to assess what everyone had eaten to trace what food was responsible. That meant he needed manpower. He sent out a group text to the entire staff, asking anyone who was available to come in.

He threw on his clothes from the day before, then went directly to the medicine cabinet. He took two aspirin and slurped up some water from the sink. As he straightened up, he felt like someone was taking a nail gun to his brain. He downed four more aspirin, then rolled on some deodorant and swished his mouth with Listerine, hoping that would deal with beer sweat and beer breath.

After he used his fingers to comb his hair, he hurried to the door. He reached for his keys. They weren't on the hook. What had he done with them? He needed to get out of there. He searched his small house. Twice. Then he realized the keys were in his pocket.

He also realized dealing with an emergency in the clothes he'd thrown on the floor last night wasn't the way to go. He wanted to get to The Gardens, but if he was going to get everyone through the latest crisis he needed to present himself as competent and in control. He changed into a suit as fast as he could.

At least he lived close to work. In twenty minutes, he was standing in the screening room with most of the staff sitting in front of him. Several who had the weekend off were already there, and he'd had texts from most of the others saying they were on their way.

"Like I said in the text, we may have an outbreak of food poisoning on our hands," Nate told them. "In any case, an unusual number of the residents have reported symptoms. What I want is—"

LeeAnne burst in. "No one has ever gotten sick from my food. No one!"

He'd need to talk her down. He turned to Amelia. She'd been waiting for him in the parking lot to give him an update, and they'd come up with a plan. "Get everyone divided up to go door-to-door like we talked about. We'll meet back here to exchange information."

Yesenia stood as Nate walked toward LeeAnne. "You should all know that especially for the older residents, this could be very serious," she told the group. "For one thing, we have to worry about dehydration."

"There are cases of bottled water in the kitchen. I'll bring them out here. Load up before you go," LeeAnne barked, rallying. "I'll get some bags, too."

"Anything else they should bring?" Nate asked the nurse practitioner.

The door opened again, and Briony stepped inside. Just what he needed.

"Not yet. I want to see anyone with symptoms, so get me that info as soon as possible," Yesenia answered. "If there are people who don't think they can keep down water, give them ice chips."

"Okay, I have The Gardens divided into quad-rants. Line up and I'll give you your assignments!" Amelia called.

Nate walked over to Briony. "What are you doing here?"

"I wanted to talk. I—"

He cut her off. "I don't have time for you."

CHAPTER 15

Briony spotted Hope near the end of the line of people. She joined her. "Can you tell me what's going on? I came by to see Nate, and there was this." She waved her hands, trying to encompass all the people. She'd been so focused on Nate when she'd walked in, she hadn't registered what he'd been saying.

"A lot of our people have gotten sick. We're going to try to figure out if it's food poisoning," Hope answered.

"I want to help. Can I help?" Nate might not want her there, but she needed to do something. She at least wanted to check on Gib.

"We're breaking up in pairs and going door-to-door. Do you want to come with me?" Hope asked. "Nate's calling people from the health department, and LeeAnne is staying here to show them everything in the kitchen. She won't let me stay. I think she needs to slam and bang things and doesn't want me to see it. She's so upset that her food might have caused all this."

"Yes. I definitely want to come." Briony sent Caleb a text saying she was going to be longer than she planned, that she needed to help with an emergency situation.

He texted back a few moments later, wanting details on what kind of emergency. Briony texted back about the possible food poisoning outbreak at the retirement center. He'd absolutely understand that as a reason for her being late coming back.

But then, Caleb being Caleb, he wanted to know what he could do. She shot back an answer, telling him she thought they had enough people and that she'd be back as soon as she could. "Going out to talk to residents now. See who is sick," she added, so he wouldn't keep messaging her. He wouldn't want to keep her from that.

She and Hope reached the front of the line, and Hope wrote down the numbers of the houses they should visit. They each grabbed bags of bottled water from a nearby table.

"Wait!" someone called. Briony turned and saw LeeAnne coming toward them.

"You're here," she said to Briony.

"I am."

"You left my boy in quite a state."

"I know. I know," she said again, struggling, and failing, for a way to explain. "I didn't mean to."

LeeAnne gave her a sheet listing all the foods served at brunch—a long list. "Check off what each person ate, whether they're sick or not," she instructed, then strode over to another pair of volunteers.

Hope gave Briony a curious look but only said, "We're starting over on Jacaranda Way."

Briony was relieved she didn't have to come up with an explanation for the girl. She was probably only nineteen or twenty. She didn't need to hear such a sad, sordid story. And, truth, Briony didn't want to see the way Hope would look at her when she found out what Briony had done. Although LeeAnne hadn't seemed to hate Briony. When she'd said Briony had hurt Nate, it was like it was something Briony should know, not like a condemnation.

"Good. I'll get to see Gib," Briony said as they walked. "The cat I'm taking care of seems to have made friends with him. He keeps coming over to visit."

"Gib is great," Hope answered. "I'm glad he's started socializing again. He stayed away from the community center for a while. He didn't even come to the dining room for meals." She grimaced. "I guess it would be better if he'd stayed home today." Her cell buzzed, and she checked it. "Nate wants us to text him and Yesenia with everyone who's affected. He says we should tell everyone that we'll be bringing in food from outside for dinner. We'll deliver something bland to everyone who's sick."

"Wow. He thinks of everything," Briony commented. "How long ago did he find out this happened?"

"Not even an hour ago." They turned up the walkway of the first bungalow on their route. "He's amazing." She banged on the door. "Samantha takes out her hearing aid when she's home by herself. The feel of it in her ear annoys her."

Briony was impressed. "Do you know so much about everyone who lives here?"

Hope banged again. "Not all. This is the street I walk down when I'm coming or going to work. When it's nice out, people are on their porches. We chat." She raised her hand to knock again, but the door swung open.

The tall, thin woman inside held up one finger as she put in her hearing aid with her free hand. "Hope! What a lovely surprise. Would you like to come in? I found a pattern to crochet an adorable little octopus, and you're getting one. You can look through the yarn and choose the color."

"That's so sweet, but I'll have to do it later. We came by to see how you're feeling," Hope told her. "Some of the residents got sick after lunch. We're afraid it might be food poisoning. Are you doing okay?"

"Fine," Samantha answered, placing one hand over her stomach. "I hope no one's seriously ill."

"Yesenia's been treating people, and Jeremiah should be in soon to help," Hope explained. "Can you tell us what you ate at lunch? That will help us figure out what food is responsible."

Briony pulled a pen out of her bag and began checking off the foods as Samantha named them. "Let me read you what else was served," she suggested when Samantha finished. "It would be easy to leave something out, like a condiment or dressing." She ran through the list and checked off a couple more items. Then she and Hope said good-bye and headed to the next house. The couple who lived there had eaten at home.

"How do you feel about doing the next one by yourself?" Hope asked.

Briony was curious, but Hope hadn't asked her any questions when LeeAnne had brought up the situation with Nate, so she decided to return the favor. "Sure."

"Thanks! I really appreciate it!" Hope exclaimed. "I'll do the one next door alone, then we can meet back up."

"See you in a few." Briony hurried up the walk-way and knocked on the door. "Max, hi." The boy was dressed in pajama bottoms and a T-shirt. "This must be your grandfather's place."

"Yeah. I just got here. I didn't bother getting dressed." He flushed with embarrassment. "I was worried. He called and said he thought he had the flu," Max answered.

"I don't think it's the flu. Several people who ate brunch at the dining hall have suddenly gotten ill. It seems like it's food poisoning," Briony explained.

Max's eyes widened. "H-how serious is that? Does he need to go to the hospital?"

"I'm going to have Yesenia, one of the nurse practitioners, visit him."

"Okay, yeah, I know her. How l-long will it be?"

"I'm not sure. It depends on how many others have symptoms. But I know another nurse is coming in, so I don't think it will be too long," she answered. "Do you think I could see Rich for a few minutes? It would really be helpful if I could find out exactly what he ate."

"Sure. Yes." He swung the door open wide, then frowned. Briony looked over her shoulder, trying to figure out what he'd seen. Hope was already waiting on the sidewalk. "What's H-h—What's s-sh-." He swallowed hard. "What's s-she doing out there?"

"Hope's going door-to-door checking on people, same as me," Briony told him.

"But why is s-h—" He hummed a little, then started again. "Why is she just standing there?"

"We're comparing notes every few houses." Briony wasn't going to tell him that Hope hadn't wanted to go to his grandfather's. "Can I come in?"

"Y-yes. S-sorry." Max stepped back so Briony could enter. Rich was sitting on the sofa with a plastic bucket next to him. But he had his notebook out and his pencil in hand. He wasn't feeling bad enough that he wasn't ready to jot down lines for one of his poems.

Briony ran down the list of foods and Rich told her what he'd eaten, then she gave him the water and encouraged him to drink it slowly.

"Can you think of anything that rhymes with 'diarrhea'?" he asked when she stood to leave. *Aiarrhea, biarrhea, ciarrhea.* Briony kept running through the alphabet, trying to think of something. "Not offhand," she admitted. "Maybe 'dysentery' would be easier!"

"Or 'the trots,' " Max suggested.

"Ah! Good idea." Rich started to scribble, and Max grinned.

"You're a good grandson," Briony told him, then she returned to Hope.

"No one was home at Archie's. He's who lives next door," Hope said.

"Can you send a text saying that Rich is sick?" Briony asked. She didn't want to do it herself. She didn't think Nate would be happy she was still around. Besides, she didn't have Yesenia's number.

"Oh no! How bad is it?" Hope asked as her thumbs flew over her phone.

"When I left he was trying to compose a poem

about diarrhea. Max was there, taking care of him," Briony answered. "He's a good kid." She looked at Hope. "I guess I shouldn't say 'kid.' He's your age. Actually, aren't you in a class together?" Nate had been asking Max about that at Family Night. It felt like weeks ago now.

"Yes. Although I doubt he knows that. When he sees me, it's like he doesn't even recognize me. Or at least he pretends not to. Maybe he doesn't want to talk to the help."

"That doesn't seem like Max," Briony said.

"How can you even say that? You barely met him," Hope protested. "Didn't you see him the other night? He wouldn't even answer when I asked if he wanted an appetizer. And he walked off about two seconds after that."

Briony tried to remember exactly what had happened, but she couldn't. Hope sounded very sure, though.

"Okay. Yesenia's got Rich on the list of people to see. Let's get going." Hope started walking, and Briony fell into step. She was glad the next house was Gib's. She was anxious to see how he was.

When she knocked on the door, he called back, saying he was coming. Just from hearing his hoarse, weak voice, Briony could tell he was one of the people who'd gotten sick.

It felt like it took forever for him to answer. When he did, his face was tinged with gray and sweat dotted his hairline. "Let's get you back inside where you can sit!" Briony exclaimed. "Hope and I came by to see if you'd gotten sick after brunch. It sure looks like you did." She stepped inside, looped her arm through his, and slowly helped him walk to the living room.

"Who else has gotten sick? What about Richard, and Regina, and Janet? And Peggy?" Gib had thrown Peggy's name in last, like it wasn't important, but after what Nate had told her Briony knew Gib had to be more concerned about her than any of the others.

"We don't know yet." Hope handed him a bottle of water. "Someone will be checking in on all of them, though."

"Where's the beast?" Gib asked Briony.

"I would say 'home,' but every time I think he's at home he's actually over here."

"He likes to bring me presents. That's the latest." He nodded at the side table. Beside the lamp sat a—She wasn't sure what. She hoped it wasn't something dead that Gib hadn't felt well enough to dispose of. She cautiously picked up the thing, trying not to touch any of the sparse white hair. To her relief, she realized it was mostly made of latex so thin it was almost transparent.

"What is it?" She gave the thing a little shake.

"Not sure. He must have played with it awhile

before he brought it over. Or else he found it in the trash," Gib answered.

It *did* look like it had been batted around with some sharp little claws and possibly chewed on a little. "You want me to throw it away?"

"Nah. I'm starting a collection. That cat is a character." Gib cleared his throat. Briony could hear how dry it was.

"Maybe try a little more water," she suggested. "Then I need to find out what you ate."

After she ran through the checklist with him, she told him they had to move on to the next house. "Would it be okay if I come back later?" she asked. "To check on you. I can let you know how Peggy and the others are doing."

He looked pleased. "If no one else needs you more. And since you seem not as crazy as you first appeared to be."

"Did you tell Nate that Archie wasn't home?" Briony asked as they started to the next house. "He's got to be anxious to know if he's one of the ones who got sick. His granddaughter will go nuclear if he did. She already wants to move him out."

"I texted him." Hope looked at Briony in what felt like an appraising way. "He told you about that? Huh. He usually keeps his problems to himself. LeeAnne has to drag things out of him. You must have gotten close pretty fast."

Briony wasn't going to touch that. They

finished their area about an hour later. As she and Hope headed into the community center, Briony felt her stomach tighten, hoping she wouldn't run into Nate again. She still needed to talk to him, but today was not the time. She'd go with Hope to turn in the lists of what everyone they'd seen had eaten, and if there wasn't anything else for volunteers to do she'd leave.

She needed to spend some time with Caleb anyway. She wondered how long he was planning to stay. Until it was time for her to go home? Wherever home was. She had no apartment to go back to. Caleb had found a place for them in Portland. She could feel her pulse start to race at the thought.

"You okay?" Hope asked as they walked into the dining room. People were gathered at several tables, filling brown bags with bananas, yogurt, crackers, and more water. They looked like they had the job covered.

"Yes. Fine." Briony pulled in a deep, steadying breath. "Since we're back, maybe I'll have a water." She opened a bottle and took a swallow. She wasn't going to let herself have a panic attack. Not now.

"We're about to run out of yogurt over here!"

Briony knew that voice. She scanned the room. Yes, there was Caleb. Somehow, he'd found The Gardens and was pitching in. Why did Caleb always have to be so . . . so Caleb?

She had to get him out of there. It was bad enough that *she'd* shown up when Nate was dealing with an emergency.

"I've got you covered, Caleb!" a twenty-something woman called as she walked toward him carrying a case of yogurt. Caleb, being Caleb, had already started making friends. This friend was gorgeous, with long, dark hair and dark eyes that reminded her of—

Briony grabbed Hope's arm. "That's—That's—"

"That's Nathalie."

"Nate's sister," they said together.

Perfect, Briony thought. *Just perfect.*

Nate and LeeAnne finished carrying the last of the meat and fish out to the Dumpster and tossed it. The Department of Health had taken samples of everything served at lunch and told them to dispose of the rest.

"What a waste." LeeAnne shook her head. "There was nothing wrong with any of that. I know bad when I see it, and that food wasn't bad."

"I agree. Somebody must have gotten to the food on the brunch buffet. The ventilation system, the treadmill, now this. And I have no idea who's behind the sabotage."

"You don't go out enough to have enemies," LeeAnne joked weakly. "And it's not like you have any enemies inside The Gardens. I'd know. Between me and the staff, I hear everything."

"There's got to be something I'm missing."

"Well, now the health department's on it. Maybe they'll see something we haven't. Fresh eyes." LeeAnne and Nate started back toward the community center. "We're set for dinner with the catered stuff and the bland foods for everyone who's sick. Are we serving breakfast as usual?"

"I don't know." He hated saying that. "I'm not sure people will be ready to eat in the dining room so soon. But it's possible getting things back to normal as fast as possible will reassure everyone. Let me think on it and get back to you."

When they returned to the kitchen, they both washed their hands. "I'm going to go check on how it's going with the care packages, see if anyone came across residents who they think need a personal visit right away. I'm going to check in on them all as soon as I can."

"I'm lucky. All I have to do is clean up this disaster." She gestured at the mess left behind by the health inspectors. "If you see Hope, tell her I've stopped having tantrums and it's safe to come back here and help."

"Will do." Nate straightened his tie, preparing to show everyone he encountered that he was in control of the situation. Even though he wasn't. Not by a long shot. He strode into the dining room. It looked like there was good progress getting food and more water assembled for delivery to those who'd gotten sick. They could switch over to making up dinner deliveries for everyone else as soon as the caterer got there, which should be within half an hour.

His gaze snagged on one of the tables, and he stopped short. His sister was tying bows onto the packages. How'd she even known what was going on? He hadn't told her or his mom. It would only have meant two more people to reassure. Or that's what he'd assumed. But here Nathalie was, actually helping. He started toward her, then stopped again. She was standing next to that guy from last night. Briony's fiancé. Ex-fiancé. What the hell was he doing here?

If he was here, that meant Briony hadn't left. He quickly spotted her in the far corner, chatting with Archie, who was sitting in his wheelchair, a natty fedora pulled low over one eye. Regina and Janet hovered over him, and he looked like he was enjoying the attention. Nate switched course and headed over, wanting to touch base.

Before he reached the little group, he was intercepted by Eliza. Because that's the kind of day it was. *You needed to talk to her anyway,* he told himself. *Might as well be now.* "Eliza, how did it go with the specialist? What did he think of the ankle?"

"The ankle? That's the least of my grandfather's

problems at the moment. I had to rush him to the emergency room. He had food poisoning. Along with most of the people here."

"The number isn't that high," Nate protested. He glanced over at Archie. "He looks well enough to flirt at least."

Eliza wasn't amused by the mild joke. "He should be in bed. But he's stubborn, and he's somehow become incredibly loyal to this place, even though he's been here less than a month. He insisted on coming over to see how things were going."

"He's made a lot of friends," Nate began. "He's been—"

She didn't let him finish. "I'll be sending you this emergency room bill along with the one from the orthopedist, once we're able to see him."

Nate didn't argue. It was pointless to remind her The Gardens had an excellent medical staff on-site who would have taken expert care of her grandfather.

"The doctor said it was lucky I got him in as fast as I did. My grandfather was badly dehydrated. They immediately got him on an IV of fluids, with Toradol for the pain and Zofran for the nausea. He was in horrible shape."

"I'm very sorry to hear that."

"You were very sorry to hear about his ankle, too. Very sorry isn't very helpful."

What could he say to that? It was true. He'd

done everything he could to deal with the food poisoning and the malfunctioning treadmill, but it wasn't enough. There could be more sabotage to come, even with the new cameras. And even if he did find who was behind it, it wouldn't take away the pain Archie, and so many others, had gone through. "The health department people have been here. They're investigating. So far, they haven't found any cleanliness issues. They've taken samples of the food we served at brunch. I should have more information soon, and I'll pass it on to everyone as soon as I do."

"You're free to speak at the meeting for the families of all the residents that I have planned for tomorrow night. I thought we could use the screening room, unless you have a problem with that."

"A meeting?" Nate repeated.

"To discuss the problems The Gardens has been having," Eliza told him.

He quickly assessed the situation. A meeting wasn't a bad idea. He needed to talk to all the families. But he didn't want Eliza running it. Too late, though. If he tried to take over, she'd make a thing out of him being unwilling to let the families be heard.

"I think that's a great idea. You're certainly welcome to use the screening room," Nate answered. "I can have refreshments—" Eliza gave a snort of derisive laughter, and Nate winced. "Or not. But I'd appreciate having a time to talk and address questions."

Eliza nodded. "I'm sure there will be many. I'd like the contact information for the families."

"That's confidential. But if you'd like to compose an e-mail, I'll be happy to send it out." That would at least give him a heads-up before he got in front of the group.

"Fine. I'll have it to you within the hour. I'll also be speaking to the residents directly. I'd like to talk to staff members, too. Unless you have an issue with that."

"Not at all. I'll tell everyone you may have questions for them." He didn't want that, either, but it wouldn't be good to look like he was trying to hide something. He needed to schedule another meeting with the staff. They'd need reassurance and explanations, too, and he wanted to thank everyone for going above and beyond today. He shot another glance at his sister. She was still at work on the bows. It's like he'd stumbled into an alternate reality. "Would you like me to set up a place for you to work on the e-mail? I can get you a laptop if you don't—"

She cut him off. "I have everything I need at Grandpa's. I suppose he'll be all right over here for now."

"If he wants to go home, I'll make sure someone takes him over so he won't have to maneuver the wheelchair on the streets."

"Don't bother. Just have him call me." With that, she walked away.

He shouldn't be irritated that she didn't say thank you. He was the one who was in the wrong. Her grandfather had been injured—twice—on his watch. But he had to push down a burst of anger as he watched her leave.

The anger immediately rose up again as he walked over to Archie. Briony's face was animated, her eyes bright, as she talked to the group, looking like she completely belonged. This time he didn't attempt to shove the anger down. He forced himself to exchange a few polite words with Regina and Janet and to ask Archie how he was feeling, then he turned to Briony. "I need to talk to you." He led the way out into the hall. "I told you to leave," he said as soon as he shut the door behind them.

"You told me you didn't have time to talk to me," she protested, but her cheeks flushed. "I stayed to help out."

"And you called your whatever he is to help, too?"

"No! I texted him to tell him I was going to be back later than I thought. I said I was helping out with an emergency at a retirement home. I didn't say you owned it. I didn't tell him to come. But he found out this place was near Storybook Court, and, of course, he came over. He's perfect. That's what a perfect man does. He helps in an emergency."

"If he's so perfect, why'd you leave him at the altar?" Nate demanded. "Because that's what you did, right?"

Briony lifted her hands, then let them fall in a helpless gesture. "Yes."

Yes. That's all she's going to say? Yes. "What did you tell him about us? Or did you lie to him, too? Say I was a neighbor or something?"

"I told him. Not the details. But I told him I slept with you."

"And?"

"And he understood."

"He understood. He *understood.* Well, I sure as hell don't."

Her chin came up. "You knew I was just out here on vacation. You knew this, this *thing* between us, was just for fun."

"Yeah. I'm having a great time," he bit out.

She pulled in a long breath. "Nate, I came over here because I know I owe you an apology. Things happened really fast between us. You know that. When we first met, it's not like I was going to blurt out, 'By the way, I'm here because I fainted on the way down the aisle and was too ashamed to stay and face my fiancé—ex-fiancé—and the wedding guests and my parents.' We were going out for a friendly drink, remember? Not a date. Then it got . . . well, you know how it got."

"What about the next time? You couldn't have mentioned it before we were screwing up against that wall over there? Oh, wait. No explanations were needed. It was just fun. At least it's just fun if you're a—" He stopped himself before he said the word, but they both knew what he'd been about to say.

And who cared? It was the truth. You had to be a slut to do what she'd done. That's why he wanted her out of his sight. "You apologized. Thank you. Now I think it would be better for you and Caleb to leave. If you still have the urge to help, there are places all over LA that need volunteers."

Nate turned away and strode back to the dining room, not checking to see if she was following. Nathalie was still over there with Caleb, tossing her hair all over the place and shooting him little glances. In about five minutes, she'd be crying because he'd rejected her. That's about all it took. A little attention from a guy and she assumed it was forever. Didn't their parents' marriage teach her anything?

"Just so you're aware, this guy was about to get married a week ago," Nate told his sister when he reached her.

"I know," Nathalie answered.

She knew? Well, at least Caleb did the stand-up thing and told her right away. Unlike the way Briony had dealt with Nate.

"Can you believe what happened to him? And he came all the way out here to try and fix things," Nathalie continued. "If I was Caleb, I'd never forgive her. Never." She looked over at Caleb. "I'm the possessive type," she confessed.

She was in full-on flirt mode. But that was Nathalie. She was a flirt. At least she understood the situation. That's the only reason he'd come over there. "I'm going to go check on the kitchen."

"Wait." Nathalie caught him by the elbow. "I thought it would be nice if we took Caleb and his ex out for dinner tonight. As a thank-you for helping out."

"No!" Nate shot back.

He heard an equally horrified "no!" from behind him. Briony.

"Thank you, but no," Briony said, more calmly this time. "Caleb came out so we could spend some time together. Some time alone."

Mac jumped up on Gib's bed and cuddled up close to him. The man reached out and stroked his head. Gib's skin felt unpleasantly damp, but Mac didn't move away. His friend needed him, and Mac was going to stay close.

There was the smell of illness coming from all directions. Later, he'd see what he could do for the other humans. He might only be one cat, but he was MacGyver. He'd do what had to be done.

CHAPTER 16

N ate, why didn't you tell me about the food poisoning?" Nathalie asked as she tied bows on the last few care packages.

"You have enough going on. Work. The kids." That wasn't the big reason, but her lack of interest in The Gardens wasn't something he wanted to talk about when staff and residents were within earshot. "Where are the kids, by the way?"

"At Mom's. That's why I was over here. I was walking back to my car and I met Caleb. He was trying to figure out where to go to help with 'the emergency.' Which I didn't even know about. We came over to the community center together. People were working on the care packages, so the two of us jumped in. If you'd told me, I would have been here earlier."

Yeah, but would you have jumped in if there wasn't a guy involved? he couldn't stop himself from thinking. "How is Mom?" he asked. He wanted to know. He also wanted to change the subject.

"Same as always," Nathalie answered. "Happy to see the kids. She likes being Grandma. So, are you going to tell me why you didn't call me about what was going on?"

He knew her, and she wasn't going to let it go. Not now that she had her teeth in it. "Want some coffee?"

She tied the last bow and gave it a little pat. "Sure. Looks like there's not much more to do until the caterer comes with the food."

LeeAnne and Hope were working on the kitchen when Nate and Nathalie came in. Nate gave LeeAnne a look, and she got it. She pretty much always got him. "Hope, I want to see what's what in the walk-in." Hope didn't ask questions. She and LeeAnne quickly left.

Nate poured him and Nathalie both coffees and sat down with his sister at the table. "Okay, what didn't you want to say in front of people?" His sister also got him, when she bothered to pay attention. "No offense, Nathalie, but—"

"No offense. That's a great way to start. I can tell it's going to be wonderful now," she snarked.

Sometimes she made him feel like they were both still thirteen, but he didn't let himself get sarcastic back. "I didn't call you because you're not part of the day-to-day running of the place." That was diplomatic.

"But this wasn't day-to-day. You had people you barely know helping out."

"Not really. Briony . . . Briony's become a

friend." He wasn't going to get into the Briony situation with his sister. She might be more than willing to give him way too many details about her relationships, but that's the last thing he wanted to do. "She's met some of the residents. I guess Caleb wanted to help out since she was."

"She wasn't even around when we were putting the packages together." Nathalie looked around the table, and he got up for the cream. "He came all the way across the country and she disappears," she continued. "That's not the way you act if you want someone back."

She managed to distract herself, he thought as he set down the creamer. Unfortunately, he didn't want to talk about this, either.

Nathalie poured a dollop of cream into her cup, then hesitated as she raised it to her lips. "Is this safe?"

How could she even ask that? "Yes, it's safe. Everything in the place is safe."

"Well, obviously not." Nathalie put the cup down.

"You can drink it, Nathalie. Don't be stupid. If you don't trust me, trust the health inspectors. They've been all over this place, and they didn't find anything."

"Then what happened? People got sick right after eating here. At least that's what I heard— from people other than you."

"Someone's been sabotaging the place, okay? The food poisoning's not the only thing that's happened. The ventilation system was tampered with, which means replacing carpets and drapes and probably furniture in the library and TV room. Books too, unless there's a way to get the smell out. And one of the treadmills jumped up a bunch of levels and threw one of the residents off. He only sprained his ankle, but I wouldn't be surprised if his granddaughter sues. And after what happened today, she might get some other families to go in with her."

"Oh, Nate. Why didn't you tell me?"

She didn't sound accusatory anymore. Just sympathetic. And maybe a little hurt.

"I'm the manager. It's my job." Nobody had said they wanted in when he took over after his dad left. And it's not like Nathalie and his mom hadn't seen him struggling with his online classes when it was taking almost all his time to keep The Gardens running.

"But this is huge. Did you tell Mom?"

He shook his head. "Come on, Nath. You know how she is. She barely holds it together when she doesn't have anything to deal with except knitting, and cooking, and watching TV. And the other night . . ."

"Spit it out."

"She said she smelled Dad's cologne," Nate admitted.

Nathalie drew in a sharp breath. "She brought up Dad?"

"Yeah. When she started talking about the smell, I immediately started thinking 'brain tumor.' You know how it can make you smell things that aren't there?"

"Jesus, Nate. You have to tell me this stuff. She's my mother, too."

"I'm going to get her in to see the doctor," Nate reassured her. "I'll let you know what she says. But I started thinking that Mom was missing him. It's right around the anniversary of when he left."

"Like I don't know that."

"I didn't know you still thought about it."

"Of course I still think about it. Just because we never talk about it doesn't mean it didn't happen."

"She told me that she has a bottle of cologne he left behind and some other stuff in the crawl space." Since they were talking about it, they might as well talk about it.

"I thought she got rid of everything. I wanted to keep his watch, you know, something I'd seen him wear so much, but she wouldn't let me."

He hadn't known that. He hadn't asked to keep anything. He'd obediently helped put everything in trash bags, then hauled them out to the dumpster.

"My brain is *psheew*." She made an exploding gesture over her head. "So, you're getting Mom to the doctor, just in case. What do we do about the sabotage?"

He noted the "we." "I got new surveillance cameras put in. The security team knows the situation. Maybe the health department will turn up something we've missed," Nate told her.

"And the lawsuit or lawsuits?"

"For now, all there is to do is wait and see. I'll talk to all the families and address their concerns as well as I can." He thought about mentioning the meeting that Eliza was planning. But he had it handled. Nathalie might have enjoyed tying on bows for an afternoon, but he knew she didn't really want to be involved.

Caleb took Briony's hand as they walked down the Santa Monica Pier that night. Her blood started to thrum in her ears as her heart sped up. But not in a good way. Her instinct was to pull away, but she wasn't going to do that to him. He'd come all the way out to LA when he'd be justified in hating her.

She forced herself to tighten her fingers slightly, and he smiled in response. "Beautiful sunset," he said.

"Gorgeous," she agreed. That's how their conversation had gone since they left The Gardens, nothing more than an exchange of pleasantries. But what did she want? She'd told him she didn't want things to go right back to the way they were. And she didn't want some deep discussion of her feelings the day of the wedding or the underlying reasons for sleeping with Nate.

She knew what she didn't want. But what *did* she want? She didn't know. That was the problem. Same as it always had been. She didn't know what she wanted.

She tried to focus. Did she want to be with Caleb? Her body kept saying no. But it's not like her body always knew best. Her body had wanted to hurl itself at Nate. And Nate hadn't turned out to be such a great person. He'd barely stopped himself from calling her a slut, as if he hadn't been right there with her doing all the supposedly slutty things. Except he hadn't been engaged a few days before.

She had. To Caleb. She was supposed to be using this time to figure out if there was a future for her and Caleb. Briony had been with Caleb more than three years. Was it all because she'd grown up feeling like she couldn't take care of herself? Was it because her parents thought he was good for her and she pretty much went along with what they thought? She realized her palms were starting to sweat. "Sorry," she murmured. She slid her hand away and tried to casually wipe it on the side of her skirt. It left a sweat stain on the pale green fabric.

"Are you okay?" Caleb asked. "Are you feeling panicky right now?"

"A little," she admitted.

He led her over to a bench. "Why don't you sit for a minute. I'll get you something to drink."

Briony let her head drop forward. She listened to the sound of the ocean, hoping that rhythm would steady her. Instead, she found herself thinking of Nate. They might have been looking at this spot from the restaurant patio above the city.

Today, Briony had hoped she'd be able to explain things in a way that would make him understand, at least a little. She'd wanted to tell him how terrifying it had been in the church when the floor wouldn't support her and everything went blurry. He hadn't wanted to hear it. He'd wanted her out of his sight as soon as possible, like he found her disgusting.

Briony heard footsteps approaching and lifted her head. She managed to smile as Caleb handed her a bottle of water. He was considerate. He wasn't someone who condemned someone else for one mistake. Look what she'd done to him. And here he was, wanting to give her another chance, to give them another chance.

"Feeling any better?" Caleb asked after she took a sip of her drink.

"I think so." She owed him—them—time. This was a beautiful spot, a romantic spot on the beach, the perfect place to find out if their relationship was worth trying to rebuild. "What do you—" *No,* she ordered herself. *Don't do it. Just because you're with Caleb don't start dithering and asking him to decide everything.* "Let's go on the Pacific Plunge!"

Great. That's what she'd come up with? She'd gone on a carousel a few times and that's it. Her parents—or was it really only her mom with her dad going along?—thought amusement park rides were too dangerous. And that one? It went straight up, then straight down, with people screaming all the way. She didn't want to go on anything that made people scream. Maybe she should pick something a little less crazy. The Ferris wheel maybe?

"Doesn't seem like your kind of thing. How about I win you a teddy at the ring toss instead?" Caleb suggested.

Irritation bubbled up inside her. "This is me not being weak or wishy-washy. I make one decision without consulting you and you're already wanting me to change back to the old me."

"You want to go on the Plunge, we'll go," Caleb said. "Let's get tickets."

As they walked to the ticket booth, Briony spotted a food vendor. "I'm going to get a corn dog." Avocado toast was more her style. She stuck to a pretty healthy diet. But tonight, she was going for new things. "Want anything?" she asked.

"We just ate a nice dinner," Caleb protested.

"I know. This isn't dinner. It's junk." She grinned at him, feeling the shaky, panicky feeling begin to evaporate and a wild reckless-ness taking its place.

"And they call it junk for a reason."

"I'm not planning to live on it. But we're at the boardwalk." Briony bought herself a corn dog, then she saw an Icee stand. Icees were pure sugar—and she wanted one. She made herself a mix of sour apple, lemonade, blue-berry, and cherry, every flavor glowing with artificial color and not really looking like something meant for ingestion. She took a sip. *A-maz-ing.* There might have been a little forbidden-fruit factor, but still.

She strolled back over to Caleb and joined the ticket booth line. Briony studied the prices. "Let's get wristbands. It'll be cheaper if we're going on more than a couple things."

"Are we going on more than a couple things?" Caleb asked.

Briony felt a pang of conscience. This was his vacation. He should have a say in what they did. But no one asked him to come. And she'd had a miserable day. She wanted to have some fun. Without being judged for it. "I want to try everything!" Not so much, but she was not turning back. Maybe the Plunge would be like the Icee. The drink looked noxious but turned out to be delicious. The Plunge looked petrifying but might turn out to be . . . only somewhat terrifying.

"Two bands," Caleb told the teenage girl behind the counter.

Briony took a bite of her corn dog. "There should be more food on sticks. I think I need a caramel apple. I wonder if they make deep-fried caramel apples? Because deep frying did wonderful things to this hot dog." She sucked down some more of her Icee. She was feeling a little manic. Could the sugar be hitting her that hard already?

"I recently read that men should limit themselves to nine teaspoons of sugar a day, and women should time themselves to six," Caleb commented.

"Way to be a buzzkill." She took another hit of Icee. "Am I right?" she asked the cashier. The girl looked at her like she was crazy. "You too," Briony told her.

"What's going on with you?" Caleb asked, handing her one of the wristbands.

"Nothing. I'm just having fun. Fun, ever heard of it? The question is what's going on with you?" She started for the Plunge, walking fast.

He didn't answer, just stayed at her side. She stopped abruptly at a trash can. "I can't bring this on the ride." She took the last few bites of the corn dog and tossed the stick, then pulled the lid off her 32-ounce Icee. It was still about three-fourths full. She brought it to her mouth, tilted her head back, and gulped, then slammed the cup into the trash. "Two points!" she cried.

About two seconds later, she got brain freeze powerful enough that she wanted to sink down to her knees, but she got moving again, joining the line for the ride. She was having fun, dammit, and a headache, a head-busting headache, wasn't going to stop her. It wouldn't last long.

From above came the shrieks of people plummeting straight down to the ground on the ride. *Shrieking with* joy, Briony told herself. *Sheer joy.* She didn't look up.

When it was time for her and Caleb to take seats in the gondola, that stupid little voice in her head started chanting, *Mistake, mistake, mistake.* Three teenage boys took the remaining seats. Briony looked at the line. Most of the people waiting were teenagers. Teenagers had no concept of mortality. That's the only reason they could think of this as fun!

She almost bolted, but the restraints locked in place. *Good.* She'd feel like a failure if she got off now.

Mistake, mistake, mistake! the little voice shouted as the gondola started to rise. Briony realized she was gripping the bar in front of her with both hands.

Caleb reached out and gave her clenched fingers a squeeze. "Don't worry. These rides are braked with either compressed air or permanent magnets."

She'd always liked how competent he was, how he was one of those guys who knew how things worked. But she didn't want a lecture during her first real amusement park ride. She deliberately loosened her fingers and looked at the view stretching out beneath her. The ocean sparkled in the moonlight. She—

The ride came to an abrupt stop. She couldn't prevent herself from grabbing onto the bar again. Then, whoosh! The gondola was hurtling down. She was in free fall! And a shriek was coming out of her throat. It really was a shriek of joy! Joy and a little bit of terror.

"That was a complete rush!" she exclaimed as they climbed out of their seats.

"This is such a first-world idea of entertainment," Caleb said. "Tricking your body into producing adrenaline, because our lives are so safe."

"Buzzkill," Briony muttered, almost, but not quite, under her breath. She didn't think she'd ever used that expression before tonight.

"Briony, you realize that you're trying to pick a fight with me, don't you?" Caleb asked, his green eyes serious.

"What I'm doing is trying to have a good time." *And trying to pick a fight with him,* the little voice commented. "What you're doing is trying to make me feel guilty by bringing up third-world countries and recommended sugar usage," she added.

"I was making conversation," Caleb protested. "I was trying to stay away from talking about, huh, why you slept with someone less than a week after we were supposed to get married."

"You said it was nothing, a fling, a stress reaction." They were getting some curious looks from the people nearby, but she didn't care.

"I was trying to be understanding, and I do get it. I don't like it, but I get it," Caleb answered, his tone extremely calm. "But, so you know, being left at the altar wasn't a stress-free experience for me, and I didn't go out and take someone to bed to deal with it."

"Of course *you* didn't! You're perfect! Too perfect to drink an Icee one night just for fun. Too perfect to eat a corn dog."

"You're making up reasons to push me away. You don't really care if I don't feel like eating junk."

"I'm riding the Scrambler next," Briony announced as she started for the ride. "You're welcome to come," she added over her shoulder. "See? Not pushing you away!"

Mac trotted down the street. It was past dinnertime, and he was ready for his num nums. That's what Jamie called them sometimes.

Soon he'd head home for some food, but there were a few more places he needed to stop. One of the women who liked to pet him was already waiting outside the front door of the first. "Hello, you handsome creature," she blah-blahed, then bent down to give him scratchies.

When the door opened, the woman took a step back. If Mac hadn't been fast, he'd have ended up with a kink in his tail from the pointy heel of her shoe. "How can you sleep wearing that?" she blah-blahed at the man. "Your sweat suits are bad enough. Those pajamas could cause blindness. I may need to go get my eclipse glasses."

Mac slipped inside as the humans continued talking. They wouldn't need to talk so much if they had working noses.

"I got 'em at the thrift store," the man answered as he let the woman in.

"Doubtless. If I had them, I'd certainly have given them to a thrift store," she commented.

Mac was surprised to see lots and lots of toysies on the living room floor. He sprang on

301

the closest paper ball and gave it a double whack.

"You should try one of the thrifts sometime. They have lots of beige clothes, too," the man said. "I know that's the only color you like."

"Your eyes have clearly already been damaged. My cardigan is sage. My blouse pistachio. And my slacks are ash gray." She looked over at Mac. "The way he's playing is adorable. Just watching is like an infusion of pure joy. Now, tell me how you're feeling."

"Everything bad that went in has now come out. Plus some good stuff," he answered.

Mac noticed that the smell of both humans was changing as they stood together. It wasn't that they smelled happier exactly, but they smelled better. A little like Jamie and David when they'd been apart and came back together. And a little like something about to go kaboom. Maybe they should get some playtime in. He thwacked a paper ball at the woman. It ran over the toe of her shoe. She ignored it.

That was not acceptable. He took the paw to three more balls, one after the other. *Thwack! Thwack! Thwack!*

The woman laughed. "All right, you win!" She kicked one of the balls toward him. It didn't go far. "I'm better at throwing." She picked up the ball. "Early drafts of so-called poems, I assume," she said to the man.

"Don't read that!" he burst out.

"I wasn't planning to, but now I'm intrigued." She began smoothing the paper out. Clearly, she did not understand how to play. Mac demonstrated by shooting another paper ball at her. *Thwack!*

She didn't even glance at it. She stared at the flattened piece of paper, which wasn't even a toy anymore. "A sonnet? I'm impressed. I didn't know you ever attemp—" She stopped mid-blah-blah. "Is this about me?"

The man's smell sharpened with anxiety, and an emotion Mac couldn't identify. It was sort of like when Diogee wanted a bite of pizza and wasn't sure he'd be given one. If Mac really wanted pizza, he just waited for the right moment and jumped on the table.

"Is it?" she repeated.

This man usually talked a lot. But this time he just nodded.

CHAPTER 17

Y̶ou," Nate said when he saw MacGyver curled up on Gib's recliner. "You're the cause of all my problems, you know that?"

"That's my buddy you're talking to. He's been keeping me company all day." The cat moved to the arm of the chair while Gib sat down, then moved onto his lap. "He left a few times, but not for long. What's your beef with him?"

"Nothing. Not his fault," Nate muttered. "How're you doing? Do you need anything? I have soup I can heat up for you." He gestured to the rolling cooler he'd been taking from place to place as he checked up on everyone who'd gotten sick.

"Nah, I'm good. Hope brought dinner around earlier." He looked down at Mac. "Wait. What kind of soup?"

"Chicken or vegetable broth. Nothing that will upset your stomach."

"Chicken." He scratched Mac under the chin. "You feel like some chicken soup, cat?"

"I'm not serving soup to that—" Nate got a grip. If he heated up soup for Mac, maybe Gib

305

would have a bowl, and getting some more liquids in him would be good. "On it."

"Before you leave. But sit for a minute."

Nate sank down on the couch. It had been a long one. Gib was the last person he needed to see before he called it a day. Although he should probably go back to his office. He needed to work on a speech for the meeting Eliza was getting together.

"You look worse than I feel. Maybe I should be the one making you soup," Gib commented.

"I'm fine." Except that his hangover headache hadn't completely gone away and he still felt queasy.

"Like hell you are," Gib answered. "You're not going to be fine until you find whoever's sabotaging the place. We both know the food poisoning has to be part of it."

"Yeah. Too close to the ventilation system and the treadmill to be anything else," Nate admitted. "You didn't see anything unusual when you were at brunch, did you?"

"I've been keeping an eye out whenever I'm over at the community center, but everything seemed normal. No guests I hadn't seen before. Regular servers. Archie going from table to table, so the women could coo over his injury." Gib's mouth twisted with disgust at the memory, making Nate sure Peggy had been one of those women.

"I saw Peggy on my rounds," he said, since he was sure Gib would want to know. "She's feeling much better. She said she didn't eat much at brunch, because she'd had some oatmeal first thing when she got up. She just wanted the company."

Gib snorted. "The company."

"She also said your buddy over there paid her a visit. Which reminds me." Nate pulled a key chain out of his pocket. "He brought her this, and she asked me to give it back." Mac gave a huff as he handed it over to Gib.

"How'd she know it was mine?"

"From the picture." The chain's fob was a picture of his grandson and granddaughter dressed up as M&M's for Halloween encased in Lucite.

"Surprised she recognized them."

"The way you show off pictures?"

"You want a beer or something? You can fetch whatever you want out of the fridge."

Nate groaned. "Do not speak that word in my presence." Gib laughed, then pressed his hand to his head with a wince. "You need some aspirin?" Nate asked.

"Think we both could use some. On the kitchen counter."

Nate walked into the kitchen. "Water okay? Or I have some ginger ale in the cooler. It's good for settling your stomach."

"Water," Gib answered. "Did you and Mac's keeper go out drinking last night? She came over this afternoon, wasn't looking so hot, either. Maybe that's why she didn't stop back by."

Nate returned and handed Gib the water and pills. He'd already taken his. "You were expecting her?"

"She said she'd come stop over later and check on me. Maybe she sent Mac in her place."

"Briony's the kind of person who does whatever she wants whenever she feels like it," Nate answered. "Maybe something better came up."

Gib raised his eyebrows. "You think she had nothing better to do this afternoon than check up on a bunch of people she barely knows?"

Nate shrugged. "I can't explain her."

"What happened?" Gib asked. "And don't say 'nothing,' because I'm old, not stupid."

It was completely inappropriate to talk to a resident about his personal life. Of course, it was completely inappropriate to talk to a resident about sabotage at The Gardens, too. And Nate could use someone to talk to. LeeAnne would listen, but she had enough to deal with.

"It turns out she has a fiancé."

"What the ever-loving hell?"

"Had, I mean." Although he was out here and they were "spending some time alone." So maybe *had* would be back to *has*. Maybe it

308

already was. Nate still didn't get how the guy could be so okay with Briony having sex with someone else. "She left him at the altar the day before she came out here. That day she came over to get Mac, that was two days after she was supposed to get married. Anyway, we, uh, hooked up. Then he showed up. And she acted like there was no reason she should have mentioned him, since she was only going to be out here for a few weeks and we both knew it wasn't anything serious between us." Nate raked his hands through his hair. "And I should not be talking about this to you. It's unprofessional."

"Good thing. Professional is boring, and I have to get my excitement secondhand."

"Since you won't ask Peggy out," Nate reminded him.

Gib ignored the comment. "What did you think was going on between you and the girl? You haven't known her for long."

"I know. It's like I've turned into my crazy sister. She's always going out on one date and thinking she's in a relationship," Nate burst out. "Not that I thought I was in a relationship with Briony. But I liked her." There. He'd said it. "I'd started thinking I wanted to at least keep in touch after she went back home. See if it was something that would just fade or if . . . Doesn't matter now."

"Let me get this straight. She's not engaged anymore. You like her—and it's not like you're coming in here every few days telling me that about some woman. What's the harm in staying in touch? It fades, it fades. It doesn't, that tells you something."

"I was interested in that before I found out about the whole left-a-guy-at-the-altar thing. Who does that? And who sleeps with a new guy a few days later?"

Gib gave a dismissive wave of the hand. "I had a dog once. Loved the dog. Had to put him down. Thought I wouldn't get a new one for at least a few years. Then the vet calls me up. Says he's treating a pup who needs a home. It was only a month or so later, but bam. Had a new dog. And I was glad I did."

Nate stared at him. "That has almost nothing to do with what we're talking about. Her fiancé didn't die."

"What I'm saying is, she probably wasn't looking for a new guy. But she met you when she met you."

"And didn't mention any of this."

"She might have. He showed up before she did."

"You have an answer for everything." Nate was starting to feel a little guilty. He didn't completely agree with Gib, but he didn't need to have handled the situation the way he did.

"There's no point in talking about it anymore. We had a fight, and I basically called her a . . ." He hesitated, trying to think of a milder word. "A harlot."

"Did you actually just say 'harlot'? Who are you—Archie Pendergast?" Gib asked. He shook his head. "You could try apologizing. Might work. Might not."

Nate stood up. "I'm making you and the cat your soup. Then I think I'll go home and cut off my head. The aspirin isn't helping."

The Pepto-Bismol wasn't helping. Briony lay in bed, staring up at the ceiling. *Don't puke, don't puke, don't puke,* she thought. That would be a horrible end to a horrible day. She hated throwing up. Well, everybody hated throwing up, but she *really* hated it. And if Caleb heard—

If Caleb heard, he'd probably come hold back her hair. But she'd know what he was thinking. He'd be all superior, thinking that he'd known she'd get sick after eating a candy apple, two cake pops, a frozen chocolate-covered banana, and some cotton candy on top of the giant Icee and the corn dog. The cotton candy was probably a mistake. The paper cone really wasn't a stick. But she didn't regret one bite or sip of anything else. "Non, je ne regrette rien," she muttered, because if you said something in French it had to be true.

311

Maybe more Pepto. But it was so disgusting. And so pink. It was wrong for something to be disgusting and pink. Pink was a happy color. Her bridesmaids' dresses were pink. The thought made her stomach roil. *Don't puke, don't puke, don't—*

Mac leapt out of nowhere—*how did he do that?*—and landed on her belly. She scrambled out of bed. *Don't puke on the floor, don't puke on the floor, don't puke on the floor.* She wished she could make it to the downstairs bathroom, but that was impossible. She flew into the master bath, dropped to her knees in front of the toilet, and let go.

It was possible Caleb wouldn't hear. Even though she hadn't had time to shut the bathroom door, the bedroom door was shut. *Please, please, please.*

Okay, maybe she was going to get a little bit of luck. She flushed the toilet and cautiously climbed to her feet. She took one step toward the door. Too soon. She scrambled back into position for round two—and heard a soft rapping on the bedroom door. "Briony? Are you okay?" Caleb called.

Could she tell him it was Mac vomiting? she wondered wildly. No. He'd never believe it. "Go back to bed. I'll be fine!" she called back. She knew better than to try to walk to the door.

"Can I get you anything?"

Why did he have to be so nice? "No. No, no. I've got everything I need. Thank you," she made herself add.

"Good night, then."

"Good night." And then it was time for round three.

She'd just gotten herself back in bed, with Mac settled on her head, thank all that was holy, instead of on her stomach, when her cell buzzed. There was no way she was going to fall back asleep anytime soon, so she checked it. There was a text from Vi. That was a good friend. Someone who texted you 1 million times, even though you never answered.

OMG. I just heard that Caleb is in LA.

Not just LA. He's here. At my cousin's.

Are you back together???

No. But I couldn't send him to a hotel. He's in the guest room.

Details.

He said he wanted to spend some time together. That I owed him that. That we owed it to each other.

Can I say he's a saint?

Do you really think he's a saint?

Well, yeah. Doesn't everyone?

So I'm crazy. Who wouldn't want to be with a saint?

I wouldn't.

You don't like Caleb? You didn't say anything! For years!

'Cause I do like him. I just wouldn't want to be his girlfriend. I'd feel bad every time I watched Real Housewives. I'd feel like I should be feeding the hungry or recycling or doing something worthy. But you're pretty much a saint, too.

No, I'm not!

Tell me something bad you've done.

I'm not good because I'm a good person. I'm good because I'm scared.

???

I'm scared of breaking rules. I'm scared of disappointing my parents. I'm afraid of falling off the jungle gym and splitting my head open. I'm good because I'm scared to be anything else. But yesterday I did something crazy!!! Caleb and I went to the Santa Monica Pier. And I suggested we go on this insane ride that falls straight down from the sky. I. I did that.

Why? You don't do rides.

I wanted to do something new. Something my mom would never have let me do. Notice how I'm twenty-seven and I'm still talking about what my mom would let me do?

How was it?

It was wonderful. Free fall, in a good way. Then when we got off Caleb said it was first-world entertainment. Because people in most of the world don't think it's fun to get an adrenaline rush by pretending they're about to die.

That's so Caleb.

I know!

Do you think you might get back together?

I like him. I kinda love him. He's such a good guy.

Don't forget handsome. With beautiful teeth.

And that. But I don't think I want to be his wife.

Who's going to tell your mother? She's the one I heard about Caleb from. She says he went out there to get you back.

You tell her.

No.

Please?

No.

I think it's a maid of honor duty.

It so isn't.

Well, first I have to tell Caleb. But after the way I treated him tonight, I'm not sure he'll be all that disappointed.

What did you do? I can't imagine you doing anything that would make someone even a little annoyed. Except for when you left him at the altar. And he was very understanding about that.

I made him go on that crazy ride, then some other ones. I didn't even ask him what he wanted to do. I ate junk food. I called him a Sugar Nazi. He said Nazis were nothing to trivialize.

That's so Caleb.

But he's right. And what did I do in response? I stuck my tongue out at him, like I'm a three-year-old. I probably should have rephrased. Also, he heard me throw up all the junky, sugary food. Humiliation.

Did he hold back your hair?

I'm sure he would have if I'd opened the door.

He's a saint.

No one wants a saint to watch them puke.

True. Also, it sounds like he's already forgiven you.

Damn. You're right. And he also forgave me for sleeping with someone else.

You cheated on Caleb? You cheated on Caleb!!!! and you didn't tell me?

Not cheated on. It was someone I met out here. Post not marrying him. So that's not cheating. But it's also not saintly. I'm really not saintly at heart, the way Caleb is.

Details.

Not now, okay? I just can't.

Okay. Pout. Hey, who is going to stop me from doing stupid things if you keep doing stupid things?

Can we take turns? Or am I only good as a designated driver?

You also hold my purse while I dance.
Thanks. So much.
I was kidding. You know I was kidding.
I know. I think I'm about to sugar crash. Hard.
Talk to you later then.
Love you.
Love you, too.

MacGyver kneaded Briony's hair. It made him less lonely for Jamie. He missed his person. But she'd be proud of how well he was taking care of things. He let his eyes close. Usually, he'd be heading out for an adventure at this time of night, but he needed his rest. He'd only gotten in two short naps during the day. His list of people to help kept getting longer. He was starting to think most of the other cats in the world were slackers.

His eyes popped open. He hadn't gotten his num nums tonight. He stood up, opened his mouth wide, and yowled.

"Mac, have mercy," Briony begged.

Mac yowled again—longer and higher.

She got out of bed. Mac leapt down to the floor and led the way to the kitchen. He was willing to do a lot for the humans who lived around him, but he was not skipping dinner.

CHAPTER 18

Briony checked her phone. After nine. *Damn, damn, damn.* She'd wanted to get up before Caleb and make him breakfast. It wouldn't be much of an apology for the way she'd acted yesterday, but it would be a start.

He'd be up by now. He never slept in. She'd been counting on Mac to be her alarm clock. He never missed getting up for breakfast. She took a few seconds to brush her teeth. Her mouth felt like something had died in there and was rapidly rotting. Then she hurried downstairs.

Where she found Caleb making French toast as Mac and Diogee watched. He must have fed them. They'd be rioting if he hadn't. "Good morning. Let me say that I acted like a complete brat last night."

"Not going to argue with you," Caleb answered cheerfully. Another thing about Caleb? He was always cheerful in the morning. It should be considered a lovely personality trait, but Briony found it annoying. For years she'd had to pretend she was cheerful the second she woke up, too, because it seemed only fair.

"I'm sorry. And you were right. I was pushing

you away. It wasn't a plan. I didn't decide to try to make you hate me. Which I guess is even worse. I acted that badly without even trying."

Caleb flipped the bread. "I don't hate you."

"Good. I don't want you to hate me." Tears suddenly stung her eyes. "It would be so horrible if you did. Even though it would be a completely reasonable response."

Caleb turned off the stove, then walked over to her and wrapped her in his arms. She held on to him tight, burying her head in his shoulder. A part of her didn't want to ever let go, ever let him go. But that was the fearful part of her who was afraid to see if she could manage her life without him. He deserved so much better.

She let herself cling to him for a few more moments, then let go and stepped away. "I don't want to marry you," she told him, blinking back tears. "That's not going to change. I wish I'd realized that's how I felt earlier, so much earlier, but I didn't. I almost didn't realize it in time."

"And that would have been so much worse," Caleb told her. "It's going to be okay, Briony. We're both going to be okay."

"You'll meet someone amazing, because you're amazing. You're so thoughtful, and sweet, and—"

Caleb held up the spatula, stopping her. "Please, don't. Just, don't."

He was always so willing to forgive, to take the

high road, but that didn't mean she hadn't deeply hurt him. She wanted to apologize a million more times, but that was only so she'd feel better. She wasn't going to make him reassure her over and over.

"You want one piece or two?" Caleb turned the stove back on.

"I may never eat again. Just make what you want for you." Briony sank down into one of the kitchen chairs, then jumped back up. "I told Gib I'd check up on him!"

"What?"

"Gib. One of the residents at The Gardens who got sick. I told him I'd check up on him before I went home yesterday, and I completely forgot. I need to go over there. I won't take long."

"Take as much time as you need," Caleb answered.

"What are you going to do?"

"Go home, I guess. Finish packing up. Move and start my new job."

"You can stay . . ." Briony offered. "You can have a vacation—"

"I don't think I'm ready for that. I'll start checking on flights out."

She felt like crying again. This felt like more of an ending than it had that day in the church. "I'll go get dressed." It was all she could think of to say.

"I know At Your Service is a great catering company," LeeAnne told Nate. "But I hate that someone else is feeding my people."

"I do, too. But we need to get the official health department clearance before we can serve again," Nate answered. "It sounded like we could get it as soon as this afternoon."

"I'll be ready as soon as you get the word," LeeAnne promised.

"I had to go ahead and hire At Your Service for dinner. I didn't want to have to scramble if we don't get the go-ahead," Nate told her.

LeeAnne sighed. "Yeah, I get that."

She sounded so beaten down. She sounded the way Nate felt. He was overwhelmed. Eliza's meeting was that night, and he had nothing to report. No, that wasn't true. He could share the results of the air check—excellent. He could announce that the new gym equipment was already in place. And he hoped he'd be able to report that the health department had cleared the kitchen for operation. But what he couldn't do was reassure the residents and family that The Gardens was safe. He couldn't tell them that the person behind the sabotage had been caught.

"Why don't you take the day off," he suggested. "You've got the kitchen completely back in order, and there's nothing you can really do right now."

"I'll go home for a while," LeeAnne agreed.

"But nothing's going to stop me from coming back tonight. I'm going to be front row center. And I won't be the only one. The staff's got your back, Nate. I hope you know that."

"I do. And I appreciate it," Nate answered.

LeeAnne grabbed her bike helmet and her backpack. "I can stay," she offered.

"Nope. You can't. The boss has spoken."

She gave a snort as she headed for the door. "Front row center," she said again, then left him alone in the huge kitchen.

He had to get himself together. No matter how he was feeling, he had to present a confident front to the staff. Make that the staff, the residents, and the families. He could start by making the rounds again. He'd checked in on everyone who'd gotten sick yesterday. Today, he was going to try to touch base with everyone. He knew Eliza would be out there talking with everybody she possibly could. Nate wasn't going to let her be the only one doing the talking.

Gib first, he decided. He needed a little time to get that confident front he needed up and running, and Gib was a good person to practice on.

But when he reached Gib's place, he saw Briony coming out the door. She froze when she saw him, and he realized there was something else he had to get done. "Can I talk to you for a second?"

"I know you don't want me here. I only came

because yesterday I told Gib I'd check in on him and then I forgot. I had to come back, but I'm leaving now," she told him.

"I'm sure he was glad to see you," Nate answered. "I still want to talk to you. Is now okay? It won't take long."

"All right." It sounded like the last thing she wanted to do. He didn't blame her.

"Let's go into the garden." He didn't want to try to have this conversation standing in the middle of the street.

"All right," she said again.

"It's back this way." He didn't speak as he led the way to the gazebo. She didn't, either. When they reached it, he sat on one of the curved white benches. She hesitated a moment, then sat beside him.

"I'm sorry about yesterday, about what I said."

"It's okay," she said quickly, but he thought it was more about her eagerness to get away from him than because she actually accepted his apology.

"It's not okay. I'd just had a conversation with Eliza that pissed me off, and I took it out on you." That was somewhat true. Briony seemed to know he wasn't being completely honest. Her expression was dubious.

He wasn't going to tell her how much it had hurt when her ex-fiancé showed up. How he'd had to go drink an insane amount of beer to cope. "I knew it was a casual thing," he added. "I knew you were going back home soon. I shouldn't have reacted the way I did. It's not like you owed me your life story."

"If it had gotten serious, which it wouldn't have, because I don't live here, I would have told you. Maybe not on a first date, but I definitely would have told you."

Nate nodded. "How is it going now that he's out here?" He both wanted and didn't want to know.

"We resolved some things last night. Actually, this morning," she answered.

Did that mean they'd gotten back together? That they'd already slept together? He reminded himself it was none of his business. Briony wasn't his girlfriend. But a hot wave of jealousy was smashing through him. He fought to keep it from showing.

"I told him it wasn't going to work between us. He wanted us to give it another chance, but I realized that even though I'd had every intention of going through with the wedding, I really didn't want to marry him."

He noticed that she had dark smudges under her eyes and she looked exhausted. "That must have been a hard conversation."

"Yeah. He didn't make it hard. He was understanding. Caleb's always understanding." Nate still didn't get how Caleb had been able to be understanding about Briony sleeping with another guy, especially so soon. "But I could tell I'd hurt him, and that was hard to see." She swallowed, and he thought she was fighting back tears. "And I treated him so horribly last night." Her words were coming faster now. "I was being a complete coward. Instead of telling him how I felt, or even actually admitting to myself how I felt, I just acted like a monster."

"Trying to drive him away," Nate said.

She let out a sigh that sounded like it started deep in her belly. "Exactly. At least I finally managed to be an adult and actually talk to him this morning—instead of behaving badly or passing out on the way to the altar."

"You really fainted?"

"Oh yeah, right down to the floor. And then I didn't even have the guts to stick around. My parents arranged for me to stay at my cousin's and put me on the plane. The next day, I met you. And I know it must seem heartless for me to be willing to sleep with another guy that fast. I still can't believe I did it. It's not my norm. Believe it or not, I'm usually a person who does the right thing. Probably because I'm too scared to do the wrong thing, but whatever the reason, that's me. I don't even jaywalk." She rubbed her forehead with her fingertips, like she was trying to erase a memory.

Did she wish she'd never met him? Or at

least that she'd never slept with him? Did he?

"Maybe behaving badly is more the real me than I want to admit," she went on. "I didn't treat you the way I should have. Then last night, I was horrible to Caleb, and after he'd been willing to forgive me for everything." She grabbed his hand. "Just know I'm sorry. If I could change the way I did everything, I would."

She started to pull her hand away, but he wouldn't let her. "Hey, this is supposed to be my apology. That's why I brought you out here."

"Apology accepted," Briony told him. She looked around. "You picked a beautiful place for it. Did you design the garden?"

"Yeah. I wanted to put it in myself, but—" He shrugged.

Briony gently pulled her hand away from him. This time, he didn't try to stop her. It's not like they were still . . . in a thing. "I saw the signs about the meeting when I was on my way to Gib's," she told him.

"Organized by Eliza," Nate told her. "I think it's going to be bad."

"You have a lot of support here. You have to know that."

"That was before so many people got sick, before the treadmill, and the ventilation problems," Nate reminded her.

"Well, I visited a lot of residents yesterday, and I didn't hear anyone bad-mouthing you or

The Gardens," Briony said. "I'd like to—Would it be okay if I came tonight? As a friend. I know I haven't been around long, but I care about what happens."

Nate realized that he'd like to look out at the crowd and see Briony there. "I'd appreciate that."

"Good. Now I have an awkward question for you."

"And all the rest of our conversations have been so smooth and painless."

"Well, I remember a few that were." Briony looked him in the eye. "Here's the question: How would you feel about Caleb coming to the meeting, too?" She held up one hand to keep him from answering too fast. "He's a lawyer. A good one. And it might be useful to have a lawyer listening to whatever Eliza is going to say."

"I doubt he's going to want to do me any favors," Nate answered. And he wasn't sure he was okay with Briony's ex helping him out even if Caleb was willing.

"If you knew him, you wouldn't say that. So, is it okay if he comes?"

He'd rather pretend the guy didn't exist. But that would be impossible even if Nate never saw Caleb again. And a lawyer might not be a bad idea. He wouldn't have to announce there was a lawyer present. He could just present Caleb as a friend of Briony's.

"If he's up for it, that would be great."

CHAPTER 19

Nate's coffee was so hot it burned his tongue, but after only a few seconds he took another sip, then muttered a curse at his stupidity. He didn't need coffee at all. His nerves were already frayed, and he was so keyed up his blood pressure was probably high enough to give him a nosebleed. In a little more than two hours, the meeting at The Gardens was starting up, and even though he'd prepped for every question, it was easy to imagine the night being catastrophic for him and The Gardens.

He took another swallow of coffee. Still too hot. Because he'd only waited about another three seconds. He was an idiot. He had to get it together. If he was honest, he had to admit that a small part of his anxiety was coming from the fact that Briony and her ex should be walking in anytime for a strategy session. He wasn't looking forward to spending time with Caleb, even though he appreciated Caleb being willing to help him out. He felt like Caleb had slept with his girlfriend, even though, one, Briony wasn't his girlfriend, and, two, Caleb was engaged to Briony before Nate even met her.

He picked up his coffee again, needing to do something with his hands, but this time he stopped himself before he drank any. The door swung open, and when Nate looked over he saw Briony, Caleb, and his sister walk in. What was Nathalie doing here? He was stressed out enough. He didn't need any of her drama tonight.

"Why didn't you tell me about the meeting?" Nathalie demanded as soon as the three of them sat down at Nate's table.

"That's probably not the most important question right now," Caleb answered before Nate could say anything.

"It's important to me," Nathalie protested.

"I didn't tell you because I have it handled."

"You have it handled? Then why were you meeting with these two?" Nathalie jerked her chin toward Briony and Caleb.

"I'm getting some legal advice. You're not a lawyer," Nate answered.

Nathalie crossed her arms. "I'm coming tonight. You can't stop me."

"Nathalie, do you realize you make everything about you?" Nate demanded. "Everything. I'm trying to deal with a crisis, and you're about to throw a fit because you feel excluded. Which means I'll have to do what I always do—talk you down. And I really don't have time for that right now."

"I'm not throwing a fit. All I was doing was

telling you that I'll be at the meeting. I can't believe you're getting mad because I want to show you some support."

"Fine. Thank you. I'm happy you'll be there." He'd tried to sound sincere, but his words came out with an edge.

"Yeah, that sounds believable."

"Drinks!" Briony exclaimed. "We need drinks. Nate, you already have yours. What does everyone else want?"

"I'll have a caramel macchiato," Nathalie answered. Nate knew there would be a lot more coming and told himself not to act annoyed. He needed to get in a good headspace before the meeting. "Large, skim, extra shot, extra hot, extra whip, sugar-free."

"You might have to say that one more time," Briony said.

"Just get her a caramel macchiato. She can—"

"Not a problem. I got it." Caleb rattled back the order. "Skim, extra shot, extra hot, extra whip, sugar-free."

"Thank you." Nathalie managed to beam at him and scowl at Nate almost simultaneously.

"And Briony? Flat white?" Caleb asked.

Briony caught her lower lip between her teeth. "I think I'll go for a chai latte."

"You know the powder they use—" Caleb started, then gave his head a hard shake. "Got it." He stood and headed for the counter.

"I'll help him carry." Briony hurried after him.

It was obvious they were giving him and Nathalie some privacy, probably because they didn't want a front-row seat to a brother-and-sister squabble.

"If you want to come, you should come." He couldn't stop himself from adding, "But you've never wanted to before. You saw me breaking my back trying to keep the place going right after Dad left and you didn't even bother putting in an appearance at the holiday party."

"That's so not fair. I was only nineteen."

"Obviously, so was I. Twins, remember?" She really did make him revert to an obnoxious kid.

"You told me it was okay to go away to school."

"And it was. It was, Nathalie. I was always more interested in the place. I—"

"That's so not fair!"

"I don't mean it in a bad way. I just mean when I was a kid I liked hanging around over at The Gardens with Grandpa. When I wasn't inhaling deeply while listening to *Black Butterfly* on repeat."

Nathalie laughed. "I almost forgot you had that stoner metal phase. It's like you were a different person."

"I was. But I still listen to it sometimes," he admitted.

Briony and Nate returned to the table. Nathalie took a sip of her drink. "Perfect," she decreed.

"Nate, I invited Nathalie to meet with us this afternoon, and I told her it would be a good idea for her to come tonight. It'll be good to remind everyone that The Gardens is a family business, and that you have the support of your family," Caleb said as soon as he sat down.

"She's welcome to be there." Nate looked at Nathalie, so she'd know he meant it.

"Good. It's important that neither of you appears upset when Eliza or anyone else is giving a negative opinion. I don't want either of you to look defensive," Caleb continued. "Now, Nate, I know that you're letting Eliza run the meeting, and I think that's fine. But I think you should introduce her, make it clear that you're still in charge and that you're allowing her to have her say because it's important to you that everyone's concerns are heard."

Good advice, Nate thought. He was starting to feel a little calmer. Having proactive things to focus on helped. He pulled out his phone so he could take a few notes. When Caleb had been talking for about ten minutes, the cell started playing "Ghostbusters."

"It's my mom," he said. "I need to take it. I'll make it as quick as I can."

"Of course," Caleb answered. He was so polite. So helpful. Like he had no problem at all that Nate had slept with Briony. His attitude mystified Nate, but he was grateful.

"There's someone in the house," his mother said as soon as Nate answered.

"Where are you?" Nate managed to keep his voice calm. He didn't want to panic her.

"I just got back from the store. I went to the kitchen door, and it was unlocked. I know I locked it. I know I did, Nate." Her voice quavered.

"Where are you now?" he repeated.

"I'm in the garage. I don't want whoever it is to see me."

"Are you sure you locked the door? If you went out the front when you left, you—"

"I'm sure! And I'm sure there's someone in my house."

"Hang tight. I'll be right over," Nate promised.

"What's wrong?" Briony asked as soon as he hung up.

"Did something happen to Mom?" Nathalie cried.

"She says someone's in the house. I need to get over there. I know someone's been watching the place, but I never thought they'd go in."

When he stood, the other three rose as well. "We're coming with you," Nathalie told him.

He didn't argue.

The Coffee Bean & Tea Leaf was close by. They were able to reach his mom's house in less than ten minutes. Nate led the way to the garage. "Mom?" he called as he stepped inside.

"Did you check the house?" his mother asked.

"I wanted to check on you first," he told her. "Nath, will you stay with her while I do?"

"Of course," his sister said.

"You want me to come with you?" Caleb asked.

"No. I got it." He could deal with Caleb helping him prep for the meeting. But letting him help with this? His ego couldn't take it.

Nate hurried around to the kitchen door. He tried the knob. The door was definitely unlocked. But if someone had gone in to rob the place while his mom was out, they wouldn't still be in there. He pushed open the door.

This wasn't possible. It wasn't possible. It couldn't be possible. "Dad?"

His father sat at the kitchen table, in the chair that had always been his when he lived there. Nate had taken it over after his dad took off. Looking at it empty had gotten to his mother. "What are you doing here? You don't get to just walk in like you live here!"

"When your mother went out, I couldn't resist taking a look," his father answered. "Spare key was where it always was. In the mouth of the little stone frog." Nate couldn't stop staring. His father looked almost the same. He had a few streaks of gray at his temples and maybe the lines in his forehead were a little deeper, but that was it.

"You've been in here before, haven't you? Mom thought she smelled your cologne." Nate could smell it now. He'd thought he'd forgotten the scent, but it was powerfully familiar. "I need you to leave. You completely terrified her. She called me hysterical because she thought someone broke it."

"I want to see her," his father said. He actually took a swallow of the coffee he'd made himself. "I want to see all of you. I was just trying to decide when would be the right time." He shook his head. "You almost caught me the other night."

"That was you?"

"That was me."

"You can't just arrive and announce you want to see us. You left. You've been gone for years. You can't—" He faltered, unable to come up with more words. "You can't," he repeated.

Then the kitchen door opened, and Nathalie stepped inside. "Mom's having fits out there. I told her she must have left the door—" Her hand flew up to her mouth, and for a moment she just stared at their father.

"I already told him he needs to go," Nate said.

Nathalie lowered her hand. She took one step into the room. Then another. "Daddy?"

He stood up, opened his arms, and Nathalie raced into them.

"I think I should go back in there." Nate picked at a splinter in the picnic table in his mother's backyard.

"It hasn't been very long. I'm sure it feels like it has, but it hasn't even been fifteen minutes." Briony felt like *she* was still trying to get her mind wrapped around what had happened since Nate went to investigate the situation in the house. She couldn't imagine how he must be feeling.

"You should have seen Nathalie. She ran right over and hugged him like he'd been wrongly imprisoned the last ten-plus years."

Briony nodded. It was the fifth time Nate had said something similar. She wasn't sure how to respond, how to help.

"And then my mother saying she wanted to talk to him alone. My mother's barely been able to do anything on her own since he left, because he destroyed her. But she insists she wants to talk to him alone." Nate raked his hands through his hair. He'd done it so often it was almost standing on end. "I really think I should get in there."

"Maybe give it a few minutes longer." Even though Nate and Nathalie were grown-up, Briony was sure there were things their mother wanted to say to their father alone. "We're really close. If she needs you, all she has to do is call out and you'll hear her. She won't even have to open the door."

He stood up. "Nathalie should be here."

"She'll be right back." Nathalie had been shaking with emotion when she and Nate came out of the house. Caleb had suggested a quick walk. He'd recently read an article about how a walk or jog activated what scientists called calming neurons. He'd tried to get Nate to come along, but Nate refused to let his mother's house out of his sight and Briony had stayed with him.

Nate sat back down. "It never even occurred to me the man I spotted watching the house was my father."

Briony nodded. He'd said that several times, too.

"What is he doing back here? Why now?"

"I don't know, Nate. Maybe that's what he's talking to your mom about now," Briony suggested.

"That bastard!" Nate was on his feet again. "He heard about the offers I've gotten on The Gardens. He came back because he wants the money! He's behind the sabotage!"

"Wait. You're going too fast for me. Why would he sabotage a place your family owns?" Briony asked.

"Don't you get it?" Nate looked feverish, his

eyes glittering. "I kept saying I wouldn't sell. So, he's sabotaging the place to force my hand. If people start moving out, The Gardens won't be able to make a profit. He thinks that'll make me take the offer. He's here to get his cut—once I have no choice but to sell."

"I guess it's possible—"

"It's more than possible. He did it. Nothing else makes sense." He strode toward the house. Briony hesitated for a second, then chased after him. He burst into the kitchen. His mom and dad jerked their heads toward him. "Nate, your father and I aren't—"

"Get out now!" Nate ordered his father. "If you do, I won't press charges."

His father slowly stood, raising both hands in a placating gesture. Did he do it? Did he actually sabotage the business Nate had worked so hard to run? More than that. That Nate had made a home for so many people.

"I just wanted to see you, to see all of you," Nate's father said. "I don't think I can walk back in like nothing happened. I didn't handle this the right way. I should have called, written, asked permission. I guess I was afraid you'd say no. I almost chickened out. I tried to come a few times before. I actually—"

Nate cut him off. "This is bullshit. You didn't come here for me or Mom or Nathalie. Not after all these years. You came here for money."

Briony saw guilt on the man's face but confusion, too. She put one hand on Nate's arm, wanting to let him know that she was there for him.

"What money? What are you talking about, Nate?" his mother exclaimed.

"Ask him! He knows."

"I don't," his father answered. "I honestly don't." Looking at his face, Briony was tempted to believe him, but she didn't know anything about him. Wow, was the resemblance between him and Nate strong, though.

When Nate spoke, he looked only at his mother. "I've gotten some offers from a real estate developer on The Gardens. I turned them down. It's ours. It's our family's. But he—" Nate gestured toward his father but still didn't look

at him. "He never cared about it. Somehow he found out about the offers, and he's been sabotaging The Gardens so I'd have no choice but to sell. And give him the money. He still owns half the place, at least technically."

"Someone has been sabotaging The Gardens?" Nate's father asked. "What happened?"

Finally, Nate looked at him. "You know. You know exactly what happened." He walked across the room until he was only a foot away from the man. Briony stayed where she was, wishing she could do something but feeling completely helpless. "Now, you are going to leave. Or I'm going to make sure you're arrested. People could have died. Do you know that? Maybe you thought food poisoning wouldn't really hurt anyone long term, but elderly people have died from it."

"Nate! Stop it!" Nathalie cried. Briony hadn't even heard her and Caleb come in. "Dad couldn't have done that. He wouldn't have."

"Right. Dad's such a great person. Never hurt a fly, right?" Nate asked his sister. "Oh, except Mom. And you, even though you're acting like he's some returning hero instead of the guy who deserted all of us."

"I don't understand what's happening," Nate's mother said, rubbing a spot on her ring finger. Where she used to wear her wedding ring, Briony realized.

"A bunch of people got sick after brunch on Saturday," Nathalie explained. "Nate thinks someone intentionally tampered with the food."

"And health department inspectors are investigating. If you left any evidence behind, they're going to find it," Nate told his father. "You better run back to Mexico or wherever it is you've been."

"I didn't do anything to the food." Nate's father looked at his mother. "April, I swear to you, I didn't do anything to anyone at The Gardens.

I didn't even know there'd been offers on the place."

"I think maybe we should table this conversation for a little while," Caleb said. "There's a meeting for residents and their families happening at The Gardens shortly. Nate, you need to focus on that for now."

"Who is this?" Nate's mom began rubbing her finger faster. "And who is she?"

"That's my lawyer, Caleb Weber. And my friend Briony. She wanted to be there for the meeting, for moral support," Nate answered.

"I don't understand why this is the first I'm hearing of any of this. Isn't this meeting something I should be there for?" Nate's mother asked.

"If you're feeling up to it, I think that would be helpful," Caleb answered. "It'll show Nate has the backing of his family."

"I want to be there, too," Nate's father said.

"No," Nate told him. "You're not family. Not anymore. You opted out when you left."

"Nate!" his mother exclaimed.

"That's not true. He's still my father," Nathalie insisted. "And yours."

Briony felt for everyone, even Nate's father, not that that meant he hadn't almost destroyed his family, although Nate's mom and sister seemed willing to at least talk to him.

"Well, I don't want him there tonight. It

would take too many explanations. The residents don't know him. It would just confuse things," Nate said.

"I'll do whatever you want," his father answered. "You don't want me there, I won't go. But I would like to talk to you sometime, when it works for you."

"Yeah, I don't know when that'll be." Nate checked the kitchen clock. "I need to get over to the community center, make sure it's all set up."

"I'm going home to get the kids. Caleb thinks it would be good for them to be there. Is that okay, Nate?" Nathalie asked.

"Sure. Fine. If the kids want to be there, it's fine." He turned to Briony. "Are you coming with me?"

"Of course." If he wanted her, she was there.

CHAPTER 20

Nate stood at the back of the screening room, Briony by his side. If someone had told him two days ago he'd be grateful to have her there, he'd have said they were crazy. But he was.

"You've got your cheering section right up front," she said softly.

He nodded. LeeAnne was front row center, as promised, Hope beside her. Gib was in the front row, too, along with Nate's mother, Nathalie and the kids, and Caleb.

"But Eliza's up there, too," Nate pointed out. She was dressed as demurely as ever, in a pale pink blouse and another of those skirts that fell to mid-calf. Her hair was pulled back with what his mother called an Alice band. She looked completely sweet and trustworthy. Nate was afraid she'd be hard to resist.

"She's about to start the meeting," Briony said.

"Wish me luck," he said, and she gave his hand a quick squeeze before he walked to the front of the room. He glanced at Eliza and saw she wore a sour expression that undercut the sweetness of her little outfit. He smiled at her, then took a moment to look around the room, giving everyone gathered time to quiet down. There wasn't an empty seat, and there were even some people standing in the back.

Peggy gave him a thumbs-up from her seat by her daughter. Rich, Regina, and Max, who were all sitting together in the second row, all smiled back at him. LeeAnne didn't smile, but she looked ready to do battle with anyone who opposed him, and Nate thought Hope would join in.

"Welcome, everyone," Nate said. "I'm glad you're all here. We have some important things to discuss. I'm going to bring Eliza Pendergast, Archie's granddaughter, up to kick things off. This meeting was her idea, and I want to thank her for organizing it." He started a round of applause, then returned to Briony.

"Thank you all for coming," Eliza said. "I wanted to have this meeting because I'm very concerned about the conditions here at The Gardens. I believe it's dangerous for all our loved ones. My grandfather—" Her voice quavered, and she had to stop mid-sentence.

Nate wondered if she was just playing to the crowd but reminded himself that she loved her grandfather and that she had completely legitimate reasons to be worried about him staying at The Gardens.

"My grandfather fell off a treadmill in this facility's gym. The treadmill malfunctioned,"

Eliza continued. "Fortunately, my grandfather only suffered a sprained ankle, but it could have been so much worse. For example, he could easily have broken a hip. Did you know—" She glanced down at the index card she held in one hand. "Did you know that the CDC reports that one in five hip-fracture patients dies within a year of their injury? One in five. And yet basic upkeep of the exercise equipment is clearly not a priority here at The Gardens."

There was a low murmuring from the crowd, and Nate wanted to jump in with the documentation that showed how often he had the gym equipment tested. But he needed to wait. Everyone here needed to see that he took Eliza's concerns, and theirs, seriously. That meant letting her talk.

"My grandfather was also one of the victims of the food poisoning epidemic this Saturday. He, along with more than eighty percent of the community here, ate brunch in the dining room. More than fifty residents became ill." Eliza checked her notecard again. "The elderly often have weakened immune systems, which means they may not recover from food poisoning as easily. They are also at greater risk of dehydration. Did you know dehydration is even more dangerous for our older family members than the rest of us? It can lead to a drop in blood pressure, and that reduces blood supply to essential organs. If the kidneys don't get enough blood, for example, it can lead to renal failure. Renal failure can lead to death."

Eliza drew in a long, shuddering breath, and again Nate wondered if she was faking her response to get a reaction. He again reminded himself that she'd been through a huge amount of stress and worry in the last several days.

"Twice in less than a week, my grandfather could have died," she announced. "Twice. For this reason, as much as my grandfather loves this place and despite the good friends he has already made, I feel like I must find him another place to live. I honestly believe that staying at The Gardens puts his life in danger."

That was enough, Nate decided. He joined Eliza in the front of the room. "Thank you, Eliza, for bringing these issues up." He took her by the arm and escorted her back to her spot beside her grandfather.

"I wasn't finished!" she hissed.

"I want to give everyone a chance to speak," he answered loudly. He spread his arms wide. "Who has questions, concerns, or comments? I'm happy to answer anything." He let his eyes briefly find Briony, then looked around at the rest of the group. "Tamara?" he called. Peggy's daughter looked like she had something to say.

Tamara stood. "What really bothers me is that

until I got Eliza's e-mail I didn't know anything about the food poisoning or anything else. You're usually so good at keeping in touch, Nate. Why didn't I hear about this?"

"You're right. I should have gotten in touch with all of you, and it's on my list of things to do," Nate answered. "Honestly, all my attention was on making sure everyone got the care they needed and on finding out what had caused people to get sick." He avoided using the words *food poisoning.*

"I'm really not sure I feel comfortable having my mother stay here," Tamara said. "All this . . . it's frightening. I might need to look at other options."

At that, Peggy stood. "Tamara, you know I appreciate how much you care about my well-being. But where I live is my decision. And I love The Gardens. I've been here for three years, and it's my home. Until this week, there's never been anything that's happened here that gave me the slightest bit of worry." She met Nate's gaze. "I'm not worried now, because I know Nate will take care of the problems. I trust him completely." She sat and tugged at her daughter's wrist until Tamara sat back down, too.

"Thank you, Peggy. And Tamara, for sharing your thoughts. Who else?" Nate asked.

He continued answering questions for more than an hour, making sure to give information from the air quality report and making it clear that not just the treadmill Archie had been on during his accident, but every piece of equipment, had already been replaced. He also reassured the group that everyone who'd gotten food poisoning had already recovered.

"Anyone else?" he asked, wanting to make sure no one had been left out. He'd also stay afterwards to talk to people individually. Not everyone would have wanted to raise issues during the meeting.

Nate's mother raised her hand. He smiled at her. "Yes, Mom?" he said. "You all know my mother, right?"

There was a smattering of applause as she stood. "I just wanted to say that Nate has been running The Gardens since he was nineteen, and every year I've been more proud of him and what he's accomplished." That got more applause, although Nate noted that Eliza and a smattering of others didn't clap.

"Thanks, Mom. That means a lot to me," he told her. And it did. She'd never really commented on the job he'd done. She just assumed he had everything handled, which was its own kind of praise.

As soon as his mother sat down, LeeAnne stood up. "A few hours ago, the health department gave the kitchen the go-ahead to start serving," she announced. "So my crew and I got busy baking. If you have a favorite pie, I bet we've made one. I say we all go into the dining room and eat."

"Are you sure it's safe?" Eliza called. "I'm not sure my grandfather's system could take another bout of food poisoning."

"I'm not willing to risk it," someone near the back agreed.

"I never turn down LeeAnne's pie," Gib said.

"I can guarantee you she uses only the freshest ingredients, and that you'll think you're eating a blue-ribbon winner from the state fair." Nathalie looked over at Lyle and Lyla. "What do you say, kids? Want pie?"

"Yes!" Lyle gave a fist pump.

"Is there blackberry?" Lyla asked LeeAnne.

"Of course."

Lyla smiled at her. "And whipped cream?"

"I don't whip it until right before it's served, but I never serve pie without it," LeeAnne told her, loudly enough so the whole room could hear.

"I could eat a whole pie myself!" Amelia called. "Hooves to tail."

"What exactly is in these pies?" Tamara sounded appalled.

"Joking. She was joking," Briony told the crowd.

"Well, let's go get in line." Nathalie stood and headed for the door, the kids, his mom, and

Caleb on her heels. Nate was relieved to see that more than half of the people in the room followed.

His twin drove him crazy a huge amount of the time. His mom, too. But right now all he could think about was how much he loved them.

Mac strolled from table to table, checking on his people. Nate and Briony both smelled much better than they had, not as happy as they had been, but much better. Gib smelled much better, too, with only a whiff of the illness that had been so strong when Mac visited him the day before. He didn't smell the way he did when the woman Mac liked, Peggy, was nearby. Mac needed to work on that.

The man and the woman who had smelled a little like they might go kaboom when they were together now smelled happier, too, and not like they were about to make a bang loud enough to make Mac's ears ring.

Caleb, the man who was living in Mac's house, smelled fair. He wasn't as happy as he could be, but he smelled better than he had yesterday, too.

Mac was satisfied. He'd made progress. He had to be patient. It took a long time to get humans to understand what they should do. They couldn't help it. They just weren't quite as intelligent as they needed to be to manage their own lives. They were more intelligent than dogs, no doubt about that, but not quite intelligent enough. They should all be required to live with a cat.

He wandered over to the man who didn't like him. He was sitting in a chair with wheels. Mac gave the man's ankle a good rubbing with his head, and the man released an odor that showed he disliked Mac even more than he had. Mission accomplished!

Mac's whiskers twitched. That about-to-kaboom smell was back. He took in a long breath, flicking the air into his mouth with his tongue. No, it wasn't exactly the same scent, and it was coming from different humans, young ones. Would he ever stop finding people who needed help?

He bunched his legs under him, then leapt onto the table to investigate. The young female stumbled back with a cry, and coffee sloshed out from the pot she held. "H-Hope! Are you all right? Did you b-burn yourself?" the young male blah-blahed loudly.

"You know my name?" the young female asked as she rubbed her skirt with a napkin.

"O-of course. We've had th-three classes together. And I k-know you from h-here, too," the young male answered.

"But you act like—It's like I'm invisible. I thought you just didn't think the person serving you was worth paying attention to," the young female said. "You never even say hello."

"S-saying anything around y-you is h-hard." The young male grimaced. "I s-stutter when I g-get n-nervous. I used to d-do it all th-the t-time." He shook his head hard, hummed a few notes. "S-sorry. I w-wasn't—I d-didn't mean to offend y-you."

"I make you nervous? Why would I make you nervous?" she blah-blahed. Since Mac was already on the table, he began to lick whipped cream off the nearest plate.

"Y-you're s-so pretty." Mac could smell the blood coming to the surface of the young male's face. "A-and s-smart." He shrugged. "Y-you n-never t-talk to m-me, either."

"Because I'm stupid. I assumed you weren't speaking to me because I was so far beneath you. I mean, I take the bus, you drive a BMW 335i convertible. I work serving you food."

"You work making people like my grand-father happy. He thinks you're awesome." The young male's blah-blahs had briefly become smoother. "S-so d-do I."

"You make him happy, too. It's so great the way you visit all the time, Max."

"Y-you know my n-name, too!"

She smiled. "We've had three classes together. And I know you from here, too."

He smiled back. "Hi, H-Hope."

"Hi, Max."

Briony collapsed into bed. That day felt like it was as long as three. So much had happened. She couldn't even imagine how Nate must be feeling, after that meeting and his dad reappearing after so long. She flipped off the lamp on the bedside table and snuggled into the mound of pillows. A few seconds later, Mac jumped up beside her and started to purr. "There's m kitty," Briony murmured, already starting to drift off.

Then her cell buzzed. It was probably Vi. Or Briony's parents. She checked it. There was a message from Ruby.

I feel like I've been missing my favorite Korean soap. Right when it got really good. ☺ Are you okay?

Sorry. Sorry, sorry, sorry! So much has happened.

So did you talk to Caleb and Nate?

Yeah. Had a big fight with Nate, where he basically slut-shamed me.

No way!

Yeah. But he apologized later. And it seems like things are kind of okay. Good, even. Between us anyway. Nate's trying to do damage control at The Gardens. Someone's been sabotaging the place. Nate thinks it's his dad. Who, BTW, has been out of the picture for about ten years. Abandoned the family, then just turned up again.

This is such a soap. Except real people. With real feelings. Which makes everything less entertaining and more horrible. What about Caleb? You notice you talked about Nate first again.

Caleb and I are officially over. He wanted to spend some time together, see if we could work it out. But I realized pretty much right away that it wasn't going to happen.

Did he take it okay?

You have to meet Caleb. He really is practically perfect—for some other woman. He's been amazing. I know he's hurt, but when Nate needed a lawyer, Caleb was right there.

Nate needed a lawyer?

Seemed like maybe some people at The Gardens might sue. Some people got sick from food poisoning—part of the sabotage. And another man got hurt on a treadmill— also sabotage.

Wow. If I can help, let me know. It would give me a chance to get a look at all these people I've been hearing about.

I will. So tired. Talk soon, okay? Sorry I dropped out of sight.

Sounds like you had a few good reasons. Good night, sweetie.

Night.

CHAPTER 21

Nate made sure to get to the dining room as soon as it opened for breakfast the next morning. It was the first time a full meal would be served since the brunch that caused the food poisoning. He wanted everyone to see him there, eating. If he had to eat three breakfasts to make that happen, fine. Maybe Briony would like to come over for one. It had felt good to have her standing next to him last night.

A few days ago he thought he'd never wanted to see her again, but after he'd had a little time to recover from the gut punch of her very newly ex-fiancé showing up at her door, and after he'd actually listened to what she had to say, he'd found that the anger had drained out of him. And the attraction he felt for her came rushing in to fill its place. More than just attraction, though. There was appreciation, too, for what a decent person she was, despite what she'd done. She'd quickly come to care about the people who lived at The Gardens, and she'd been there for them. She'd been there for him, too, as soon as he'd let her. He shot her a quick text, hoping she'd take him up on the breakfast invite.

"Nate!" Rich called to him. He turned and saw Rich and Regina coming toward him. They both usually ate a little later. Something was wrong, he realized as they reached him. Rich's face was tight with worry, and Regina looked like she'd dressed hurriedly, her hair brushed, but not perfectly styled the way it usually was.

"Good morning. What's up?" Nate asked, making sure to keep his voice level and calm.

"Max just called me. He'd been checking social media to see if there were any mentions of The Gardens after last night's meeting," Rich told him. "A bunch of things popped up. There are new one- and two-star ratings on some sites. Senior Living, Geek Geezers, Assisted Living Search." He turned to Regina. "What was the other one?"

"Retirement Home Compare," she answered.

"Max says he wants to help turn it around. He'd been texting with Hope. They're both studying marketing, and they are going to come up with some social media strategies. Can you meet with them this afternoon?" Rich asked.

"Absolutely."

"I want to help," Regina said. "I may not be up on all the social media outlets, but I know my way around a computer. There must be something I can do."

"You never know when you'll need a poet. I can write limericks about how great The Gardens is." He pulled out his notebook and pencil. "There was a place called The Gardens."

"Maybe something about how it wouldn't make hearts harden?" Regina suggested.

"Possibly, possibly," Rich said. "How about we meet up at three?"

Nate nodded. "Let's use the bungalow next to Gertie's. I'd like some privacy, and it's empty until next week. Unless the woman moving in goes to any of the sites you mention. Sounds like the reviews would keep anyone away."

"We're going to take care of that," Rich promised. "Now, I need coffee if I'm going to finish this poem. And I'm sure you'll want your peppermint tea," he added to Regina. He linked his arm through hers, and they started for their usual table.

Nate stared after them, momentarily distracted from their news by their behavior. Regina had offered a line for a limerick, when usually she'd have made a comment about how the form shouldn't even be considered poetry. Rich had remembered the tea she drank, and he'd taken her arm. Nate didn't think he'd ever seen the two touch before. Had something started up between them? It wouldn't be completely crazy. They actually shared a lot of interests—crosswords, art, literature.

He got his brain back where it belonged. He needed to check out those websites. He chose a table by one of the windows and pulled out his cell. When the waiter came by, he asked for the fruit salad. If he was going to be eating three times in the next few hours, he needed to pace himself.

By the time he got his food, his appetite had disappeared. The reviews felt like an attack, a personal attack. Why wouldn't they? Nate spent the majority of his time working to make The Gardens the best place it could possibly be for the residents. Before those few days with Briony it was pretty much all he did, that and problem-solve for his mom and sister.

His thoughts veered to his father. That kept happening, even with everything else he was dealing with. It was like a wall inside him had crumbled, the wall he'd erected years ago to keep out all thoughts about his father. *Focus,* Nate told himself. *He's not worth even a few seconds of your time. You've got more impor-tant things to deal with.* His father was nothing to Nate after being gone all these years, after deserting his family.

"Nate. Hello."

He'd been staring blankly down at his plate, and now he looked up and found Briony sitting across from him. "Hey, you came."

"You asked." She smiled. "How're you doing? You were so deep in thought, I hated to inter-rupt you."

"I'm glad you did. I was thinking about my father. And I don't have time for that right now. I just found out there's a smear campaign going against The Gardens on the interwebs," he told her. "If you can call it a smear campaign when what people are saying is true."

"Oh, Nate, no!" Briony reached for his hand, then hesitated and pulled it back. He got that. He had no idea where they were. They were in a good place, a friendly place, but more than that? Now wasn't the time to try to figure it out.

"Yeah. My average rating—I mean The Gardens' average rating is already way down. A bunch of one-stars will do that fast." He forced himself to take a bite of the fruit salad. It was amazing, like everything LeeAnne made. She'd drizzled on some kind of yogurt dressing. He realized his appetite was back and took another bite. "Have some, until someone takes your order." He spotted a server already coming toward them.

"Thanks." She picked up her fork and stabbed a star fruit. "What are you going to do? Any ideas?"

"Hope and Max are coming over at three. They're getting some suggestions together. They're both getting marketing degrees."

"Guess Hope was wrong. She seemed to think Max never talked to her because he felt superior to her, with his family being so wealthy and her working here in the kitchen."

"She was insanely wrong," Nate answered. "I'm pretty sure Max doesn't talk to her because she's so pretty it makes him nervous and when he gets nervous the stutter he had as a kid comes back. He stuttered some when he was talking to you on Family Night."

"And she was being rude to him, because he wasn't talking to her. It's like that story with the guy who sold his watch to buy his wife hair combs and she sold her hair to buy him a watch chain," Briony said. "Actually, no. That doesn't quite make sense. It's like the reverse of that, kind of. No, not really that, either." She frowned, then shook her head. "They were both acting badly, because they were both making assumptions about how the other one felt. Forget the whole hair and watch thing."

Nate laughed. "I love to hear you ramble."

"I don't ramble. Much. Except sometimes." She pressed her fingers to her lips. "Stopping now," she mumbled, and he laughed again. "Can I come to the meeting? I want to do something to help. You should ask your sister, too. Caleb told me she really feels bad that she hasn't been involved and wants to do more."

"She'll be at work this afternoon. And after that she'll probably be off hugging my father." He could hear the bitterness in his voice and tried to explain it to Briony. "She can do what she wants, but I *cannot* understand how she could forgive him. She didn't even ask for an explanation."

"Were they really close, before he left?" Briony asked.

"Yeah. Closer than I was to him. My grandfather expected him to be more interested in The Gardens, and I agreed. But shouldn't that make it harder for her to forgive him? Shouldn't she feel more betrayed when he left, because they were so close?"

"I'm not the best person to ask about what emotions are appropriate," Briony said, with a wry smile, then her eyes widened. "He's here. Your father."

"Here?" He thought he'd be able to choose when—and if—he wanted to deal with the man. He couldn't believe his father had had the balls to come over here. Although Nate shouldn't be surprised. His father had had the balls to come home after all these years. He'd walked right into the house, even though no one was home, like he still lived there.

"What are you going to do? Are you going to talk to him?" Briony asked.

"Is he coming over?" Nate didn't want to turn around and check.

"No, he's just standing over by the door. But he's looking over here."

Nate stood up. "I may as well get this over with."

"Should I head home?" Briony asked.

"Have breakfast. I'll come find you when I'm done."

"Good. I want to know how it goes."

At least there was that. She'd be waiting for him, once he got this over with. Nate turned and walked over to his father, who started speaking immediately. "I know I said I'd wait to talk to you. But I can't let you keep thinking I could be behind the sabotage. This place means something to me, Nate."

Nate gave a harsh bark of a laugh. "Yeah. You've really shown that."

"It was started by my grandfather, run by my father, and now by my son. I would never do anything to hurt The Gardens," his father insisted.

"You walked out on this place, same as you did the family," Nate told him.

He didn't speak for a long moment. "You're right," he admitted.

"I don't want to talk in here. Let's go outside." Nate didn't wait for him to agree. He headed out the door and out of the community center.

"Do you believe me?" his father asked once they reached the sidewalk.

"No. Maybe you're telling the truth. Maybe not. But I can't take your word for anything. It's worthless." Nate began to walk, unable to stand still. His father fell into step beside him.

"Fair enough. Fair enough," his father repeated. "Let me ask you this. Before you knew I was back, who were you thinking was behind the sabotage?"

"I had no idea," Nate answered. "I couldn't, I can't, come up with one other person who'd want to destroy this place. You have a reason that makes sense. Money."

"How can I convince you that—"

"You can't," Nate told him. "I'd have to trust you, and I don't." He stopped abruptly and faced his father. "Do you have any idea what you did to Mom? You wrecked her. She's in her fifties, and she acts like she's ninety. She has no confidence in herself. You smashed it. It's like she's afraid to do anything. She hardly goes out. She doesn't have friends. She has me, and Nath, and the grandkids."

"That's actually a lot," he answered.

"And Nathalie. She's a mess. She goes from loser guy to loser guy. It's like she picks the ones who will disappoint her. The way you did."

"What about you, Nate? What did I do to you?"

"Nothing. I was too busy taking care of everything to even miss you," Nate answered. "What I want to know is what you have planned now. If you're telling the truth, and you didn't come back hoping to force us into selling The Gardens, what are you here for? Are you thinking you'll get back together with Mom? What exactly are you doing here?"

"I wanted to see you. I don't have a plan other than that. I hope you'll let me get to know you again. You and Nathalie. And my grand-children."

"You don't get to call them yours. As far as they're concerned, they don't have a grand-father." His sister's ex was out of the kids' lives, and so were his parents.

"So now I have a plan. My plan is to stick around long enough to change that. I'm renting a room in a house not too far from here. I'm looking for a job. I don't really care what it is. It's just a way to be here."

"And Mom? You didn't say what you want from her."

He shook his head. "That's up to her. If she's willing, I would like to get to know her again, too. None of the choices are mine. I know that."

"Right now, I have enough to deal with. If I want to see you, I'll let you know."

His father nodded slowly. "All right," he finally said. "Your mother knows how to reach me." He started to turn away, then hesitated. "The place looks good, Nate. The place looks really good. Your grandfather would be proud."

Nate stood there and watched him walk away, then he returned to Briony. "What happened?" she asked.

"Can you ramble about something for a while?" he asked. "I'd like to sit here for at least a few minutes and not think about my family or The Gardens."

"Sure. I can do that."

Mac watched Gib as he picked up the present Mac had brought. He didn't hold it to his nose. Not good. Mac had been able to smell the present from at least a block away, but he doubted Gib would be able to understand what was special about it unless he took a good whiff. Maybe not even then.

"Well, I know you must think this is pretty special," Gib blah-blahed. "And for that reason, I thank you. What you imagine I'll do with a pink sock with daisies on it I'll never know. Even if you'd brought two, they wouldn't fit and they aren't my style. But you deserve a sardine for the effort."

Sardine. That was a word that made Mac pay attention. He trotted to the kitchen ahead of Gib. He wound himself between Gib's ankles as Gib took out the beautiful red-and-blue can. Then *pop!* That wonderful sound. Mac gave an impatient mew as Gib pulled the top back much too slowly. Then he placed three of the sardines on a plate and set it in front of Mac. Oh, Holy Bast, they were good, salty and oily and oh, so fishy.

Gib must have loved the present to give Mac this kind of award. But Peggy . . . she was almost as bad as Jamie. Jamie was a little worse. Sometimes she threw his presents away. Peggy had just returned hers.

She'd really liked the sparkly he'd brought her, though. He'd seen it around her neck. Then the other human had taken it away.

Well, Mac knew where that other human was. He'd just go and get the sparkly back. After a few more sardines. He gave a long meow to tell Gib he'd like seconds.

Nate told himself to stop reading the new reviews of The Gardens while he waited for everyone to arrive for the meeting. It wasn't productive. He didn't think this meeting was going to be that productive, either. He appreciated Hope and Max wanting to develop a strategy for combating the negative publicity, but that was only a Band-Aid. What Nate needed was to find the person behind the sabotage.

His father still seemed like the most likely person. It was too much of a coincidence that he'd shown up at the same time as the sabotage, and it sounded like he needed money. He was renting a room, and he didn't even have a job. But could his dad really have been willing to kill someone to get what he wanted? Nathalie would say no. His mother too. Nate wanted to believe the answer was no, but he didn't feel certain of anything where his father was concerned.

A knock pulled Nate away from his thoughts. He put on his game face. He wanted everyone to see confidence when they looked at him. When he answered the door, he found Briony, Caleb, and a fiftyish woman in turquoise cowboy boots on the porch.

"This is Ruby. My first LA friend," Briony announced. "She thinks she can help out. She's in the movie biz and thinks getting some video of the place and some testimony from the residents who adore you, as most of them do, would be a good idea. People would rather watch than read."

"I appreciate it. Come on in." Before Nate could shut the door behind them, Max, Hope, Regina, and Rich turned up the walkway.

"LeeAnne will be here in a minute. She's bringing leftover pie," Hope told him as they came inside.

"I hope there's some of the butterscotch-and-chocolate-pudding pie left," Max said. Nate noticed he didn't get hung up on a single word. He must be more comfortable with Hope now that they'd actually spent some time talking. Didn't surprise him. Hope was a sweetheart.

"If there isn't, I'll make you one," Hope told him. "LeeAnne has been slowly trusting me with her secret recipes, and that's one I know."

"That would be awesome." Max smiled at Hope. Briony caught Nate's eye and smiled at him. He decided the meeting was worthwhile, even if they only ended up with a Band-Aid. It had gotten Hope and Max, who was also a sweetheart, or whatever the guy version of that should be called, more time together. And it had given him more time with Briony before she left. He didn't even mind that Caleb was here.

"Sit down, everyone." The TV lounge and library were back in use, but they hadn't moved the furniture back into storage yet.

"Is there a secret handshake? It feels like there should be a secret handshake." This time it was Gib who'd arrived just as Nate was about to close the door. "I'm not sure how much help I'll be, but I wanted to be here."

"Thanks." Nate hadn't even mentioned the meeting to Gib, but here he was. Nate was struck by how tight he and Gib had gotten over the years since Gib had moved in. In truth, the man was his closest friend. If his food poisoning had been more serious—Nate didn't want to think about it.

"Hold the door!" LeeAnne called. She wheeled a cart loaded with pies toward him. Amelia followed, with one of the Nespresso machines cradled in her arms.

Amelia gave Nate a wink as she passed by. "In case we need help espressoing our thoughts." She laughed. She almost always laughed at her own jokes.

"Is that everybody?" Nate asked, hand on the doorknob.

"Your sister is taking off from work early to come," Caleb answered. "You mom wanted to be here, but she's going to watch the kids."

Did that mean his father would be spending time with the kids? Nate didn't think that was a good idea. Not until he knew for sure who was behind the sabotage.

"We told—" Regina began.

"Peggy and Janet," Nate finished for her. "I see them coming down the sidewalk."

"I'm surprised either of them wanted to come since Archie's not going to be here," Gib muttered. "He's not, is he?"

"I think Archie would be on our side," Regina said, and Rich gave a snort from the seat beside her. "But we don't want his granddaughter to know what we have planned. We don't want her to be able to take countermeasures."

LeeAnne and Amelia began taking coffee orders, and Hope jumped up to help. Max immediately got up, too.

Peggy gave Nate a quick hug as she entered the bungalow. "I'm so sorry about my daughter," she told him.

"I completely understand how she feels," Nate answered. "If you were my mom and I heard about what had been happening around here, I'd be worried for you. I don't know if I'd want you staying here."

"But it wouldn't be your choice," Peggy said. "And it isn't my daughter's."

"You're staying then?" Gib asked.

"Of course I'm staying. This is where my friends are. That's the most important thing in the world to me." Peggy and Janet took seats in the dining room chairs Nate had moved into the living room.

"My sister's pulling up. We should be able to get started in a minute." Nate realized her car hadn't been running rough the way it had last time he'd seen her drive it. He'd been meaning to check the filters and take a look at the vacuum hose to see if it was loose or broken. She must have gotten it together and taken it in to Jiffy Lube.

"Car sounds good," he commented when she rushed up to the porch.

"Dad took a look at it for me when I dropped off the kids. It was just a clogged filter."

"I was going to do that." Even though he'd nagged her to get it checked, he'd known she wouldn't. It had been on his list of things to take care of. Maybe he should be grateful his father had given him one less thing to worry about, but he found himself feeling resentful. He shouldn't be able to slip back into his mother's and sister's lives so easily.

When Nate finally shut the door, he found that there was an empty seat next to Briony, which made him unreasonably happy. "First of all, I want each of you to know how much I appreciate you being here," he said as he sat down.

"Stuff it. Let's get down to business," Gib cut in.

Well, he's back to his regular self, Nate thought. *Rich and Peggy too.* He wanted to do another check on everyone who'd gotten sick, but if the residents here were indicators, they should be doing great.

"I guess that means we're up." Max handed a cup of black coffee to Nate. Hope or LeeAnne must have told him that's what he would want. "Hope and I came up with a plan that hits all the major social media platforms."

"We set up a Buffer site, so we'll be able to manage everything as efficiently as possible," Hope added.

"I've been working on some limericks about The Gardens," Rich announced.

"That's something I'd like to get video of. Are you comfortable reciting them?" Ruby asked. That got laughs from everyone.

"Try to stop him," Regina answered, her voice warm with affection.

"Video of any residents who are willing would be great," Max said. "We'd want to get things like the Wii bowling league and the art class."

"And just people hanging out, socializing. Oh, and people in the gardens, definitely. They're so gorgeous." Hope flashed a smile at Nate.

"They're really special," Briony agreed.

"We need to get some positive reviews up as fast as possible," Max said. "If it's okay with you, Nate, Hope and I would like to go door-to-door with a laptop and help people do reviews if they're willing."

"I don't know. I don't want anyone to feel pressured," Nate answered.

"We could come up with a list of people we know would be willing," Janet suggested. "We could approach them, and if they give us the okay we could bring the kids in."

"I can help people go to sites and put up reviews, too," Regina added.

"That granddaughter of Archie's is around all the time. She's going to find out what's going on," Gib said.

"She's as hard to get rid of as a bedbug," Amelia agreed.

"And even crazier," Rich said.

"I wouldn't call her crazy," Nate protested.

"She was wild-eyed when she saw me wearing that locket," Peggy said. "She looked like she wanted to rip it off my throat. I tried to explain that it just turned up in my room, but she wouldn't hear it."

"And there's something off about the way she acts around her grandfather. She's so touchy-feely." Janet took a bite of her blackberry pie.

"What do you mean?" Nathalie asked.

"If you ever came around, you'd know." There was a little edge to Gib's voice, but Nathalie either didn't notice it or was ignoring it.

"She just doesn't act like most granddaughters, that's all," Janet explained. "And he calls her 'honeybuns.'"

"'Honeybun,' he said," Peggy corrected.

"That's what he claimed, but I heard him say it again. It was definitely 'honeybuns.' And *that* is *not* normal," Janet insisted.

"You sure it's not just because you want him to be calling you 'honeybuns'?" Rich asked.

"You men don't like how much attention Archie gets. We all know that. But it's because he's so charming. If you were half as charming, maybe you'd get half the attention," Janet snapped.

"Oh, I've seen Rich be charming, on occasion," Regina said. Janet looked back and forth between her and Rich, eyebrows raised.

"I think we're getting a little off track," Nate said.

"I don't know that that's true," Rich replied. "Eliza's the ringleader. I don't doubt she suggested people leave those negative reviews you got."

"I wonder if we could get Archie to do a testimonial for The Gardens," Hope said. "He's always saying how happy he is here. That might make people think twice about what Eliza has to say."

Mac opened his eyes and stretched. His tummy had been so full after the sardines that he'd needed a nap. He'd been missing way too many naps lately. But now it was time to get back to work. First, he wanted to get back that sparkly for Peggy.

It wasn't hard to find the scent trail of the woman who had it. She was close. In moments, he reached the house he needed, and slipped through the convenient tear he'd made in the screen around the porch. He followed the sound of the blah-blahs coming from the man who didn't like Mac.

The man most of the humans called Archie was walking back and forth across the room. If he had a tail, it would be twitching. But he didn't deserve a tail. The woman, Eliza was her name, lay on the sofa, watching the man. Mac could see the sparkly around her neck. He'd never understand why so many human females seemed to enjoy wearing collars. But humans weren't sensible. He'd realized that when he still had his kitten fluff.

"Would you sit down? You're making me crazy with all that pacing."

"You'd be pacing, too, if you had to sit in a wheelchair every time you went out the door. When am I going to be able to get out of this place?" Archie walked faster.

"I didn't expect so many people to stand up for Nate at the meeting, not after the food poisoning. But we're making progress. Just think about the payoff."

Mac narrowed his eyes, allowing him to gauge the perfect distance for a leap-and-grab maneuver. He took three steps forward, then launched himself onto the arm of the sofa. The woman's eyes widened in surprise as she discovered him poised above her. He didn't give her time to move. He looped one paw under the sparkly's chain, then with a whip-flip it was over her head.

He gave a hiss of irritation as his prize tangled in Eliza's hair, but it was a minor problem. He grabbed the sparkly between his teeth and gave his head a hard jerk. Eliza cried out as it ripped free, taking a little hair with it.

"Grab him! He's got my locket. We can't let anyone see inside it!"

"Why did you keep wearing the damn thing after the last time?" Archie yelled, starting after Mac. Pointless. Mac was way too fast. He made his escape through the tear in the screen before

Archie had a chance to get one finger on him. Mac zeroed in on Peggy's scent and ran toward her with her present.

He heard Archie and Eliza coming after him. Good. A little entertainment. Mac veered toward a flowering tree close to a house and leapt onto the lowest branch without slowing. From the tree, he jumped to the roof. He heard Archie and Eliza shouting as he made his way from roof to tree to roof, making a game of not letting his feet touch the ground. When he reached the house where he smelled Peggy, he went straight down the chimney. When he popped out into the room, he saw lots of his people, just the way he'd known he would. He'd smelled them too.

"Mac! How did you know to come—Oh, never mind," Briony blah-blahed loudly.

Ruby, one of the first humans he'd taken charge of, laughed until Mac could smell tears coming from her eyes.

"You rascal. Come over here." Gib clicked his tongue at Mac.

Mac ignored them all. He needed to complete his mission. He sauntered over to Peggy, raised up on his back legs, and lay the sparkly in her lap. Then he licked his paw and began to wash the soot off his face.

"I don't believe this!" Max exclaimed.

"He's truly an exceptional cat," Briony said as

she fished a tissue out of her purse and handed it to Ruby.

"Not the cat. Archie and Eliza! They're running down the sidewalk!" Max told them.

Nate leapt up and rushed to the window. Briony and the rest of the group followed, clustering around him.

"How's he running on that sprained ankle?" Gib asked.

It had to be more sabotage. That was the only explanation Nate could come up with for the two of them running over here in a panic.

"Do you think they heard about the meeting?" Regina asked.

"I'm going to find out. Everybody, wait here." Nate didn't want a crowd, not until he found out what was going on and decided what needed to be done. He hurried outside, but before he was halfway across the small front lawn, Archie's knees buckled. Eliza tried to catch him, but he collapsed onto the pavement. She let out a shrill scream that seemed to go on forever.

Nate ran the last few feet and crouched down next to the elderly man, scanning him for signs of a head injury, a fracture, a stroke.

"Do you need us to call nine-one-one?" Briony called.

"Yes! Get them over here." Usually he'd get The Gardens' doctor to make an assessment, unless there was an obvious reason for an ambulance. But he didn't want to take any chances with Archie.

"That's not necessary," Eliza said breathlessly. "It's not necessary," she repeated, this time loudly enough for Briony to hear.

Nate stared at her. She was so protective of her grandfather. He was surprised she hadn't already called an ambulance herself. She was probably in shock, not thinking clearly.

"My ankle gave out. There's no need for the meat wagon," Archie protested.

His voice was strong. That was something. But Nate wanted to be absolutely sure Archie was okay. He looked over his shoulder at Briony. "Call!"

She nodded, her cell already in her hand.

Nate felt Archie begin to struggle to his feet. "Arch, no. Stay down until the paramedics get here." He grabbed Archie by the shoulders, but Archie was surprisingly strong. He managed to shake Nate off and stand.

"Damn it, Archie. I told you not to try and get up." Fear made Nate's voice sharper than he intended.

"I'm fine," Archie insisted.

"At least let's get you inside where you can sit down." Nate guided one of Archie's arms around his neck and, keeping his pace slow, started helping Archie over to the house. "What happened?" he asked Eliza, who was helping support Archie's other side.

"You saw. He just toppled. If he hadn't hurt his ankle on that machine of yours, it never would have happened." She glared at him.

"But why were you two running in the first place?" Nate asked.

"That's not what's important right now. I want to get my grandfather comfortable," Eliza snapped. "Not that that's even possible after what he's been through." Together she and Nate maneuvered Archie through the open door and into the living room. They eased him down onto the sofa.

Everyone formed a ragged circle around Archie. Nate didn't have to remind them to give him air. They were all careful not to crowd him. "What can we do for you?" Janet asked, taking one step forward.

"How about some water?" Nathalie offered. She started toward the kitchen.

"I'll get it!" Janet hurried off, and Nathalie returned to the group.

Nate caught a flash of movement in his peripheral vision, and a second later Mac soundlessly landed on the back of the sofa. "That cat!" Eliza shrieked. "That horrible cat!" She lurched toward Mac. He hissed, his ears pressed flat against his head.

Briony quickly positioned herself between

Eliza and MacGyver. "I know you're upset, but don't take it out on Mac."

"That cat stole my necklace! It was a present from Grandpa. He went chasing after that horrible animal to get it back, even though I begged him not to." Eliza clasped her hands together, her knuckles whitening. "He could have had a heart attack. He could have broken a hip. Who knows what that fall did to his ankle." Her voice got higher with every sentence.

"Eliza, why don't you sit down?" Nate suggested. "You've had a—"

A cry from Briony interrupted him. "Mac! No! Don't!" she yelped.

Too late. Mac had already jumped down onto Archie's chest.

"Mac won't hurt him. He likes—" Gib began.

"Get it off him!" Eliza shouted.

Briony and Nate both reached for Mac, but he slipped between their hands. One of his paws shot out and swiped across Archie's head—taking a chunk of hair and skin with it. Archie let out a bellow.

"Oh, my god. Mac! What did you do?" Nate heard Briony exclaim, horror lacing her voice. He didn't look at her. He couldn't stop staring at Archie, his brain trying to process what he was seeing. There was no blood on Archie's scalp. It was covered with . . . thick blond hair.

"What? What?" Nathalie said. She swallowed

hard, but only managed another "what?" Nate knew how she felt. He looked down at Mac. The cat was batting something that sprouted splotchy white hair around the floor.

"Grandpa?" Eliza pressed her hands to her chest in a way that seemed especially theatrical to Nate. What was going on? He felt like he'd walked into the middle of a movie.

Briony took a deep breath, then gingerly picked up the thing Mac was playing with. She held it between two fingers and gave it a tentative shake. "It's a . . . I think it's a sort of a wig."

"A bald cap. Well, partial bald cap, actually," Ruby said. "Nice quality. Did you use a mold block?" she asked Archie. He blinked rapidly, but didn't answer. It looked like he was trying to do some processing himself. "You must have. The edges were impressive," Ruby continued. "And the makeup? Expert. I could get you a job on a movie tomorrow. Except that you're obviously scum."

Archie blinked a few more times. He was clearly having trouble assessing the situation too. Suddenly, he sprang to his feet. He took two long strides toward the door, then realized Caleb had positioned himself in front of it and stopped.

Nate had to admit he was really starting to like Caleb. He might even forgive the guy for having sex with Briony while the two of them were engaged.

"Lookin' pretty spry there, Archie," Rich commented. "I don't know about you," he said to Gib. "But it's been years since I could move that fast."

"My knees crack as loud as rifle fire if I try," Gib answered.

"You're a fake!" Janet's face flushed as she glared at Archie.

"And he's way too young for you, sweetheart," Eliza told her.

"But you aren't, are you, *honeybuns?*" Peggy asked. "You're his girlfriend."

How did this make any kind of sense? How would Archie get anything out of pretending to be an old man? Was he hiding from someone? The police?

No, Nate realized. Giving the appearance of an old man had given Archie complete access to The Gardens. He was behind the sabotage. He'd been able to run on his injured ankle because his ankle wasn't injured. He'd faked it and blamed it on Nate's equipment. But why? Who was this guy really?

"I think it's time to take a closer look at the present Mac brought you," Nate told Peggy. At the sound of his name, Mac began to purr.

"I'm not sure I can open it." Peggy turned the locket over in her fingers. "My arthritis and the tiny clasp don't work together."

"Here, let me." Briony reached out her hand, and Peggy passed her the necklace.

Nathan shot a glance at Archie. He didn't look like he was going to try and bulldoze his way past Caleb. He sat slumped on the couch, head in hands, defeated. Eliza now sat beside him, eyes hot as she watched Briony open the locket. She didn't look defeated. She looked furious.

"What's in it?" Gib asked, leaning forward.

"A picture of Eliza and one of Archie without his old-guy getup," Briony answered.

"Hey, I know him!" Ruby exclaimed, looking over Briony's shoulder. "It's Kenneth 'The Closer' Archer."

Archie groaned, but didn't lift his head. "From the bus stop!" LeeAnne exclaimed, staring at him. "The 'Everything I Touch Turns to Sold' real estate agent. I can't believe I didn't recognize him. I see his smarmy face every time I head toward House of Pies."

Nate's body began to tingle, like someone had flipped on an electric current inside him. He walked over to Archie and waited for the man to look up. "You're the realtor who's been trying to buy this place."

"What?" Peggy exclaimed, her dark eyes bright. "You aren't thinking of selling, are you, Nate?"

"No. He kept sending me e-mails and letters

and leaving messages. I told him no every way I could think of. So, he decided to try and force me to sell by ruining The Gardens' reputation."

Archie straightened up. "I made him a great offer on behalf of a client who loves this property," he told the group, as if he had a chance of getting them on his side. "Any sane person would have jumped at it!"

"He always forgets to say I'm the one who brought the client in," Eliza said bitterly. "I convinced him we were the agents for the property. The commission could have set me—us—up for life." She turned to Nate. "And you would never have had to work again."

"Fortunately, Nate's crazy enough to care about more than money," Rich said. "I'm going to write a poem for him." He reached for his notebook. "Not a limerick. An ode."

Regina patted his knee. "Perfect. A poem of praise that often expresses deep feelings. You deserve one, Nate."

Caleb left his position in front of the door and joined Nate in front of Archie—Archer—and Eliza. "You realize you're going to be charged with attempted murder."

"Those chemicals wouldn't have killed anyone," Archie protested. "They were only strong enough to make people sick. Eliza did the research."

"Shut up!" Eliza elbowed him in the ribs hard enough to make him grunt.

"As you so eloquently pointed out at the meeting, food poisoning is especially risky for the elderly," Caleb told Eliza.

"You S.O.B.! You could have killed Peggy." Nate noticed that Peggy was the only one Gib mentioned, even though he'd been poisoned himself.

"I didn't use anyth—" Archie stopped mid-word, head jerking toward the window.

Nate realized what had gotten Archie's attention. The sound of a siren coming closer.

"I guess I should have asked for the police instead of an ambulance when I called nine-one-one," Briony said.

More than three hours later, it was over. The group watched through the window as two police officers escorted Eliza and Archer to a squad car. They were being taken in for questioning.

Nate and the others returned to their seats without speaking, overwhelmed and exhausted. The only sound was Mac's rumbling purr. Nate didn't think he'd stopped purring once since he'd snatched off Archer's wig.

Gib finally broke the silence. "Good night, nurse, as Archie would say." He shook his head.

"Archer, you mean," Briony reminded him.

"Good night, nurse?" Ruby repeated.

"Archie used as much crazy slang as you and Riley do when you're pretending to be cowboys," Briony explained.

"What is it even supposed to mean?" Ruby asked.

"It's an exclamation of surprise, often used in place of a cussword." Regina smoothed her hair, although it was already perfect. "I don't believe the origin is known, although some think it started with a silent movie of that name, where Fatty Arbuckle dressed up as a nurse and flirted with Buster Keaton. Others think it started during World War One, and was simply a good night to a nurse in a military hospital."

"She's right. Of course." Rich held up his cell. "It's on a list of expressions from the nineteen-twenties. First thing that popped up when I Googled it. Should have known not to bother looking it up with Regina around. Archer used almost everything on the list while he was playing the part of an old man. He went back a few too many decades."

"I found his crazy expressions charming," Janet admitted. "I feel like such an idiot."

"We all thought he was great," Peggy told her. "It wasn't just you."

"I didn't think he was so great. But I had no idea what he was up to," Gib admitted. "You know who did, though?" He pointed at Mac.

"He's a delightful kitty cat," Peggy answered. "But that's impossible."

Gib stood up. "I'll prove it. I just need to go home and get something."

"I'll take you over," Hope volunteered.

"I'll go too," Max said.

Nate stretched his arms over his head, trying to relieve the tension in his shoulders. "Strange day."

"Long, good, bad, hard, strange," Briony said from beside him, speaking so softly only he could hear. Heat flooded his body just thinking about that night. He wished he could make everyone else in the room disappear. What he wanted most, what he needed, was to be alone with her. Not just so he could touch her, although he badly wanted to touch her, but so he could talk to her. That night in the kitchen, drinking wine, he'd told her things he hadn't thought he'd ever share with someone who wasn't family.

Being alone would have to wait. Nate could tell the others felt the need to stay together, at least a little longer. Maybe he should order pizzas for everyone, although LeeAnne would probably throw a fit if he suggested it. She'd want to cook.

Nate looked over at his sister and found her looking back at him, just as he'd known she would be. It was a twin thing. "You owe Dad an apology," Nathalie told him. "A big one."

"Yeah, Dad's never done a single bad thing," he shot back, but almost immediately he relented. No matter what his father had done, Nate had to tell him the truth and apologize. He'd been wrong to accuse his dad of sabotage. "I'll talk to him, I promise." Nathalie nodded, satisfied.

"Is anybody hungry?" LeeAnne asked. "We can move to the kitchen. I'll make anything anybody wants." Nate smiled. Did he know her or what?

"Does that include—" Rich began.

He was interrupted by Gib, Max, and Hope returning to the room. Gib carried a paper shopping bag, which he upended over the coffee table. He fished out a ragged piece of thin latex with patches of white hair and pulled it onto his head. "Look familiar?" he asked. "Keep in mind it's been used as a cat toy by our friend." Gib gestured to Mac, who'd curled up on Peggy's lap. "This will help." Gib stuck what looked like a fuzzy gray caterpillar over one eyebrow.

"He must have had to make a replacement wig after Mac made off with that one." Rich chuckled.

"He made new eyebrows too," Janet said. "I thought he'd done manscaping on them, but he must have mistakenly made the newer pair thinner."

Ruby picked a piece of sponge off the table, then gave it a sniff. Mac's purring grew louder, something Nate hadn't thought was possible. "Schram Foam Latex, talc, plus some cake foundation. He knew what he was doing."

"What is all the rest of this, anyway?" Peggy gestured to the small mound of items on the coffee table. "That looks like one of my socks." She pulled a pink sock with daisies on it from somewhere near the bottom. Then she flushed and snatched a deep purple bra. She balled it up and shoved it into her bag. Nate pretended not to notice. So did everyone else. Even Rich. Regina was obviously having an influence on him.

"You should know that Mac is a diabolical matchmaker," Ruby told them. "He got two of my friends together by stealing socks and whatnot from one of them and bringing it to the other. He also got two teenagers at Storybook Court together in pretty much the same way. Oh, and a truly annoying man, who turned out to have a heart of melted butter, ended up with our mail carrier, all thanks to Mac. I don't know how he does it, but he seems to be able to sense which people belong together. It seems like he's added detective to his résumé," she added.

"You talked to me for the first time after Mac made me spill coffee on myself!" Hope reminded Max. She flushed. "Not that that means . . ."

"I'd been wanting to talk to you since the first

day of our first class," Max told her. "I owe the cat a thank-you present."

"A few cans of sardines would do it. He can't get enough of them." Gib shot a fast look at Peggy, then looked away just as quickly.

"He brought me your key chain, the one with the picture of your grandkids," Peggy said to Gib, then looked down at Mac while she stroked his head.

"You two would make an adorable couple," Janet said. She looked over at Richard and Regina. "What about you two? Did Mac have anything to do with how you can suddenly tolerate each other?"

Regina tilted her head to one side, considering. "He did make sure I read a sonnet that had me thinking Rich had hidden depths beneath some truly atrocious clothing."

Rich laughed. "I might owe the feline a few cans of sardines, too."

"If I give him some sardines in advance, you think he'd work some cat magic for me?" Janet asked. "Since Archie is out of the picture?"

"You never had a chance with—" Regina began, then stopped herself. "I think it's worth a try. He's a very intuitive kitty, don't you think so, Peggy?"

Peggy looked at Gib. "I think he has it wrong with me and Michael."

"Michael? Who's Michael?" Janet asked.

"Gib. Michael Gibson," Peggy explained. "We went to high school for four years, and he never even spoke to me."

"Not s-speaking doesn't necessarily mean not interested," Max said.

"Really?" Peggy looked at Gib, not Max, when she asked the question.

"Really," Gib answered. "If you'd go out to dinner with me sometime, I'd buy the cat a damn sardine factory."

Peggy laughed. "Well, get out your checkbook."

Gib beamed. That was the only word for it.

"I'm glad he decided to start visiting The Gardens." Nate reached over and took Briony's hand. "Who knows how things might have turned out without him around."

One year later

Nate guided the pink Cadillac convertible into the Little White Wedding Chapel's Tunnel of Love. "How're you feeling?" he asked Briony.

"Wonderful!" She smiled up at the stars and cherubs painted on the ceiling. "I could have walked down an aisle twelve miles long without a problem. I could have danced down the aisle. Roller-skated!"

"Maybe we should renew our vows here," Jamie said from the back seat.

393

"We just finished celebrating our first anniversary," David protested, laughing.

"Who cares? I think we should renew every year. Every month! I want to celebrate pretty much constantly. Right, Mac?" She cuddled the kitty, who sat in her lap, wearing a black tuxedo tie. Nate wore a full tuxedo, and Briony had on a dress with a nipped-in waist and a wide skirt with an overlay of tulle, which he knew because he'd heard her, Jamie, and Ruby endlessly discussing it. Really, all he cared about was getting her out of it. He'd let her talk him into taking a month-long sex break so their honeymoon would be extra special.

He pulled up to the window where the minister was waiting for them. They'd debated going with an Elvis impersonator, but Briony had decided she wanted a little bit of tradition and had asked the chapel to let her bring in her own minister from back home. Nate had let her make all the decisions. He wanted to marry her. He didn't care about the trimmings, and he'd enjoyed watching how much pleasure Briony took in making dozens and dozens of choices, including having David and Jamie—and Mac—as their witnesses.

The exchange of vows took less than two minutes; then he got to kiss her. Every time he kissed her, he didn't think it was possible for it to get better, but somehow it did. This just-married kiss might hold the record for the rest of his life. Or maybe each kiss would top the last as-long-as-they-both-shall-lived.

He circled the Caddy around to the entrance of the tunnel. A Vegas-era Elvis replaced Nate behind the wheel. Briony helped Peggy get the full skirt of her long champagne-colored dress with white flower appliques—according to what Nate had been hearing—into the back seat.

"You're up," Nate told Gib. Gib got in next to Peggy; then Jamie passed Mac over to him. They'd had to have Mac as an attendant, too, since he'd played such a big part in getting them together. Peggy was actually wearing the pink daisy socks as her "something old."

Elvis started the pink Cadillac through the tunnel, and Briony, Nate, Jamie, and David returned to the parking lot. Most of the residents of The Gardens had come to Vegas for the ceremonies on party busses. Some threw hand-fuls of flower petals at Nate and Briony, while others blew iridescent soap bubbles.

Nathalie rushed over to them and managed to wrap them both in a hug, Lyle and Lyla joining the huddle a moment later. "I'm so happy for you!" she exclaimed. "Although I'm the older twin. That means I should be getting married first."

He shook his head. His sister had become so much more involved in The Gardens and so much better at taking charge of her life over the past year, but he suspected she'd always be a little on the self-centered side.

"You're going to be getting married to Caleb, so you shouldn't whine," Lyla told her mother.

"Lyla! Caleb and I haven't talked about marriage!" She looked over at Caleb, who was helping LeeAnne and her staff get the tail-gate reception food organized.

"You talk about everything else," Lyla answered. "She texts him almost every day, and they have these long conversations a couple nights a week."

"After you're asleep—so I thought," Nathalie said.

"Look! They're coming out!" LeeAnne called as Elvis pulled the Caddy back to the entrance of the tunnel.

"Our turn," Rich told Regina.

"She looks so beautiful," Briony said. "So elegant."

Regina wore a knee-length cream suit with touches of pink and a large pink hat. "She does, but not as beautiful as you," Nate agreed as he watched Max get behind the wheel to chauffeur his grandfather and Regina to the chapel's drive-thru window. Hope sat beside him, holding Mac.

"He must really love her," Briony continued. "That tuxedo could have come right off James

Bond. Except for the tie." It was bright pink and covered with black pawprints.

"That's extremely understated for him, and all to please Regina," Nate answered. "Although I got a look at his honeymoon pajamas. I hope she brought her sunglasses."

"Here come the parents," Briony announced. "At least my mom can stop sending me articles about how dangerous Vegas is."

Nate knew sticking to her decision to have their wedding in Las Vegas had been hard for Briony. He was proud of her for going with her gut, even when it meant going against her mom's wishes. And while Briony's mother looked a little nervous, she also beamed as she hugged first Briony, then him.

"Great venue, Briony," her dad said; then it was his turn to kiss the bride. "I love it. And I love you."

"I love you, too, Dad," she answered.

Then Nate's parents were up. His mom hugged him tight, tight, tight. His dad hesitated, then hugged him, too. They hadn't reached the state where a hug felt natural, but they were getting there. When his dad had had trouble finding a job, Nate had taken him on at The Gardens. He'd made him start as a busboy, which he now had to admit was kind of a jerk move, but he'd wanted to be sure his father was going to stick around, and when he did

Nate had bumped him up to assistant activities director. The ladies seemed to love him even more than they had Archie, the Archie created by Kenneth Archer. Nate wondered if the man was able to charm his fellow inmates so easily.

"Anyone else want to take a ride through the tunnel? My treat!" Rich called as he got out of the Caddy. Nate caught his dad shooting a look at his mom.

His mother shook a finger at him. "Oh no. You are still on roommate status," she said. They were technically still married, but his mother wasn't treating him like a husband. "If you continue to behave yourself, maybe we'll come visit the chapel for ourselves one day."

Nate found that he didn't hate the idea of his parents getting back together at some point. About six months ago, his dad had moved back into the family house, and Nate could see that his mom was happier with him around. She got out more, going to a lot of the events his father organized at The Gardens. They'd even started taking salsa lessons together. But his mother, like Nate, had needed time before she could completely trust Nate's father again.

"I just realized I forgot to ask you the question I always ask people when I first meet them," Ruby said to Briony as she joined them.

"Let's hear it," Briony said.

"If your life was a movie, what would it be called?" Ruby asked.

Briony raised her eyebrows. "My answer will be so different today than it would have been back then." She took Nate's hand. "What do you think? My life and your life are going to have even more overlap now."

Nate had hired Briony to work at The Gardens, too, mostly so he could get her to stay in LA when her cat-sitting gig ended, but also because with Briony doing the accounting, Nate actually had time to take care of the plants and make some additions to The Gardens' gardens.

He considered the question. "I think it's going to have to have 'Cat' in the title somewhere. We never would have met without MacGyver."

"I agree," Briony said. "If everyone would just follow Mac's orders, the world would be a happier place."

"Orders, that's about right." Jamie joined them with Mac in her arms. "He doesn't ask; he tells. He's extremely bossy."

"I've got it." Nate gave Mac's head a stroke, and Mac gave Nate one of those slow blinks of his. "The movie should be *Obey the Paw.*"

"Love it!" Jamie exclaimed.

Briony reached over and scratched Mac under the chin. "Me too. I don't want to think about what my life would be like if Mac hadn't become my people sitter."

Books are produced in the United States using U.S.-based materials

Books are printed using a revolutionary new process called THINKtech™ that lowers energy usage by 70% and increases overall quality

Books are durable and flexible because of Smyth-sewing

Paper is sourced using environmentally responsible foresting methods and the paper is acid-free

Center Point Large Print
600 Brooks Road / PO Box 1
Thorndike, ME 04986-0001 USA

(207) 568-3717

US & Canada:
1 800 929-9108
www.centerpointlargeprint.com